H I M

The Inheritance

Book 01 of The Hymn Chronicles

By

John D. Parfait, Jr.

Title: HIM: The Inheritance

ISBN:

Paperback: 978-1-917327-18-3

About the Author

John D. Parfait, Jr., holds a Bachelor of Science in Chemistry from the University of Texas Arlington and has 50 years of experience as a chemist in private industry. At age 80, John began his literary journey and published *Mudman: Tale of a Texas Swamp* in 2023. He aims to write at least ten books by age 90.

John has written poetry and three novels, specializing in Coming of Age and Fiction genres. His inspirations for writing stem from a lifelong love of storytelling and a desire to share his tales with the world. His personal motto is, "Save. Give. Achieve. Believe. At least a little of each, every day." Outside of writing, he enjoys bowling, the outdoors, and philosophy.

A proud Army veteran, John values his roles as a son, husband, father, and grandfather.

Acknowledgements

My Friend and Fellow Author, Tom Gillespie.

While helping him with his great book, Vietnam - One Week in December, 1969, in 2022, Tom became serious one day and advised me to write my own books. Because of my advanced age, I was reluctant and, having never before written a book, did not pay much attention to his advice. Tom was persistent with his encouragement, though, and in 2023 I wrote and published my first book, Mudman, Tale of a Texas Swamp. This book, Him, is my second published work and my third book is completed and will be published later in 2024. To my surprise, I enjoy writing.

Thank you Tom, my friend, for your encouragement and support, without which, it is unlikely I would ever have written anything.

Table of Contents

About the Author ii

Acknowledgements iii

Chapter 1 - Abilities 1

Chapter 2 - Aunt Rita.. 8

Chapter 3 - The Awakening 21

Chapter 4 - Flying Below the Radar....................................26

Chapter 5 - The Birthday Party 36

Chapter 6 - Randolph Barton..41

Chapter 7 - They 45

Chapter 8 - Keepaway 49

Chapter 9 - The Eliminator 53

Chapter 10 - The Debrief..65

Chapter 11 - A Trip To The Zoo 76

Chapter 12 - The Scenario 88

Chapter 13 - Little Things 96

Chapter 14 - Director Sheridan 104

Chapter 15 - The Plot Unfolds...113

Chapter 16 - Aiden 121

Chapter 17 - The Aftermath...130

Chapter 18 - A Dinner Outing 134

Chapter 19 - A Conversation With Auntie.........................140

Chapter 20 - The Nephalim 149

Chapter 21 - Too Many Unknowns 159

Chapter 22 - Andra Lincoln.. 163

Chapter 23 - Conversation With An Angel............................ 172

Chapter 24 - The Kingdom of God 180

Chapter 25 - Jehovah / God.. 187

Chapter 26 - The Killer Cult... 195

Chapter 27 - A Visit With God 207

Chapter 28 - The Angel Gathering 215

Chapter 29 - Walter 227

Chapter 30 - The End Of An Era................................... 231

Chapter 1 - Abilities

Do you ever wonder how and why things happen? It is not unusual for little things to occur in life seemingly 'right out of the blue,' creating big life-changing results in our lives we never anticipated or considered. That happened to him on a very pleasant April afternoon in Texas.

He is a happy and contented man, retired recently from a bottling plant where he was the manager of the Quality Division, responsible for overseeing the company's in-process and finished product quality. He had worked twenty-six years for the same company and was satisfied that he had something to do with the success of the plant; however, twenty-six years was enough. He wanted to do some traveling while still strong and healthy enough to do so and decided now was the time. After all, he was 51 years of age now.

There was something else pushing him to retire; the desire to do something with his life that was of benefit to mankind, and he had no idea what that might be. About four years back, thoughts of doing something better with his life began entering his mind. He had never married but had more than a few relationships in his time and has been with the same woman, off and on, for the past seven years. They live separately but are good friends and see each other regularly, every week, an arrangement that works well for both of them.

Another thing needs to be mentioned that will answer most of your questions about him. He is different. It was about the age of twelve or thirteen when that was made plain to him. His unusual difference from the other kids at school was beginning to be noticed, raising his profile to the point where his dad was forced to give him 'the talk.' Things were happening around him that challenged coincidence, causing conversation among the teachers and students.

It actually began when he signed up and began playing Little League Baseball. He proved to be a good player and a real good hitter.

He was twelve years old at the time and considered himself to be one of the guys on the team and was just that until he came up to bat for the third time in an evening game. He hit doubles in his first two times at bat, and the young pitcher on the mound did not want him to get another hit, so he decided to throw the ball at him instead of over the plate, figuring that a walk or a hit batter would result, which turned out to be correct; the pitcher walked him. The thing is, he threw four balls directly at the batter and could not hit him. To those watching, it looked like the young pitcher had lost control and was throwing wild pitches, but that was not the case. The young pitcher knew he was throwing right at the batter and could not hit him in four straight tries. The batter knew the pitcher was throwing at him, too, and realized that he could not be hit. A few more similar instances during the next few weeks raised the interest of the other players and coaches, causing his dad to take action.

The conversation with his dad lasted over an hour and was full of questions and answers, all resulting in the revelation that he was born with certain abilities. It was emphasized that exhibiting abilities to others will result in the unhappiness of everyone in the family, particularly him. He could use these abilities to his advantage as long as no one noticed, but he should keep his actions to himself, seldom use them, and take care to hurt no one. With the help of his aunt and the support of his dad, he was just another person growing up, attending school, serving in the military, attending college, and going to work every week, that is, until that pleasant April afternoon previously mentioned. Let's get back to that.

Driving in the traffic going out of Dallas on a Saturday afternoon is enjoyable, for the most part, but doesn't allow for thinking and daydreaming, which is all he wanted to do today; so, he checked to see that no cars were behind him and drove to the right lane to take the next exit and head toward a more rural area away from the holiday drivers on the highway. As he turned onto the exit road, he glanced at the rearview mirror and noticed a police car following close behind, but didn't think much of it because this was a weekend, and the traffic cops were out doing their best to keep things moving steadily and safely and, of course, earning money for the city by occasionally issuing tickets for speeding and other traffic violations. Many years ago, he considered a career in law enforcement but decided against it when it became clear that the politics and social limitations of that profession had corrupted the system, making it no place for moral and ethical individuals to thrive. On top of that, it was plain that keeping his abilities hidden in that occupation would be far too difficult.

Anyway, as he turned from the exit road to the main street heading toward the country, the flashing lights of the police car behind him came on, indicating for him to pull over and stop, which he did. He had to be careful, though, because a ditch near the street did not allow him to park all the way off the road without driving into it. Traffic was not heavy on the street, but this road led to the lake, and cars, some pulling boats, were passing by frequently. He remained in his car and took out his driver's license and proof of insurance to give to the officer.

"Something is wrong; why in the world was I pulled over?" he thought. "I wasn't speeding, but maybe one of my tail lights is out or something. Oh well, guess I'm about to find out." Looking through the side mirror, he noticed the police officer was writing something in a notebook before approaching the driver's window.

He said, "Good afternoon, officer," and handed his driver's license and insurance card out the window.

The officer, a young man, maybe in his late twenties, made no effort to take the papers and said, "Sir, step out of the vehicle."

"This is strange." he thought to himself. "Something is not right here." He looked at the officer and asked, "Why?"

"Sir!" the officer firmly repeated with authority, "Step out of the car!" and added, "Do not make me tell you again."

"Look, officer," he calmly answered. "I will not leave my car without a good reason, and your ordering me to do so is not a reason. Why are you so angry, anyway?"

The officer frowned, "I warned you, old man." He briskly spoke into his radio, "Officer needs assistance." He gave directions to our location. Then he turned and ordered, "Pull the vehicle further from the road; you are too close to the traffic here."

"What are you talking about?" the driver said, "if I drive anymore to the right, my car will end up in that ditch, and I'll never get it out. I'm sorry, officer, but there is something not quite right about you. I have done nothing wrong, and you pulled me onto this busy, narrow road, demanding I get out of my car without any reasonable explanation. I'm leaving." He started his car and put it in gear.

The officer came to the driver's window and angrily spoke, "Listen, you fucking idiot, if you drive away, I will run you down and shoot your stupid ass! You are resisting arrest and leaving the scene, meaning you are a dangerous fugitive and giving me cause to use deadly force."

The man calmly answered, "First, I was never arrested. Second, you are angry and threatening me for no apparent reason. I am concerned about that. Third, how are you going to do all that with an empty gun and a flat tire?" Then he slowly drove away.

The officer turned to look at his car; the left front tire was flat. He then lifted and looked at his gun; it was not loaded. "What the fuck?" he muttered and added, "I'll get that bastard!" But his attention was compromised, and he was standing at the edge of the road. He heard but never saw what hit him.

The driver of the truck, pulling a boat, was going about 60 miles per hour when, in the oncoming traffic, a truck transporting half of a mobile home was approaching from the other direction. The driver pulling the boat steered a little to the right to give the approaching wide load more room on the road and saw the policeman standing on the road too late. He hit the brakes and instinctively turned left to avoid the officer. After that, everything 'went to hell in a handbasket' in an instant.

The right side of the truck with the boat hit the policeman, killing him instantly, and veered into the mobile home transport. The boat behind the truck slammed into the police car, and both caught on fire and burned. The driver of the mobile home carrier saw the truck veering towards him and turned his truck to the right to avoid a collision, ran into the ditch on that side of the road, causing the truck and its load to flip over on its side, killing the driver and destroying the mobile home. All in all, a terrible accident involving twelve vehicles resulted in 5 fatalities and numerous injuries.

Remember me wondering earlier about how and why things happen and how a little thing can often have huge life-changing results? That fatal accident is an example. What was the "little thing" that began the whole tragedy? There was no license plate on the rear of the car. The officer, instead of talking with the driver about the missing plate, assumed it was a stolen vehicle because it fit the description of a car without plates recently stolen from a used car lot. Why were the plates missing from the driver's car? He had received his new plates yesterday, took the old ones off, got interrupted before installing the new ones, and totally forgot about them.

See what I mean? Little things.

What about him? He drove off, never looked back, and had a great day driving around the country, thinking about what to do with the rest of his life. He did not see the accident or even hear about it until Monday. Even then, it did not occur to him that he was there minutes before the accident happened; it was just another bad accident. He was expecting the police to come and arrest him sometime soon for driving away from that policeman last Saturday, but no consequences so far.

"I wonder," he thought, "could that officer have changed his mind? He was very angry at me for what seemed to be no good reason. Maybe he was having trouble at home or work. You can never tell what is going on in a person's mind, especially if social or business pressure is involved. Maybe he just thought it over and decided to let it go. That would be nice. Anyway, it was impressive how I thought that tire to be flat and emptied his gun. I'll bet he is still wondering about that. I'm wondering, too, about my special abilities; I have never tried to push them to their limit." He made a mental note to talk with his Aunt Rita. She would know.

Monday evening, while putting groceries in the trunk of his car at the supermarket, he noticed his car's old and new license plates lying next to his toolbox, where he had left them Friday when his neighbor came by to talk. He now realized why he was pulled over by the cop, with no license plates, and felt guilty about the way he treated the young man. Immediately, right in the parking lot, he installed the new plates and drove home, realizing he could have handled that Saturday incident better.

"Why didn't that officer mention that he pulled me over because of missing license plates, and why was he so angry with me?" he asked himself. "Oh well, no harm done. If the police contact me later, I will explain what happened and pay the fine."

The thing is, he liked thinking that cop's tire to go flat. It was a power thing. That officer was giving orders like he was the one in charge when he wasn't. It occurred to him that his abilities could be used to make a positive contribution to the world. It was not yet 'cast in concrete,' but a plan was forming in his mind about how to use his abilities to help people. Helping the world or the country was outside his reach, but he could help people. He had been a regular person all his life: responsible, hard-working, and unnoticed by society. Oh, he had friends and co-workers in his life and was close to his aunt (she was his only living relative), but in a way, he felt empty and incomplete. He had abilities beyond his imagination, which he had suppressed and kept hidden all his life, because his dad and aunt warned against their use.

"Society is not prepared for that which you are capable," his dad would warn. "They will fear you and come to hate you; never let them see the real you." So, he didn't. As a result, he was not satisfied with his life and wanted to make a better contribution to the world with the time he had remaining, however long that may be. He also had a burning desire to know more about who and what it is, that he is. He doesn't know for sure, nor does anyone else, except for his Aunt Rita. She also has the abilities. It has been a while since the last time they visited. He looked forward to seeing her again. He loved his aunt and made a mental note to call and let her know of an impending visit.

Chapter 2 - Aunt Rita

You know something? When a man makes up his mind about something, that something occupies the majority of his thoughts; that is what happened with him. Preparing to enter a new phase of his life was exciting. For the first time in years, he was enthusiastic about the future; however, thinking about doing something and actually "doing something" are two very different concepts. Many people dream about things they want or need to accomplish, but thinking is the easy part; taking action and following through is often left undone because of the work required. Humans generally do not like to work. He needed a plan and had no one with whom to talk except Aunt Rita, and that was something not to be anticipated. His aunt is conservative and quite adamant about keeping their special abilities untold, unseen, and unknown by anyone. She will be totally opposed to the idea of using his abilities for anything that might compromise their anonymous standing in society.

He woke up early, about a week later and called his aunt to check if she was going to be home today. She answered the phone and said, "Well, nephew, what possessed you to honor me with a call so early in the morning?" and then asked before he could reply, "Did someone die?"

He knew she was being sarcastic and said, "No, Aunt Rita, no deaths that I know of; anyway, you keep track of that type of information way more than me. We have not seen each other in a while and I was thinking about coming over and visiting, if you were going to be home today."

"Goodness gracious!" she exclaimed, "now you've done gone and got an old woman excited. My only nephew wants to visit with me today. I don't know what to say and not sure I can handle such special treatment."

"Come on, Aunt Rita, get off your 'high horse' and quit picking on me." he laughed. "It hasn't been all that long since our last visit."

"Four months," was her reply.

"Well, you live way over there on the other side of Ft. Worth," he answered weakly.

"One and a half hours drive," was her reply, and she added, "You would think an only nephew would spend 90 minutes of driving to visit his one and only aunt more than three times a year, wouldn't you?"

"Doggone it, Aunt Rita . . ."

Then she laughed and interrupted him, "I'm just messing with you, boy. I would love to see you today. You get yourself on over here; it has been awhile since we have been able to sit and talk, and I want to know what you've been up to since retiring."

"Okay," he said, "I'm heading your way. I have to make a pit stop for gas and should be there before eleven o'clock."

"Alright, boy," she answered, "I'll fix something for lunch."

Grabbing a paper sack with a present for his aunt inside, he walked out to his car, thinking, "I don't know why she always calls me 'boy'. She knows I'm over 50; just habit, I suppose."

Aunt Rita is 25 years older than him and is his dad's younger sister. His aunt's extra abilities became noticeable when she was aged 6 and just beginning public school. Her teacher first became aware that something unusual in her classroom was occurring because of a strange incident. Right next to young Rita's desk was a window. One warm, rainy day, when the classroom windows were closed, young Rita got up from her desk and raised the window about halfway open. A breeze was lightly coming in, carrying cool air and a few drops of rain, to which a few students objected. Young Rita, on the other hand, liked how it felt. The teacher noticed the commotion there, saw the open window, and promptly went there and closed the window.

The little girl who was doing the most complaining turned, looked back at Rita, and said triumphantly, "You're not the boss here; I am." Then made an ugly face at her. When she turned back, facing the front of the class, the window went up halfway. It was raining harder now, and the little boss girl, thinking that Rita had gotten up and raised the window again, screamed at the teacher, "She opened the window again!"

The teacher, seeing the rain coming in through the half-open window, went and again closed the window. This time, she told Rita to leave the window down and moved her to another desk on the other side of the room. Rita had not spoken during the entire event and quietly sat at her new desk. Little boss girl shot Rita a mean look and stuck her tongue out at her. This is when it got a little crazy. As the teacher was walking back to the front of the room, guess what! The window moved halfway up again, all by itself. The little boss girl turned to look at a smiling Rita, and, of course, Rita stuck her tongue out at her, which angered the little girl, who immediately got up and went to shut the window, . . .but she never got there. The floor was wet, and the boss girl, walking indignantly and fast, slipped and fell hard on the floor. The teacher turned and saw what had happened and quickly hurried to help the little girl, who was lying on the floor, unconscious, with blood flowing from her mouth. She picked up the boss girl to carry her to the school medical clinic, and as she was leaving, the window slammed shut. Startled, the teacher turned, looked at the window, and then at Rita, who was busy coloring in her notebook. The rest of the class was in disarray, some crying, some crowding around the blood on the floor and pointing to the window, saying crazy things the way kids do.

It was later determined that the boss girl was okay, except for the fact her tongue was bitten half off on one side; she had done that in the fall. The thing is, no one saw anything except the part where the window opened and closed by itself, which only a few kids saw, and even they had different versions as to how it happened.

In the aftermath, the teacher was disciplined for not immediately moving the children away from the wet floor and calling the janitor to mop away the water. All the children in the classroom had to undergo counseling for their traumatic experience. Little boss girl had oral surgery to repair her bitten tongue, but sadly, she was left with a speech impediment for the rest of her life and had trouble chewing because the feeling never returned to the repaired side of her tongue.

Although the teacher was suspicious that something about Rita was unusual, she could not make an issue of the incident because, after all, young Rita was at her desk on the other side of the room when the accident happened; however, she did talk to Rita's parents about the incident, who later conducted young Rita's first 'talk' regarding 'special abilities.' After the school year, the teacher left the area and was never heard from again. Rita had no idea of everything that resulted from the accident on that rainy day at school. As far as the accident is concerned, all she did was cause the window to open twice and close once on its own; it was fun making that mean girl mad, and all that happened afterwards was not her doing.

There were other, smaller incidents that motivated Rita's parents to remove her from public education and home school her. They understood 'special abilities'; that so-called 'gift' had cursed their family from one generation to another for many centuries. Only one child from each generation of the family inherited the abilities. Rita never married and chose not to have children; she viewed the abilities as a family curse. Her older brother married, though, and had one child, her nephew, who was coming to visit today. He was the last of the line to inherit the curse and wanted no children. He was 51, and his abilities would end with his passing. The thing is, he knows little about his powers and the time has come for him to know who he is.

He was almost to Ft. Worth and pulled into a small service station that was one of his favorite places to stop for gas. He parked next to one of the pumps and went in to grab a bottle of water and pay upfront for the gas, which is normal these days because some people fill up and drive away without paying. Now, the clerks control the pumps from the inside, and you have to pay first before pumping gas. It's a sad commentary on our society, but it is what it is, and paying upfront eliminates the drive-aways.

As he went through the door, something seemed odd; there were about five customers in the store, and none of them were moving. They were just standing next to each other.

A young man in a ski-mask was behind the counter, cleaning out the cash register and putting the money in a backpack hanging from his shoulder. Another man was busy grabbing tobacco products and putting them in a plastic garbage bag. There were three men, all wearing hoodies and ski-masks. The 3rd man was holding a gun on the customers and immediately pointed it at the intruder as he entered the store.

"Well, well, I seem to be in the right place at the wrong time," he said, casually. "Don't you just hate it when that happens?"

"You best not try anything stupid, motherfucker, or I'll cap your white ass where you stand!" ordered a voice behind him.

"Why would you want to do that?" he said, "I'm only here for a bottle of water and some gas." He looked at the big man with the gun and advised, "Come on, dumbo, put that gun down; you don't want to shoot anyone." Then said loudly to the thief behind the counter, "Hey, homie!" The young man stopped what he was doing. "Yeah you, dingbat! Turn on pump two; I need ten gallons of gas. I'm paying cash and in a hurry."

The masked man at the cash register glanced at the intruder, obviously irritated by the man's easy and disrespectful manner, smiled an evil grin and ordered, "Jingles, put that muthafucker down and take his money; he ain't gonna need no money or gas no mo."

He pointed directly at the man behind the counter and calmly said, "You are a bad person, aren't you? Why is that? Were you abused as a child?"

"Jingles!" he hollered, "I tol' ya to cap that fuckin' asshole. Put him down, right now! Boat! Get that tobacco out to the car; we're leaving."

"Sir," he said quietly to the robber, "how do you expect to do that with two flat tires? Why is it you are such a bad person, anyway?"

The man bolted over the counter, looked outside, and saw both tires on the driver's side were flat. He was confused and did not understand what was happening. Something was wrong! He looked at the calm man standing in front of him with a gun at his head, unafraid and staring straight through him. For the first time in his young life, his confidence was draining, and genuine fear crept into his eyes.

"Who the fuck are you?" he stammered.

"Why, son, that is the wrong question. Why didn't you answer me? Have you no manners? I suspect the police are on their way, now, and you will be arrested and in custody soon. I have an appointment and really have to leave. You and your friends wait here for the cops. Tell them the truth."

"Fuck you, muthafucker!" growled the young criminal.

"I'm leaving now. By the way, young feller, it's too bad about your foot, but you know how it is; shit happens." He went outside, got in his car, and drove off.

"Why didn't you shoot that asshole, Jingles?" he demanded and wondered, "What's he mean about my foot?"

"I tried to shoot him, Myron, but couldn't do it," said Jingles, and added, "Hell, I can't even move now!"

"Me neither!" exclaimed Boat.

All three masked men were frozen in place, holding their guns. The customers had run to the back of the store while the robbers were focused on him and were huddled there, not moving because the gunmen were still armed. Myron was holding his gun down by his side, Jingles was pointing his gun where the calm man had been standing before he left, and Boat was pointing his at the entrance.

In less than a minute, three police cars roared up with lights flashing and sirens blaring. Six officers spread out and quickly approached the door with weapons drawn; they saw the armed men in the store, and ordered them to drop their weapons. Myron's reflexes caused him to fire his weapon and shoot himself in the foot. Boat and Jingles nervously fired their guns without thinking and the police returned fire. All three robbers died that day. So did the store manager. Myron had murdered him earlier. There were no other casualties. All three thieves were young and under 20 years old. Two were brothers, and the other was a cousin.

The witnesses all told the police about another man who escaped in a car before they arrived. The police thought he might have been a fourth robber who got cold feet, changed his mind, and left, but the witnesses all agreed that he was a customer wanting a bottle of water and 10 gallons of gasoline.

After leaving the store, he thought to himself, "These abilities of mine are great! I was in total control back there and broke up a robbery in process." He chuckled and said out loud, "I wonder how young Myron feels about his foot about now? He shouldn't be pointing a loaded gun, with the hammer back, at his foot; now, that is dangerous." He laughed as he thought about it. "Those boys were young and mean. I hope the time they spend in prison helps them to become better men. Thank God no one else was hurt." he said under his breath and pulled into another gas station, filled up his car, got a bottle of water and continued on to visit his aunt.

Aunt Rita lives by herself in a two-bedroom house in a rural area outside of Ft. Worth. Someone must be mowing and trimming her yard for her because it looked really great. I drove up the driveway under a carport and parked. It was eleven o'clock on the dot, and I was trying to decide whether to tell her about my little adventure or keep it to myself when she opened the side door of the house and motioned for me to come on in. I walked in, and she put her arms around me and hugged me like we hadn't seen each other in years. I love my Aunt Rita; she always makes me feel special.

"I'm so happy to see you, boy; you look really good. You're going to stay overnight, aren't you?"

"I was kinda hoping you would ask so I wouldn't have to beg; I brought a change of clothes just in case."

"Aw, hush now," she said, "you know you're always welcome here. I just finished making a batch of tuna fish sandwiches for lunch; I recollect how you like them, and there's iced tea in the fridge."

"I sure do, and that iced tea is like frosting on a cake," I said, and retrieved the tea from the fridge, sat down at the table, and ate two sandwiches before saying anything else.

She came to the table and watched me steadily wolf down the sandwiches before asking, "What has been going on with you, boy? Something is on your mind. Tell me."

Aunt Rita is not one to beat around the bush for long. She sensed I had a good reason for coming to see her and wanted to get right to it.

"Aunt Rita, I want to know more about my special abilities. All my life has been spent hiding and keeping them unknown from everyone, and I'm real curious about what they are and how to use them. I am retired now, 51 years old, and want to do something worthwhile with the life I have left. My thinking is that my abilities allow me to be of help to people, and feel my purpose for being is more than tending a garden, taking cruises, or watching television for the rest of my life. I believe you can help me learn more about what these abilities allow me to do."

"You have been experimenting with them, haven't you? It's only natural that you would; I'm surprised you haven't done so before."

"Yes, I have." I replied and told her about the encounter with the police officer and the robbers at the service station.

"Did anyone see you use your abilities?" she asked, eager for an answer.

"No. The police officer didn't know what to think about his empty gun, and those three young robbers could not figure out what was happening to them. I left them standing in place for the police to arrest; they're probably in jail now."

"Tell me something, how did you feel during and after those incidents?" she asked.

"I actually felt great Auntie! I never felt in danger and was in total charge of each situation."

"I'm sure you did and were," she smiled and said. "I know that feeling well and understand the addiction of being in charge. The truth is, though, I cannot advise you about your special abilities, nephew, because yours are much different from mine. You will have to learn how to use them yourself."

"But Aunt Rita," he protested, "I'm not confident how and when to use my abilities. I want to use them to help people, but want to avoid hurting anyone in the process."

"The thing is boy, most people in a bad situation brought the problem upon themselves; they earned it, and you cannot tell what is what. Believe me, I know; I have been there. A fine line exists between the two concepts of helping and hurting; great care must be taken when deciding on one or the other, since you cannot know what the full consequences of your actions will be. Most of the time the best decision as to what should be done to help or hurt anyone is **nothing**. Observe, but do nothing; however, doing nothing does not seem to be your intent."

"Up to this point," she reminded, "you have lived your life as a type of public recluse, going to work, being a good citizen, avoiding serious trouble, and fulfilling your obligations, all the while flying under the public radar, being, for all practical purposes, invisible. You have successfully kept your abilities carefully wrapped and unopened. Now, you are beginning to unwrap them, not just to see and evaluate, but to use them. To your credit, your motives are moral, as you are a good man. The problem, if there is one, is your ignorance, which can be cured only through experience, and therein lies the danger. Much damage to people and property will occur in your quest for this experience. Allow me to give you an example."

"Imagine the proverbial bull who wanders into an antique store of fine art and furniture; he has never been there before, and understands nothing of rare, fine china and other fragile and valuable items. He is only walking through the store out of curiosity, unaware of the consequences of his actions. As he looks around, his horns knock valuable items off shelves, and his great size and strength overturns glass display cabinets and scatters their broken contents on the floor. Upon seeing all the damage he has caused; the bull wants to get to the front door and back outside again. But the store owners are afraid of the bull and upset at the mess he is making, so they attack him with brooms, screaming at him and waving their hands and arms, trying to scare him into leaving. However, their actions have the opposite effect; the bull, feeling threatened, assumes a defensive attitude, bringing his size, strength, and destructive power to full force, causing chaos and obliteration of the store. The bull then leaves to the outside and walks on down the road, never really understanding what all the commotion was about."

"All of that happened, nephew because the bull innocently inserted himself into a place where he was unwelcome and with which he was unfamiliar, a place where his strength, size, and power could only result in chaos and destruction. You, my darling nephew, are such a bull in the china shop of the world. You can live here, without serious consequences, in only two ways:

1) You must live here as an ordinary human, pretty much like everyone else, unnoticed and invisible, until your passing, or

2) You must live outside of society, in seclusion, perhaps in a cave somewhere, where your abilities will go unrevealed. I hope you realize I am being facetious when I say that."

"Aunt Rita, I am at a type of crossroads here. I believe that my unusual abilities must be kept secret and under control, but I feel that can be done with practice. I have no desire to be a 'bull in a china shop,' hurting people and things because of my ignorance of these abilities; however, neither do I want to live the rest of my life as a man with the ability to help people and wind up doing nothing! Of course, I understand the need to learn how to tell the difference between helping and hurting, but that is where you come in, isn't it? I can benefit from your experience. You can help me to learn those things."

"No, boy, I don't think so. You and I were cursed with different abilities, and I don't really understand yours. But even though I cannot help you to learn how to use yours, I think I can do something better."

"Better?" he questioned. "Now you really have my attention, Aunt Rita. What can you do that is better than helping me to understand how to use my abilities?"

"I can tell you who and what you are," she softly answered. "It is time for you to know."

There was silence in the kitchen. Both were looking, staring at each other. Aunt Rita had a soft type of understanding in her eyes, and he had confusion and questions in his. She silently rose from the chair, went to her bedroom, opened the cedar chest at the foot of her bed, removed a large book from beneath some blankets, brought it to the kitchen, and laid it on the table.

"This is where we begin," she stated and opened the book. "Nephew, we come from a very long line of abilities dating back centuries upon centuries. These abilities appear to be an ancient family inheritance. We no longer know when or even from where they originated. Sometimes, the abilities skip a few generations, but never have there been two from the same generation born with abilities. Your great-grandfather believed that only those worthy of the abilities inherited them, but that never made sense to me. How is it determined that a newborn child is or is not worthy? There is something unique about abilities; they are cumulative. In other words, each new worthy recipient not only receives his or her abilities but also receives the abilities of all those that came before."

"Aunt Rita, are you saying I have . . ."

She interrupted, "Yes, that is exactly what I am saying. You now possess all the abilities, and you are the last heir. I have no children, nor do you. You are the last and ultimate receiver, and your abilities end with you."

"Aunt Rita, do you have . . "

She again interrupted, "No. My possession of the abilities ended when you were 50 years old. You always had your inherited abilities up to that time, and they are powerful, but at age 50, you inherited the rest, the rest being mine. You now have the whole shebang. There is also an ancient poem written in the book." She turned to a page in the book and read the poem.

Neither a destroyer nor a builder shall he abide,

Nor will he unite the masses, nor by strength divide.

Nor will he curse adversity, nor else will he deride.

Expect no interference, one's fate must he decide.

Hymn paused for a moment and responded, "Aunt Rita, I have no idea what that means. You were going to tell me who and what I am; all you have told me is that I have all the abilities."

"Nephew," she said and looked at him intently, "I'm going to have to stop calling you 'boy.' You are Him, the Man. As such, need not be concerned with 'abilities.' You possess Power."

"So, I'm the man with the power," he replied, smiling. "That is who I am. Okay, Aunt Rita, what am I?"

She replied, "The single, most dangerous entity in existence."

Chapter 3 - The Awakening

"Aunt Rita, making the claim that I am the single most dangerous person in existence is a bit dramatic, is it not? I mean, all I want to do is to contribute good to society in my remaining years, and I figured that my abilities would help me achieve that goal. You're making me out to be some kind of superpower, and I'm not. Sure, I have learned to make tires go flat and to make guns irrelevant, but if I had super powers, I would know them, don't you think?"

Aunt Rita was solemn in her response. "You no longer just have abilities, nephew; you have great power, which will soon begin to manifest itself. I experienced similar power for a very long time and understand your skepticism, but the type of power you now have is unprecedented, and because of your ignorance, you are quite dangerous. Your saving grace now is you are unknown, but that will change in an instant when someone finds out about you. The leaders of governments will consider you a threat to their power, which is translated as a 'threat to national security.' They will attack you with great power and, like the bull in the china shop, you will defend yourself. Should that happen, much destruction will result, with the loss of many lives being a consequence."

"Aunt Rita, if you are correct, I have the capacity to hurt people without intention, a responsibility I am unprepared to accept. I'm just a man with special abilities who desires to use them to help people, not hurt them, and here you are saying that governments of the world will consider me their enemy because I help people. Something is wrong with that scenario. This power you claim I have is a responsibility for which I do not seem worthy. Heck, Auntie, I'm basically a regular 'live and let live' guy who pays little attention to world affairs or government politics."

"I understand, nephew, but you must accept the fact you are now the last and greatest of the generations and are the Man with the Power for a reason."

"How do I do that? What do I do now?" he asked.

"Pretty much anything you want to," she answered. "What do you want to do?"

"I'm still trying to process what has happened. With the kind of power you are talking about, I'm almost afraid to move or go anywhere. I have no idea how to use the abilities, much less great power. Do you have any suggestions?"

"Yes," she advised. There are 5 suggested rules to follow."

"Number 1) Build yourself a safe place where only you can go at a moment's notice. The Superman of the comics had great powers and built what he called his Fortress of Solitude as his get-away place. Batman had his Bat Cave. You need a place like that where no one but you can reside. You will need a place to be alone at times. Create it."

"Number 2) Start very slow and do little things for practice. See, listen, and be slow to take action."

"Number 3) Avoid offensive action and avoid being intrusive. Rather, be responsive."

"Number 4) Keep your emotions under control."

"Number 5) Always remember you are human."

"Only five suggestions, huh?" he stated. "I should be able to handle those. Which of the five is most important?"

Rita answered, "Number 5."

"Aunt Rita, do you have any idea if my power is limited? Are there things I cannot do?"

"The only unlimited power is God; you are not God. You cannot undo that which you have done, so be careful what you do. There is something else you should know that my daddy told me."

"Oh yeah? What is that?"

"Daddy told me there is an important secret to the abilities that I needed to discover. I never did."

"So, what did he say?"

"He couldn't tell me because he didn't know for sure but said it had something to do with seeds."

"Seeds? What kind of seeds?"

"He never said. His grandfather told him the secret, but he didn't pay much attention. Daddy didn't inherit the abilities, so it wasn't that important to him. Discover the secret, nephew."

"Yeah. Seeds. Right! No problem there."

"You'll find it, my nephew; you're special."

"Aunt Rita, have I ever told you that I love you?"

"Why yes, nephew, many times."

"I love you. Add that to the others."

"I'm going to stay here for the next few days. My confidence in my ability to properly handle the power is low, and I need some time to adjust and consider the consequences resulting from my use of power. Hurting people without intent bothers me more than can be explained, even more so now that you told me my actions cannot be undone. There is a lot to learn about this power, and I am beginning to understand that using it sparingly may be for the best. The question is, how is that done?"

"You are welcome to stay as long as you like, nephew, but you need to create your own 'Fortress of Solitude.' You are protected wherever you go, but others do not enjoy the same privilege."

He spent two days with his aunt doing nothing except eating and sleeping. No intense practicing the use of powers, no studying or planning his new life, and no worrying. He had pretty much made up his mind to just live as normal as possible, using his powers for small situations that may arise and flying under the radar of attention. Aunt Rita emphasized that great responsibility was the child of great power.

"I have given you all the advice I have," she said as they walked to the side door, "and now you are on your own; the world awaits you. Try to be a careful bull." She laughed and pushed him out the door.

During the drive back to his home in Dallas, his head was full of thoughts about the power, his life, and what to do with the time allotted to him. He was very curious about this power of his and noticed a soft drink can rolling across the highway ahead of his car and thought, "Why not?" The can zipped into the air in front and above his car as he sped below it, chuckling at the simple pleasure of watching a can fly up on its own into the sky. "This flying below the radar thing is gonna be easy," he whispered to himself as he continued down the highway toward home.

As circumstance would have it, physics and gravity, along with the can, combined in a beautiful waltz in the sky above his car for a moment, but the can soon began an elliptical descent to the highway below and fell into the driver's windshield of a minivan going about 75 mph. It was just an empty soft drink can, but its collision with the glass, along with the sound of impact, startled the driver into jerking the steering wheel to the left just enough to cause her car to hit the truck in the left lane. Both vehicles were traveling just above the speed limit, and, at that speed, both skidded, separated, lost control, and flipped over several times. On the other side of the highway, a man saw the accident and hit his brakes, causing the car behind to hit and turn his car into traffic. A seven-vehicle accident resulted in three deaths and multiple injuries to others. All occupants of the original collision perished, resulting in five deaths, including two children.

Little things.

He never saw what happened, even if he had looked back and seen the accident; the thought that the can he willed high into the air was the cause of everything that happened would never have crossed his mind. That is often the way of things in this reality. It is normal for people to do little things all the time, to which they give no attention, that later result in big things they never hear about. It is common in human society, and few understand or even think about that truth.

Chapter 4 – Flying Below the Radar

He had a positive feeling about the plan to keep a low profile regarding his inherited, so-called powers. It just might give him the time necessary for learning what all this means. He wondered if his being the last in a long line of 'abilities' people meant something.

"Was it chance?" he thought, "or destiny? Am I the only one in the world with this 'gift,' or do others exist, as well? What am I supposed to do with it, anyway? All I have now are questions. What was it Aunt Rita advised? Avoid offensive action; try to be defensive and not intrusive. I need to think about that."

He had an idea. Why not go to the courthouse and watch a trial to see legal justice in action? It's early morning, and the thought crossed his mind that he needed to get out in society to see regular people just doing regular things. Opposing lawyers fighting it out in a courtroom might be an interesting way to test his objectivity and patience; also, it might be informative to watch a judge exercise his great powers, so he drove to the courthouse.

He walked into the first courtroom and sat down in the back to watch. The attorneys were in the process of picking the jurors for the trial. It turned out that one of the lawyers was the defendant, is not a lawyer, and is being sued by a woman who is a prominent attorney in Dallas County. Her lawyer is also a very well-known attorney in Dallas. The defendant was a man about age 45 and was definitely out of his element. The judge was irritated at the man defending himself because he did not know what 'voir dire' meant.

"Mr. Stewart!" advised the judge, "You chose to ignore my advice to hire an attorney and decided to act as your own council, which is your right; however, I am not here to teach you the law. You are on your own in my courtroom. Do you understand?"

"Yes, Your Honor," replied Mr. Stewart. "I totally understand and apologize for my ignorance of the term."

The opposing attorney standing next to him leaned over and quietly advised him that voir dire meant to examine the potential jurors. He stated that he would go first if Mr. Stewart did not mind. Mr. Stewart was appreciative of the advice and thanked him.

While watching the process of accepting and rejecting jurors, he was surprised to observe that the opponents in this trial appeared to be good and congenial men. He liked them both. The plaintiff in the trial was a quite attractive woman in her middle thirties. She was quiet, and calmly observing the proceedings. Eventually, the jury was chosen and seated.

The plaintiff, Ms. Vogal, was suing the defendant over a used copier she purchased a month ago. She claimed it was defective when she bought it and was suing for $15,000; the defendant claimed the copier was working fine at her office for several weeks after delivery and that she signed the follow-up documents confirming her total satisfaction. A simple 'she said, he said' civil case, or so it seemed.

Mr. Stewart won the verdict because he was prepared and came across as honest and believable to the jury; she, on the other hand, was not believable and was ordered to pay court costs. As soon as the judge closed the case and dismissed the jury, two law officers arrived and placed Mr. Stewart under arrest for sexual assault. He was devastated and kept asking who made such a claim as they cuffed his hands behind his back. The officers made no effort to answer his questions, treated him badly for asking, and seated him in the jury area while they went to talk with the judge, who was not happy with what happened in his courtroom.

Ms. Vogal walked to Mr. Stewart and took a picture of him with her phone, sitting there handcuffed. She smiled and said, "You should have just paid me the $15,000 I asked for in the first place. Now, you're going to prison for a long time. Are you going to defend yourself in that trial, too? Just plead guilty and make the best deal you can. The district attorney has all the evidence he needs."

Mr. Stewart asked, "Why are you doing this, Janet? You know I never assaulted you!"

"Well, Tony," she smiled, "As I recall, you touched me inside and out, and I got you off in my car."

"Yeah Janet, that's true," Tony replied, "but that is not assault; that is consensual, uh, what's the word? uh. . ."

"Foreplay, Tony, foreplay," she interrupted and smiled, "and it is assault if I say so. Have fun in prison," and she turned to walk away.

As Janet was leaving, Tony said, "Come on, Janet. This doesn't make any sense! Why are you doing this?"

She angrily turned back, glared at him, and said, "I am a well-respected woman and attorney in this city, Tony, and you tossed me away like garbage. No one does that to me; I am not garbage, but you are, now." Then she walked over where the arresting officers were talking with the judge.

He heard the conversation between the two from the back of the room, figuring that hearing from a distance must be one of the powers. Aunt Rita's voice was in his head, saying, "Do not be intrusive." How could he avoid being intrusive? Janet Vogal was committing a crime simply because she felt wronged and wanted revenge, but it was overkill. The punishment did not fit Tony's crime of casting her aside, at least from an objective point of view. Something had to be done.

And something **was** done. It seems that Ms. Vogal put her phone in the seat next to Mr. Stewart after taking his picture and left without retrieving it. It was recording and captured their entire conversation. For whatever reason, it suddenly began loudly playing back their discussion. The courtroom was very quiet except for the phone. The judge walked to the jury area and saw that a phone was the source of the talking. Janet was taken aback for a moment but immediately knew what had occurred. She had left the recording feature of her phone on while talking to Tony, and now her confession was clearly playing for everyone to hear. She ran to the phone to turn it off, but it was too late; the judge stopped her, and they listened to the rest of the recording. It was very damning.

The judge motioned for the arresting officers to release Mr. Stewart and advised him of his right to file defamation charges against Ms. Vogal. The judge sternly advised that Ms. Vogal would also be charged with the crime of filing false charges against Mr. Stewart and there were more than a few other charges that would be looked into as well.

As the judge was talking to Tony and advising the officers, the man in the back stood up, turned, and left the courtroom. No one paid him any attention and never even thought about him. There seemed to be an extra spring in his demeanor as he walked down the steps of the courthouse that day; he felt good about what he achieved and learned a few things, too. There was no intrusion into this case between Mr. Stewart and Ms. Vogal. They each were responsible for their results. All the man in the back of the courtroom did was allow the truth to be heard by manipulating Ms. Vogal's phone.

In one of her rules, his aunt said to avoid being intrusive and taking offensive action. He did that and allowed justice to prevail.

"It is important for me to think about what I want to do before using these powers," he thought to himself. "That way, no one should get hurt as a result of their use. Little steps will pave the way for bigger ones. Little steps and patience." It was patience that would be the bigger challenge.

It was close to noon, and he was hungry because breakfast was not an option that morning; he was too interested in getting to the courthouse and observing the legal system at work. "I'll stop and get something on the way home," he decided.

Decisions. The future of people is shaped by the decisions they make, usually in their own self-interest. Deciding to stop and eat before going home today was just a simple decision triggered by hunger; he was still unaware of his powers, as evidenced by the fact there was no need to stop, as food was at his beck and call. A small place named The Burger House was up ahead, so he parked there, went in and sat down in a booth. He picked up the menu to check it out and decide what to order. Seems like a reasonable and simple decision, does it not? One can never be sure about a decision other than the fact every decision, when followed thru, always has consequences. This one was no different.

The Burger House is a busy, small restaurant that serves a variety of sandwiches but, as the name implies, specializes in hamburgers. The place was full of customers, and he was surprised when he saw the open booth down at the end of the row. The dining area was buzzing with various conversations of people eating and socializing until he sat down and picked up the menu; then, it became rather quiet. He was sitting in the booth with his back to the room, reading the menu, when a voice behind said quietly, "Sir, you are sitting in my booth."

He sat there looking over the menu, ignoring the comment that he assumed was meant for someone else; after all, he couldn't see who was speaking and had no reason to believe someone was speaking to him. It was quiet in the dining room now.

"Mister, are you deaf?" questioned a different voice. "The man told you to get out of his booth! Now move along before I am forced to throw you out!"

Although the commotion going on in the booth behind was interesting, he did not want to get involved and just sat there looking at the menu when a well-dressed man stepped into view at his right and commented, "Now, Frederick, there is no need for threats; the gentleman obviously does not understand what has happened here."

The man then moved into full view and stated, "Sir, you have occupied a booth that is reserved for me; arrangements can be made for you to eat elsewhere in the dining room, and it is necessary that you vacate my booth now.

Two other men moved into view as well and their demeanor indicated they were willing to use force if necessary. They seemed to be bodyguards or enforcers of some type.

He suddenly realized the problem. There was no commotion going on in the booth behind him; the problem was with him and the booth in which he was sitting.

"This might be interesting," he thought to himself, and without looking up from the menu, he said calmly, "No, this booth is satisfactory to me, but you are welcome to join me if you like," and he opened his hand and extended it to the seat on the other side of the table.

He glanced up from the menu for a moment and, looking the obviously important man straight in his eyes, said softly, "I have not ordered yet, so your timing is perfect. I am about to ask for some coffee; how do you take yours?"

The important man was livid; he was not used to being treated as an equal and took it as disrespect. Anger burned in his eyes as he nodded at the two men and said, "Remove this asshole from the restaurant and make him understand he is never to return!"

While sitting there, he realized this was getting out of hand and quickly said, "Wait! Hold on just a minute, guys; it is obvious there has been a terrible misunderstanding!"

"I thought so," said the important man and added, "leave now while you are able to walk; you need to learn respect for your betters."

"I forgot my manners momentarily guys, what I meant to say is, all three of you are welcome to join me for lunch. As you can see, there is plenty of room in the booth, and Mr. Fancypants here probably has a good enough credit rating to pay for whatever we want to eat. What do you say, fellows? How do you guys take your coffee?"

The restaurant was silent, except for some muffled giggles heard and being stifled in the dining area. The three men standing at the end booth were experiencing mixed emotions. Fancypants wanted to strangle him, Frederick wanted to badly hurt him, and William was thinking, "I kinda like this guy."

"Come on, Fancy, sit down; you two men sit down too, and let's all have some burgers." Fancy sat down across from him, but the men remained standing.

William said, "Sir, it is against company policy for us to sit with Mr. Marshall; we are his security team."

"Well then, go do some security stuff, but do it outside; Fancy and I are gonna sit here, talk awhile, and eat. We'll let you know when we're done." The men left the restaurant and went to do some security stuff.

The waitress came over to take their order. "We will have two coffees, please," he said, then glanced at Mr. Marshall and asked, "How about you, Fancy? You want some coffee?" Before Fancy could reply, he laughed and stated, "Aw, I'm just messing with you, man," and laughing again, he said to the waitress, "Thank you, ma'am. That will be all."

Mr. Marshall, unused to being treated so casually, tried to get up and couldn't move. Alarmed and totally confused by his situation, he looked sharply at the fellow across the table and demanded, "Who the hell are you, anyway?"

"I'm just a man trying to learn some respect for my betters," he replied.

Fancy looked directly at him, then looked away and replied softly, "That was an unfortunate comment. I was very angry and forgot myself for a brief moment. I'm sorry about that. Who are you, anyway?"

"I was about to ask you that exact question.".

"I am Forrest Marshall, United States Senator from the great state of Oklahoma," he proudly stated.

"Oklahoma? What are you doing down here in Texas making a lot of stupid noise over a booth in a sandwich shop? Do they actually reserve this booth for you?"

"Yeah, they do. I really like this restaurant and often come here to eat every time I get down this way; they serve the best hamburgers anywhere."

"Why did you come in here acting important, willing to hurt or kill me just because I sat in your booth? Are you so important that you even have a private booth in an obscure sandwich place in Texas?"

"You obviously do not understand the importance of being a U.S. Senator. Being treated like royalty gets in your head over time, and pretty soon, you start acting the part. I wasn't like that in my first term. I have changed since then, and I'm actually not proud of it right now. You know something? I never revealed that to anyone before, and just admitting the truth of it out loud somehow makes me feel … different. Mister, I'm glad I met you today. Sitting with someone and talking is something that just isn't done anymore; it is unusual to find such opportunities like this in my world. Why do you suppose that is?"

"Well, Senator, you live in a political society where being yourself is dangerous, particularly if you are basically a moral and ethical person. You must hide yourself and be what you are expected to be in order to survive there. Still, there is little reason to be mean, though. Why do you need bodyguards? Is your life at risk?"

"The truth is, I'm not sure why the bodyguards are necessary and cannot recall ever being physically threatened. Public figures are probably always at risk in one way or another, but there are times when I wonder if the guards are looking out for my best interests or just watching me."

"Do you need to be watched, Senator?"

"Need often depends upon the criterion which, in the case of high office, is great power or access to it; those in power must always understand they are watched by a greater power."

"Do you like it, Senator? The power."

"Hell, yes! Power is the ultimate high."

"How do you avoid abusing your power, Senator?"

"Well, truth be known, I don't; however, it is more true to say I can't. Using power to get something good accomplished or to keep something bad from happening has consequences that help some people and hurt others. Very often, in hindsight, you realize that doing nothing would have been better than taking action. Possessing power is a serious responsibility because using it is intoxicating and fraught with consequences. The greatest wisdom is knowing when not to use power, and there is very little of that in Washington or government in general."

"Senator, someone once informed me that all wise decisions had something to do with seeds, but they couldn't remember the phrase. Have you heard anything like that?"

"I think you're referring to the old saying that you reap what you sow. In other words, you're gonna grow what you plant, harvest what you grow, and eat what you harvest, so always be aware of what you plant. It may sound self-evident, but you're not going to grow corn by planting watermelon seeds."

"That's it! The answer for which I have been looking. Thanks, Senator."

"Why, you are more than welcome. Of course, that doesn't work in Congress, you know."

"Really? Why not?"

"Because of the way all decisions are made in Congress, none of us so-called public servants really know for sure what seeds are being planted, meaning we also have no idea of what the resulting crop will be. The truth is, no one really cares as long as the public is convinced we are looking after their best interests and the media spins it to make us look good."

"Thank you, Senator Marshall. You have been an interesting and informative lunch companion, so interesting in fact that I forgot to order any food. It's time for me to get on home, but I promise not to occupy your booth in the future."

The Senator laughed and advised, "You can forget about that. I'm canceling that reservation; it was a result of one of those power things we discussed earlier, and I'm not proud of it."

They shook hands and parted as good friends. He thought to himself while walking to the car, "It seems that people are compelled to relax and tell the truth, as they see it when talking with me one on one. That is a power to remember. This Senator from Oklahoma is basically a good man, corrupted a bit by great power, influence, and money, but I suspect he will be different after today, which will likely cost him in the next election. We can't have ethical people of high morals holding public office. No, that just won't do."

Chapter 5 – The Birthday Party

The next two months were spent learning about the powers and practicing self-control. What was it the Senator said? Something about having power and doing nothing was sometimes better than taking action. Those with power must have the wisdom to know when to use it, but more importantly, when not to use it. Sounds easy enough, as long as one understands wisdom and power.

"Doggone it!" he thought, "I almost forgot. Some of my friends are having a birthday dinner party at a local restaurant for Wayne Parsons, a longtime acquaintance of mine whom I have not seen since late last year. Wayne is celebrating his 70th birthday, and I felt obligated to attend. Probably will be fun; we are a group of about twelve who get together 3 or 4 times a year in various local places to socialize and catch up on what everyone has been doing since the last meeting. Having good friends can be inconvenient sometimes, but it is always a blessing."

He got to the restaurant on time and found that most were already there and had a table prepared for the party. Someone had been planning this, probably Wayne's wife, Holly. She was good at doing things like that. He made a trip around the table, greeting everyone, and sat down across from a couple with whom he was not familiar. Their name tags revealed them to be David and Pat Mabry.

"Guess they are visitors to the group," he thought and smiled and nodded to them. Mrs. Mabry seems pleasant, although quiet and reserved. Her husband David, though, is obviously an opposite personality, outgoing and vocal. This is going to be one of those 'patience practices' for me tonight because David has his second drink in his hand and is obnoxious. I don't like him. Might make for an interesting dinner, though.

Well, during the dinner, at his section of the long combination of tables, the conversation was being dominated by none other than

David Mabry. Turned out Mr. Mabry owned a security company and was an expert on the subject of law enforcement. Yes, everyone was bored at his diatribes regarding the current condition of law enforcement in America.

Across the table from David, he was watching the couple with interest while, at the same time, feeding questions to David about law enforcement. David was ecstatic! He was the center of attention and loved it. Of course, most of that end of the table had moved to the other side, and the attention given to David was mostly from Him.

The subject turned to 'courage under fire,' and David jumped on it like the proverbial duck on a June bug. The thing is, he had a problem with cowardice, which he defined as a defect allowing people to let their fears control them. According to David, his wife, Pat, was a prime example of that type of person. He went on about how Pat was afraid of her own shadow and never had the courage to take even the smallest of chances. He was in the process of offering more examples of cowardice, but the man across the table interrupted and asked, "David, of what are you afraid? What are your fears?"

"What?" retorted David. "That sounds like you are accusing me of being afraid of something. You might want to rethink that!" he advised belligerently.

"Not really accusations, David," said the man. "It is obvious you have fears. Many things exist that frighten you. What are some of them? I am interested to know."

David was indignant. "Mister, I'm not afraid of anything or anyone, and you better be careful how you talk to me, or I'll show you what real fear is, and you won't like it!" David was in his late 30s, well-conditioned, and projected a menacing image of a tough man, not someone to mess with.

David's voice was rising now, and an embarrassing silence had set in around the dining table. People generally dislike being around public confrontations, and this one had so evolved.

The Man paid no attention to David's posturing and stated, "Mr. Mabry, men who are not afraid of anything have no reason to say it. You do not just say it; you yell it. Are you that ashamed of being afraid?"

"That does it!" David said angrily. He stood up from his chair, got dizzy, and slumped back down in a type of drunken stupor.

His wife leaned over and spoke his name several times, getting no response but soft, low grunts from David. She quickly explained, "He does this on occasion, you know, he tends to drink too much sometimes and passes out, but he'll be alright. I'm very sorry we ruined your celebration."

The man across the table stood up, walked around to the other side, and said, "Everyone get on with the birthday celebration, and don't worry about David; I'll look after him to see he doesn't fall out of the chair. Someone bring us a couple of cups of black coffee."

"Hello, David." said the man quietly. "I know you are not passed out because you really didn't drink that much; however, you are paralyzed." David's eyes flew open immediately. "And you are going to stay that way if we are unable come to an agreement on your future behavior. Before we continue, you must know what will happen if you break the agreement."

In his mind, David immediately went into cardiac arrest; he felt he was having a massive heart attack and was dying. His eyes opened wide, his throat closed, and inside his panicked mind, he was screaming in fear! Suddenly, it stopped. He was back to just being paralyzed, and tears were flowing down his cheeks.

"Everyone has choices, David. You now have three."

1. "You have a choice to live your life as an invalid, paralyzed, never moving, never speaking, and being fed by a nurse who also changes your diapers."

2. "You can choose a life where you respect people, especially your wife, Pat, for whom you will care and provide. She deserves a better husband than you have been."

3. "You can choose to just die, rather than change."

"This is the promise, and it is binding: You promise to never communicate anything concerning me or what happened to you tonight. A moment ago, you had a taste of genuine fear and now have an understanding of what fear is. Be more tolerant of people, David; many live with fears of which you are not aware. You are strong and your criticism hurts people. Do not be a man who hurts people.

By making one of the 3 choices, you confirm the promise. Attempt to break it, and you revert to what you now are, an invalid. This is as serious as a massive heart attack, David. Blink your choice: 1, 2, or 3. Now!" David blinked twice.

Everyone was singing the birthday song, and when the candles were blown out, the cake was cut, and Pat returned with coffee and cake for both men.

David was slowly regaining his senses. "He's going to be okay, Pat; the alcohol, along with the anger, overwhelmed him a bit. David should work at managing his temper, though; it might cause a stroke one day."

"I know," she replied. "He has always been a highly charged man, but I love him and know he has a good heart. Sometimes, his pride just gets the best of him."

He looked directly into David's eyes and commented, "Maybe this will serve as a 'wake-up call' for him. What do you think, David?"

"I think never seeing you again will be a blessing," he retorted and said to Pat. "Come on, honey; let's stop on the way home and get an ice cream cone. I know how much you like them; I like 'em too," and they left without saying anything to anyone, but Pat waved.

He thought, "I guess that means David and I are never going to be friends."

He never heard from David again. Pat talked with Holly a few months later and reported that David was a changed man. He was more considerate to people and treated her "better than he treats his car, and that man loves his car," she was reported to have said.

Chapter 6 - Randolph Barton

At an obscure office in a Maryland city about which no one talks because very few know of its existence, an Information Specialist detects a series of unreasonable incidents occurring in the Dallas/Ft. Worth areas that are outside the limits of standard probability. It is not unusual for this to surface occasionally, but these incidents are striking because of their similarity to a set of incidents in 1973 from which 47 deaths resulted. The incidents were partially investigated but never resulted in solid information because the lead investigator lost her life in a boating accident on Lake Tawakoni, east of Dallas, before filing her report. The investigation closed afterward, but among notes found in her home was a reference to a threat concerning the national security of the World that will reach its peak in 50 years if left unchecked. No specifics concerning the threat were ever uncovered, but it is interesting to note that this office was created soon after her death.

The full report eventually made its way to the desk of a Mr. Randolph Barton, who read it and immediately made a call from a very secure phone. The connection was verified, and he said with controlled excitement, "We have an Ability Notice, sir."

"Come on Randy, we have had these before to no avail; why the urgency now? This line is for extreme ability notices. What makes this one extreme?"

"Two things, sir: One is the similarity to those observed in 1973, and two, 2023 is the fiftieth year, the 'peak' year, or the prophesied year of the Abilities, whatever the hell they are. The prophecy refers to the 'end of times', though."

"Hold on now, Randy, we have to be careful here. I know enough about the history of this crazy phenomenon of abilities to realize that some things are better left alone, and unless you are talking about a threat to national security, I am unsure whether to let this alone or request a general order to eliminate it. Truthfully, Randy, we know little about these abilities and even less about who or what has them. It does seem a bit extreme to say they could bring about the end of the world, though."

"I totally understand, sir. Like you, I am quite informed of the legends regarding the 'abilities'; they are among the greatest of mysteries yet to be solved. Up to this time, they have never shown themselves to be any threat to our National Security; however, one of the recent notices involved a U.S. Senator, and, as has been previously mentioned, this is the 50th year. What shall we do? Leave it alone, or take action. It is your call, sir."

"A Senator, huh? I wonder if he has been briefed? Probably not, or I would have heard about it. Maybe there is a third option, Randy. What about sending in a team to observe and report? We need to know more about who or what has the 'abilities' anyway. Do we not? I need to be more informed before making any decisions of this magnitude and certainly prior to taking it upstairs."

"Yes, sir, I understand." Randy was considering the various potential outcomes of such an investigation and asked, "What if extraterrestrial type activity is discovered? Just asking."

"As far as our department is concerned, alien involvement is preferred, because extraterrestrial activity is not our problem. In that case we will hand everything over to the UFO people and go our merry way. In any event, what interests us is para-psychological in nature and, more than likely, will be found to be of human origin. And Randy, if your suspicions prove to be correct, abilities may be far more dangerous than aliens. Be very careful not to engage; what we need now is information, because we have no idea what we are dealing with. Perhaps your observation team should include a high-level eliminator, just in case. Of course, that is your call, but think about it. I still think we are probably overreacting, but as you pointed out, this is the 50th year. That alone is a reason to investigate. Be sure to keep me updated when new information is acquired and have that recent Ability Notice sent here within the hour."

"Yes, sir. I will begin putting the team together immediately. The Ability Notice is being sent now."

Randolph Barton disconnected the call and was totally unsure of what to do next. "Dallas-Ft. Worth!" he thought. "I wonder if the team is authorized a helicopter and a limousine?"

Mr. Barton figured he needed four field operatives, including an eliminator. He didn't like using eliminators because they are highly trained assassins and were unknowns who operated outside the team; however, they had value, and this may be a dangerous outing. The other three operatives will be expert "diggers," so-called 'special investigators' who were actually information detectives with an understanding of, and access to, technology only a few people even know exists. They are the ultimate diggers of information.

Mr. Randolph Barton, though, was an administrator and had little understanding of the technical aspects of the 'Search and Find' section of his department, nor had he any interest in that area; he was a highly certified psychologist with expertise in a different science. A PhD diploma, framed ceremoniously, had a home at the bottom of a drawer in his desk, lying face down underneath a row of files. Being referred to as 'Dr. Barton' was something to which he never aspired and mostly avoided; the truth being, except for those closest to him, of which there were few, no one knew of his Doctorate in psychology.

Randy, a nickname for which he did not care, was 41 years old, a happy man, and successful by most standards, but had no significant achievements outside of college other than becoming the head of a small government department. He did have something no one else had, though, that being a total fascination of the legendary phenomenon, "Abilities," which he considered to be more important than anything that exists or has ever existed and was perhaps the most informed person on earth in their regard. Interestingly, all that is known of Abilities is captured in mystery and legend; concrete evidence has yet to be discovered. What Randy found to be incredible, though, was the odd lack of interest in Abilities by people everywhere, including colleagues he has known for years, many of whom refused to even exhibit an interest in discussing the subject. And now, he is a somewhat unknown head of an obscure government department located in an insignificant building in a small city in Maryland where he, along with his wife and four children, live as well-liked and respected members of society. Randy is a regular guy who, although happy, believes he has a greater purpose in life and feels he has somehow come up short.

And here he is now, on the verge of beginning a search for the solution to perhaps the greatest unknown mystery of mankind. "How fitting," he thought, "an unknown man on the trail of what may possibly be the greatest unknown mystery ever, with a chance of solving it." An excitement never felt before began rising within him, creating a burning desire to get the search underway.

Mr. Barton had no idea of what he was about to encounter; of course, that is no reflection on him, as neither did anyone else.

Chapter 7 - They

His last few weeks were interesting, but there was something missing, and a visit with Aunt Rita seemed like a good idea, so he called to make sure it was okay with her and drove over to Ft. Worth to stay a few days. As always, Aunt Rita was happy to see him and had a good meal waiting; that was just her style. She had another 'style,' which was getting straight to the point of whatever she thought the 'point' was, and the 'point' today was him.

"What's been happening with you, nephew? Here you have all those powers that would make kings and presidents drool on themselves, and you're not the least bit excited. What is going on with you, anyway?"

"That's just it, Aunt Rita. There is no real excitement in having great powers, but there **is** satisfaction in using them. It worries me that I might not use them in the correct way and do something terrible that cannot be undone. I never used to be very concerned about anything I did, and now I'm concerned about everything I do. I have never been so unsure of myself; something is missing, and that is where you come in."

"You are right on, nephew! Something is missing, and yes, I know what it is; but that is not important now. You have not done a very good job of 'flying under the radar' in the last few months, and they are going to come after you because of it."

"They?"

"Yes, 'They,' and you will be easy to find," she advised. "Don't bother looking them up; they are not listed anywhere. I know that because I have looked. Did you build a fortress of solitude like we discussed?"

"No. The truth is, I'm not real sure how to build such a place or where to build it."

"Nephew! Such a place will exist when you think it into existence! 'Where', is not an issue. The bottom of the Atlantic Ocean, Mars, and the Taj Mahal are at your disposal! You really must try to understand that of which you are capable. It is important for you to have a 'Keep Away' place to where only you can go when you are tired or emotionally upset and want to just get away and think without consequences, kinda like you are doing now."

"That is exactly what I am saying, Aunt Rita. Apparently, there are a lot of things in regard to these powers of which I am unaware."

"That is to be expected, my darling, and that is the best reason for a 'Keep Away' place of your own where you can learn about the powers without consequences. You need it, so do it."

"Who are the 'They' that will come after me, Aunt Rita? Is a Keep Away place necessary to protect me from them?"

"The 'They' to which I refer are the powers and forces of the world, Nephew, and make no mistake about it; they are very powerful and capable of great destruction when challenged. Their strength lies in the commitment of their leaders to protect their power without any regard to morals, ethics, or humanity, and the loss of life is a secondary consideration to the loss of power, which they will protect at all costs. They only fear that over which they have little or no control. That is, you; however, they do not yet know for sure if, who, what, or where you are. There is not much more to tell."

"By the way, you have misunderstood my insistence on a Keep Away place, my nephew. Such a place is not necessary to protect you from the world; rather, it is needed to protect the world from you. You are too moral and ethical a man to be an offensive force, but defensively? Well, let's just say our world has yet to see such as that."

"Aunt Rita, why will they not just leave me alone? The politics of the world are not a concern of mine. How leaders manage their countries has never been, and is not now, of interest. Anyway, I am in my fifties and only just beginning to learn who or what I am. It has become obvious that these unknown powers of mine are dangerous, but they are also very beneficial, and I am not a threat to anyone; never would I use my power against the nations or people of the world. Killing or harming people is against my personal beliefs."

"They are not going to leave you alone, nephew, because they are ignorant, which is not totally their fault. You may not see yourself as a threat, but you are quite dangerous. Nothing like you has ever existed. They cannot even imagine you. To them, you are just a freak with abilities who may be a threat to their power and, if found to be so, will be summarily eliminated. By the time they realize what they are up against, they will have gone too far, and it may be too late for the world."

"I am confident you will find a solution to your enigma, nephew. Always remember you have a reason for being and that a greater power than you exists. For some reason beyond my imagination, the world now requires your presence. Stay your course and your values. People and nations pretty much always get that for which they ask, and they almost always ask for that which they believe to be in their best interests. That is their right; take care not to interfere in that truth. Always allow people to make their own decisions, whether you believe them to be right or wrong; in that way, the consequences are their sole responsibility, not yours."

As his Aunt was talking, he was thinking, "Just what is it that I am, anyway? She is convinced I am some sort of superhuman with powers against which nations cannot stand. Saying that nothing like me has ever existed sounds over-dramatic and way out of the believable range. Where is she coming from with these comments?"

"Aunt Rita, I have to say . . ."

She interrupted, saying, "I know what I have been telling you is too much to wrap your mind around right now, but there is little time for you to learn on your own all that is necessary for you to know about your powers. Listen, nephew, those coming for you are not bad people; mostly, they are doing what they are paid to do. They are just the first wave, the investigators, and are only gathering information to send to their superiors. If that report signals danger, the next wave will be a collateral-damage creating machine and there will be no going back to the way life is now."

"How do I go about stopping that from happening?" he asked and then questioned, "What would you do?"

"I would create that Keep Away place, go there, and stay there until they got tired of looking for me," she answered. "But I'm not sure that is why you were chosen to be the One."

He replied, "Maybe the first wave can be convinced to send a report to their superiors that says no threat exists."

Her response was, "The thing that troubles me, nephew, is the probability that ship has already sailed. There is an old legend saying the abilities will peak in 2023, this year. That will be enough to spur them into action. You are pretty much on your own, so trust yourself and try to follow the rules of power you have been practicing."

Chapter 8 - Keepaway

That night, he thought about all that Aunt Rita talked about, particularly the Keep Away Place, and decided she was right; he needed a place to think and practice his powers without creating harmful consequences. What was it that Aunt Rita said about the Keep Away Place? Something about it existing when I think it into existence and being anywhere I wanted it to be. What exactly do I want my own personal place to be? He found a notebook in his room and began listing the things necessary for such a special place: Keepaway.

1. I want Keepaway to be private, totally invulnerable, and only accessible by me instantly at any time.

2. I want the scenery inside Keepaway to be whatever I want at any particular time.

3. I want to see what is happening outside Keepaway anywhere at any time.

4. I want to practice my powers inside Keepaway, without a noticeable effect anywhere on the outside unless desired by me.

5. I want Keepaway to be entirely undetectable in any way by anyone or anything.

6. I want to be anywhere I want to be upon departing from Keepaway.

7. I also want to be able to communicate instantly with anyone or everyone at any time from Keepaway.

8. I want to be able to use or direct my powers anywhere from Keepaway.

9. I want Keepaway to exist only when I use it and at no other time.

10. I want access in Keepaway to all that is known.

"That's a good start; I can make changes or additions as needed," he thought, and instantly, he was there! He looked around and considered adding something. "How about a private beachfront in the Bahamas," he whispered, and suddenly, he was walking on a beautiful beach. "Wow! Having this power could spoil a man," he said to himself. "Maybe Aunt Rita was right; I could stay here and let those government people do whatever it is they do." He spent the rest of the night there, slept late, took a long walk on the beach with his mind full of ideas, and then stepped from Keepaway into his room and headed to the kitchen to see his aunt.

"There you are! Where have you been, nephew? Been looking for you all morning long and thought maybe you left without saying anything."

"I spent the night in Keepaway and went for a nice walk on a beach this morning, trying to sort things out. Almost decided to stay."

"Keepaway? Beach? Stay? What in the . . .you did it, didn't you? The Fortress of Solitude. You built yours. What in the world got into you all of a sudden?"

"Well, Auntie, you convinced me with all those prophecies yesterday. The idea of a Keepaway Place started making sense to me, so I just sat down with a pen and paper and wrote one into existence. Should have followed your advice the first time you mentioned it."

"So, you gave some thought to staying there for a while, did you? What changed your mind?"

"What was it you said a while back? Everything happens for a reason. I'm not sure about that. Maybe all that is here is the result of nothing more than random chance. I actually have never had a serious thought about life in all my 51 years of living. Now, I'm wondering about everything, and the answers are not likely to be found if I am hiding in Keepaway. Why is it these powers do not include answers, Aunt Rita?"

"I suspect a better question is, how is it the powers do all they do?" she answered. "Because that is the question that applies to you. I'm curious, nephew, what is it that you believe?"

"You mean about religion, God, Jesus, Nirvana, and all that?"

"Yes," she answered. "And all that. What do you believe?"

"I have given those things little attention in my life, Auntie. I am convinced that high morals, ethics, and kindness account for good people; I like good people and don't like the bad ones. That's about it, as far as my religion goes, Auntie."

"How can you tell the difference between them, my nephew? The good and the bad?" she asked softly.

"I can't, and that is my point. You can't tell the difference between people. As to whether they are religious or atheist, it makes no difference; they are still people. Some are good, some are bad, and I can't tell the difference between them. That is my dilemma. Got any suggestions?"

"You don't need suggestions from anyone, nephew; you are a good man. Just be that."

"I wish I had the confidence in me that you have," he replied. "I'm going to head on back to Dallas; I have a lawn to mow. Thanks, Auntie, I love you." He walked to his car, got in, waved, and drove away.

Rita smiled, waved back, and said to no one in particular, "A lawn to mow. Would you listen to that! My nephew is going to mow his lawn, something he can do with a thought. That man has yet to know who he is. I hope they don't push him too hard before he learns. . . for their sake."

Over the next few weeks, Keepaway became like an addiction in that while there, everything he wanted or thought he needed was provided. He could do whatever, without being concerned about consequences; however, one thing was a concern, which was the addiction to the genuine pleasure of just being there. The understanding that everything in Keepaway was an illusion did not matter; it crossed his mind that what he considered the real world may also be an illusion, one that seemed real only because he was inside it. He created Keepaway and knew it to be an illusion, but could it be that his creation was an illusion within an illusion? Or even an illusion within an illusion within an illusion and on and on?

The thought occurred that Keepaway was the heaven to which everyone aspired, and it was his. Had he created his own heaven? Why not? Virtually everything there contributed to his happiness. As far as he knew, that which he desired of heaven was in Keepaway. All, that is, except answers. Why was it that he was given the powers? What was the purpose? To create a wonderful heaven in which to live? Not hardly. Those questions and more are what kept him solidly grounded in the world outside. Keepaway was similar to a great and wonderful amusement park, where people visit to get away from the drudgery and pressures of everyday life for a-while. A place to recharge for a return to the obligations of their existence. He was unsure exactly what his obligations were, but he felt them and intended to fulfill them. Keepaway was not heaven, if there is such a place, but it is certainly a wonderful, safe place to rest, visit, and recharge when the outer world becomes a bit overwhelming.

Chapter 9 – The Eliminator

Randolph Barton was standing behind his desk, staring out the window of his office, wondering if, when, and where the source of the abilities would be found. His new office was located in Grapevine, Texas, strategically located between Dallas and Ft. Worth and close to DFW Airport. He and his team of three had been in Texas a month, chasing clues that led nowhere. There was a fourth member of the team he had yet to meet, which was expected and even normal because, as previously noted, eliminators were independent and preferred to remain anonymous. Randolph was suspicious; the one assigned to him was a team member who reported to a higher authority, something of which he was not comfortable, but could do nothing about. The chain of command in government is held together by very powerful links.

The call came through on his cell phone as he was about to call his wife in Maryland to get updated on family life there and inform her of his intentions to come home for the weekend. Just as well because that was not destined to happen.

Randolph pressed the button and said, "Barton here." Before he completed the 'here,' a voice said, "Mr. Barton, we found Him."

"Him?" he said, the excitement rising in his chest. He sat in his chair and questioned, "It's a 'him,' is it?"

"Yes, sir, and it is confirmed."

"Do you have any reason to believe him to be aware of our presence or knowledge of him?"

"None, sir. We have him under surveillance, and his car is compromised with audio and location."

"Give me the particulars on him."

"He is Caucasian, 51 years of age, 6 foot 1, 185 lbs. ex-military (Medical Corps), college graduate (Business Adm.), never married, no kids, and retired from a bottling plant where he rose to high management level."

"Where is he now?" Mr. Barton asked.

"He is just now leaving his residence, sir. He has a favorite restaurant and is possibly driving there now for lunch. It's a small, popular restaurant called 'The Burger House,' not far from your location."

"Send me the directions. I am leaving here as we speak. Contact me if there are changes as to his destination. I don't know if you have time, but audio and video at that burger joint are essential. Has any word come in about the eliminator? I want contact with him and need to know his current location."

"Roger that, sir. The restaurant's location has now been added to your vehicle's GPS, and surveillance at the restaurant was completed earlier. The eliminator reported that he is in the area, but we have no location on him, nor do we have contact information. He is off our radar."

"Mr. Barton replied, "I am wired for audio and video; make sure I am monitored, and find that damn eliminator! I don't know from whom he gets his orders, but it's not me, and my trust there is beyond non-existent."

"Yes, sir!" was the answer.

Ever since the meeting with that Senator from Oklahoma, The Burger House has been his favorite eating place. He goes there three or four times a week and has formed friendships with the employees and some of the regular customers there. The atmosphere is laid back but regulated; no rowdy behavior or language is tolerated, and, as a matter of fact, the restaurant is quite popular with various law enforcement personnel, which creates an almost constant presence of on and off-duty police officers. As a result, it is one of the safest public places in Texas.

While driving to The Burger House, something about his car kept nagging him. He looked at the gauges and saw nothing; there was plenty of gas, and the temperature was good, but he still had the uneasy feeling that something was wrong with the car. So, he imagined the 'something' gone, and immediately, it was gone. "These powers are so handy," he thought, "but I can't help feeling a bit guilty about using them on such small problems." All his life, he was used to taking care of his own problems by himself, and using his powers to eliminate a car problem somehow seemed like cheating.

"Mr. Barton, are you on?"

"Yes, I'm on. What you got?"

"We have lost all contact with the subject's car and no idea of its exact location, but the burger place still seems likely, based upon the latest figures and estimates."

"Are we still confident he is not aware of our presence?" asked Barton.

"Yes, sir. There is no evidence he is aware."

"Good! I am continuing to the burger joint. Keep me up to date on his whereabouts as you determine them."

"Roger that, sir."

Randolph Barton could not help feeling that his subject knew about his team. The abilities that man has in his possession are almost entirely unknown by anyone, if government officials are being truthful. Barton's trust level of government superiors was low right now. He must find out by himself and make the most accurate report possible. Talking with the Abilities Man seems absolutely necessary, and he is determined to do that today. An unknown kept rattling around in his mind, though. "Where in hell is that eliminator!" he thought.

Being able to fix car problems was filling his mind as he pulled into a 'customers only' parking space and turned off the engine. "I wonder if I can make all kinds of repairs and improvements in vehicles just by thinking them done? I probably can," he chuckled, "but that seems like cheating, too, and not something of interest. Think I'll just let people deal with their own car problems."

He went in and saw that the booth down at the end was open, got the waiter's attention, and pointed at the booth. The waiter smiled and nodded, so he walked over and slid into the booth, his back to the dining area.

The waiter came over, gave him a menu, and asked what he would like to drink. He replied, "Just bring me a coffee and two biscuits now, Daniel; I'll order something to eat later."

"Right on, sir." said Daniel, smiling, and added, "I'll be right back with your order."

He couldn't help but laugh. That young man always seemed to be smiling or laughing and 'cutting up' with his customers. He was a natural waiter, relaxed, and at home around people.

Daniel returned with the coffee and reported, "I brought you fresh coffee and . . ." (suddenly, a man approached and sat down on the other side of the booth across the table.) Daniel continued, ". . .and hot biscuits will be coming out of the oven in a few." Then he turned and went to another table.

"This should be interesting," he thought as he looked at the visitor across the table and then said, "So, you like coffee and biscuits too. You didn't have to be so rude about it, though; there is plenty to go around."

The intruder was a blond-haired man about 30, less than 6 feet tall, 180 lbs. or less, well-groomed and dressed, and casually looking straight at him. He was just staring, without talking, trying to read the man. After a few seconds, he decided to initiate a conversation with the intruder.

"Something in your eyes says you are not a good man, and your poor manners endorse that deduction. Are you a bad man, Blondie, or just having a 'bad hair day' because of the wind?"

"The intruder flashed a grin and commented, "You, my friend, appear to be a man who does not frighten easily, and I can guarantee you that is about to change. What is coming for you is beyond your imagination; however, you have choices. Well, the truth is, you have two. You are to come with me now, willingly, or you and everyone in this restaurant will perish. You run, and everyone dies; you stay, and everyone dies, and even if you pass out from fright, everyone dies, and there is nothing you can do to stop it except leave peacefully with me. You have five minutes. Choose wisely. I will wait outside."

"You know what, Blondie? I really would like you to meet my aunt. She could tell you some things. We're not leaving. I have hot biscuits coming out of the oven about now and have been looking forward to them for two days. You will understand what I mean when you catch their aroma. The melting butter, along with three different types of jelly, will make you want to come back for more; I guarantee it."

Daniel was on the way with a plate containing two hot biscuits. He set them down, along with the jelly, next to his coffee and asked, "Can I get you anything else, sir?"

"Yeah, Daniel, warm up my cup, and bring a coffee for my visitor. Bring a ticket for him, as well; he likes to pay his own way."

Daniel glanced briefly at Blondie and left to get fresh coffee.

"What do you think, Blondie?" he asked while cutting the biscuits in half and spreading blackberry jam on one of them. "I suspect you are now beginning to regret not ordering some biscuits for yourself. Now, normally, I would share with a visitor, but I don't like you. Order your own biscuits."

Blondie looked at him in disbelief, not understanding the man's calm demeanor regarding the crisis he was facing and angry about being dismissed casually and without respect. He firmly said, "Listen, you sonofa…" but promptly closed his mouth and just sat there quietly, panic beginning to show in his eyes.

He looked directly at Blondie and advised, "You may not talk or move while I am enjoying these wonderful biscuits with jelly. Here comes Daniel with our coffee, so sit very still, be very quiet, and behave yourself."

"Oh, I almost forgot! How much time do we have left? Right! You can't talk. Oh well," he sighed, then closed his eyes and took a bite of his biscuit, obviously savoring the moment. Daniel brought the coffee for the visitor, filled the half-full cup, and left without saying anything. He finished the first biscuit, then stared into Blondie's eyes.

"I see confusion and fear in your eyes now, Blondie, and I suspect you are beginning to understand the reality here." He took a bite of the second biscuit, this time with grape jam, sipped his coffee, and continued. "How was it you put it, 'what is coming is beyond imagination' is what you said. To whose imagination were you referring, Blondie? Yours? Certainly not mine. Tell you what, young man, you have caused a great deal of despair for others in your life with no idea what it means, and you need to understand. Sleep now for a few minutes, and upon waking, tell no one what happened today, or you will sleep again there, forever."

He glanced up, and another well-dressed man was standing and looking down at him. "My name is Randolph Barton, sir, and I very much want to speak with you. I was told that you were alone, but see, you have a companion. It is my desire to talk with you alone. Forgive my manners, but would you mind asking your companion to leave? I have important business that must be attended by the two of us alone."

"Mr. Barton, did someone enter the restaurant with you? In front of, or behind?" He had sensed the presence of someone or something.

"No one that I noticed, sir."

"Barton, I suspect this visitor of mine is unfortunately stuck there for a while; can you put off our visit until tomorrow when a personal meeting can better be arranged?"

Barton replied, "I am afraid not, sir. Right now, just may be the only time we have, and it is quite important that we speak."

A voice came on in Barton's earpiece, "Sir, I hope you are getting this. We have lost all surveillance of the restaurant and can neither see nor hear anything in there."

Barton said, "You are Him, aren't you?" Without any effort to conceal his actions, Mr. Barton removed both his earpiece and camera, then tossed them into a garbage can placed next to the restroom. "I have been urgently wanting to talk with you. So, who is this visitor of yours, and what is wrong with him?"

"In all honesty, Randy, I don't know the man. He is known here as Blondie for obvious reasons, and he overstepped his authority earlier, which is causing him to rethink his future as a government employee. I don't care much for his manners."

Barton looked closely at the napping visitor and then slowly sat down in the booth next to him. He turned his attention to the man across the table and asked, "What was it this man wanted?"

He answered, "Blondie demanded that I leave with him or everyone in this restaurant, including me, would perish in five minutes."

"How long ago was that?" queried Barton nervously.

"I don't know, for sure," the man answered, "I have not been paying any attention to the time. Probably five or six minutes, though. You think maybe his timing was off?"

"Why would he make such a horrible demand?" asked Barton.

"You know something, Randy?" he stated and looked directly into the eyes of Barton, "You know much more about that than I. Do you not?"

Randy looked at Blondie again and admitted, "Yes, I think so. I have never met him, but am quite sure he is employed as an 'eliminator' in certain departments of our government."

"An eliminator? Does it really mean what it means, Randy?"

"Yes, it does. Eliminators are expert snipers, proficient in the use of explosives and many other ways of killing. They are like lone wolves who do the bidding of the government elite and are well-paid for their service. All eliminators are wealthy beyond their needs."

"Why would this one threaten to kill everyone in the restaurant just to eliminate me? The people dining here have no involvement with me other than proximity. Has he no regard for human life, Randy?"

"Sir, people like Blondie are carefully created to follow orders; they are rigidly trained to have no moral compass. Nothing is more important than completing a mission; they totally believe any and all collateral damage resulting from the success of their mission is justified and necessary. Eliminators are human machines and have proven to be useful for governments and major corporations in situations where National Security is at risk."

"Randy, are you insinuating that my government considers me a threat to national security?"

"It seems so, sir. They don't send eliminators for less."

"They, Randy?"

"Those who run the country, sir. They possess great wealth and power with which they manage the country and perhaps the world while assuring that which is in the best interests of the people is maintained."

He thought about the phrase "in the best interests of the people," and asked, "Randy, are you not one of the 'they' who runs things?"

"No, sir. I am a small cog in the machinery that researches and provides information to a superior who reports to his superior. The level of my position in that 'food chain' is unknown to me, but probably somewhere in the middle would be my guess. It is unlikely 'They' even know my name."

"Is it not reasonable to believe that has changed and is undergoing changes as we speak, Randy? You have been in the company of a threat to national security for over ten minutes, a threat that was supposed to have been eliminated a short time ago. Add to that, our conversation is dark and unheard by anyone, and neither you nor their eliminator has reported back. Your profile is very high about now. They not only know your name, but they know the name of everyone in your family, including that of the guppy in your children's fish tank. What do you suppose they are planning at this moment?"

"Sir, I suspect they will come here with great force."

"And I will be elsewhere," he said, and then asked, "Randy, I am interested; what will you tell them?"

"Honestly, sir, at this moment, I have no clue. Do you want to tell them something?"

"Advise the 'they' to let me be," he warned. "Don't worry about Blondie," he said as he got up to leave. "He is waking in fear and will be of no further use to them, nor can he ever communicate anything about you or me without grave consequences. Blondie now has a moral compass. I perceive you to be a good man, Randy, and I look forward to talking with you again." Then he got up from the booth, waved goodbye, walked out to his car, got in, and drove away. No one seemed to notice.

Randolph Barton sat in the booth, confused and wondering what had just happened. Those in the restaurant were eating, talking, and laughing, totally oblivious to the conversation that occurred in the booth down at the end. Daniel came by with fresh coffee, picked up the money on the table left there by 'Him,' and asked, "Will there be anything else, sir?"

Mr. Barton handed him a twenty-dollar bill and said quietly, "No. Thank you, Daniel."

Daniel's face lit up with a big grin at the generous tip. He thanked Mr. Barton for his kindness and walked away a happy young man.

Mr. Barton scolded himself, thinking, "I sat right across from him and did not ask one pertinent question about him, all the while spilling confidential information in answer to his questions without any reservation to holding back anything. The man didn't do anything special with the abilities attributed to him except for disabling the eliminator, but that could be explained by some hypnotic or psychological application. In any event, there is something quite different about that man! I genuinely like and trust him, though, and have no idea why."

Blondie was awake now, silent, with tears running down his face and dripping into his coffee as he quietly sipped it, oblivious to his surroundings. When Mr. Randolph questioned him about what happened and why his threat to kill the man never resulted, all he could say was, "I'm sorry, I cannot talk about it right now." There was genuine emotion and a sense of penitence about Blondie, things that are unheard of and not known to exist among eliminators.

"Blondie!" said Mr. Barton quite sternly, "the Calvary will be here any minute now, so pull yourself together immediately, and prepare for their questions."

"Martin," said Blondie softly, "My name is Martin."

Mr. Barton looked intensely at Blondie a moment and thought, "Something is seriously wrong with this man, but whatever it is, he is no longer an eliminator. I wonder what the abilities man did to him?"

The first five agents to enter were in full body armor, guns ready. Someone ordered everyone inside to calmly exit the restaurant because a bomb threat had been issued. The two men in the booth at the end were the only ones left when four men in suits arrived. One man sat down across the table from Martin and Barton; the other three were security personnel.

He identified himself, "I am Agent Bohannon, gentlemen. What in the hell happened here? What went wrong?"

"I am Randolph Barton. What happened here is this: someone had an agenda not contained in the original plan, an agenda comprised of killing everyone in this restaurant, including me, just to take out one man. Thank God, it failed."

Agent Bohannon countered, "We are not in agreement with that sentiment. This particular man is a security threat to the world if our intelligence is correct, and billions of people may die if he is not stopped. Twenty patrons of a restaurant or billions of innocent people is a no-brainer all the way. You had some time to talk with him, Barton. Did he say anything?"

"The most important thing he said was a warning, of sorts."

"A warning?" questioned Bohannon.

Barton replied, "Yes. He said to advise the 'they' to let him be."

"The they?" he said. 'The They' and nothing else? Who or what was he talking about?" Bohannon demanded.

"Well, Mr. Bohannon, I suspect he was talking about you."

"Me!" Bohannon retorted, "What the hell are **you** talking about?"

"You, Mr. Bohannon. You are a part of the 'they' who are trying to kill him, and all of you have now been warned to let him be. Can you do that?"

Bohannon paused for a moment and replied, "No, Mr. Barton, I cannot. The committee will never agree to that and wouldn't keep the promise if one was made. There is too much power at stake, and I am convinced this abilities man is a threat to the National Security of our country and must be removed."

Barton surmised, "That is quite unfortunate, Mr. Bohannon; however, it is unlikely you have experienced anyone like this abilities man in your lifetime. The real threat to our country's National Security is the ignorance and self-importance of people like those composing the 'committee' you referenced a moment ago. There is something important you should realize, Bohannon; you are actually like the people in this restaurant, earlier: expendable. He saved them, you know. What kind of man does that? Perhaps a man of integrity, a moral man? Maybe he saved you, too. Think about it."

"What I think, Mr. Barton, is you seem to know more about this abilities man than you have been willing to reveal. They will want that information."

"And I will tell them all I know and believe," Randy answered, "but it is my fear their minds are already set on a violent course, and all I understand about him probably pales in comparison to what is actually there. I must say, though, in all sincerity, it is my opinion we should let him be."

Chapter 10 – The Debrief

Martin was quiet and unresponsive during the discussion between Barton and Bohannon. He was being bombarded by thoughts of leaving, making a new life, and never being seen again. All he needed was fourteen minutes of freedom to secure that plan, but since he would be closely guarded until after being debriefed, no such freedom was available. Martin was afraid of the questions he would be asked, and he was afraid of the abilities man.

That biscuit-eating man was different, unlike anyone else. He looked like nothing, a typical loser who sat in that booth drinking coffee and eating biscuits and jelly while his world was about to come down around him, like hell itself. The Burger House was previously wired with explosives because it was abilities man's routine to eat there two to three times a week, and Martin had arranged to be informed whenever he showed up. There was no clear kill shot from outside the restaurant, so the building was wired to explode if the man could not be lured out into the parking lot. Martin's plan was to kill him as he left the building, and he was sure he would choose to go outside rather than have an explosion kill all the people inside. But no, the man had to stay until he finished eating those damn biscuits!

Time was running out because Randolph Barton was on his way there, and Martin had orders to kill the man before Barton arrived. Martin decided to shoot the man right there in the booth and leave before the building exploded because the detonation was now going to happen, come hell or high water, and he had about two minutes to get it done. That is when the worst happened: Martin had a stroke or something that caused temporary paralysis. His silenced gun was in his lap, and he could neither move nor talk; all he could do was sit there and watch the man sip coffee and eat a biscuit while the seconds ticked away to annihilation. Intense fear filled him as the man looked deep into his eyes and said something about his staying somewhere forever; then, he faded into a dark, lonely place of despair. After what seemed to be an eternity, he awoke, able to move, and with tears falling from his eyes. He was sitting in the booth next to Mr. Randolph Barton, sipping coffee and telling Barton his real name.

Two hours later, Martin and Mr. Barton were in separate rooms waiting to be questioned about their encounter with the man they were now referring to as Mr. Abilities.

The discussion with Martin went nowhere because he remembered nothing about his time in the restaurant with Mr. Abilities, except the man really liked biscuits and jelly. He never said anything about the place of despair because he was never asked and would have lied if asked, anyway. All he was sure of was this: he never wanted to go back to that place and would do all it takes to assure he doesn't. He broke into tears several times when asked about Mr. Barton and the explosives he placed in The Burger House and was particularly sensitive about any reference to his plan to kill everyone there, if that's what it took to eliminate Mr. Abilities. Martin apologized many times for not only that but also for the deaths caused by previous missions in which he was involved.

The only important information revealed from Martin's interrogation was this: apparently, talking with Mr. Abilities is a danger to be avoided at all costs, which made the debriefing of Randolph Barton of great interest to the powers that be. They were very interested in what Mr. Barton had to say. Martin was dismissed with the usual paperwork signings, security declarations, and direct orders to be available until all debriefing was concluded.

Martin neither spoke nor looked at anyone as he walked through the long hallway and exited the building. Three taxicabs and a limousine were waiting at the curb, but Martin paid them no attention and walked unhurriedly to the third building across the street to the right, a lady's clothing store, picked totally at random as a place to begin his planned disappearance. He knew he was being watched and needed to get out of sight. Instantly, unknown to Martin, three red dots appeared on the back of his coat as he hesitated briefly to allow two young women to walk past the store in front of him and then proceeded to the entrance door. As the ladies passed, one of them retrieved a gun from her shopping bag, aimed point blank at the back of his head, and pulled the trigger. Unknowingly and summarily, without a thought of looking back, Martin walked into the building and, for all practical purposes, totally disappeared.

It is interesting to note this fact: From the moment Martin walked from the government office building as a free man to the moment he disappeared into the clothing store, fourteen minutes elapsed.

Randolph Barton was comfortably seated in a room awaiting his debriefing and had been waiting for almost two hours. Unknown to him, a group of 16 people were closely observing his every move, which seemed rather superfluous since he was sleeping and had been for most of his time there. Randy was accustomed to being an 'in charge,' Type A sort of man who gave orders and planned the direction of important offices of government. Now, as he napped in a comfortable chair, never has he been more at peace with himself, a peace that was about to be challenged by self-righteous professional people with an agenda.

"Mr. Barton! Wake up! They are ready for you now."

He was jolted out of a restful sleep by a voice coming from a speaker. Sounded feminine, but you can never tell for sure these days. Say something like, "Yes, ma'am" to a female-man or "Yes, sir" to a male-woman, and the next thing you know, your job is on the line. Kinda makes one wonder, "Why?" every once in a while. A rather dangerous question that and one almost never asked of those in authority. "How did we get from what seems like yesterday to today?" he pondered and thought, "Interesting."

A young man appeared and escorted him to the debriefing room, where two women and a man were seated at a table. He pointed to a comfortable chair across from them, where Barton sat down, smiled, and formally introduced himself.

"Hello, I am Randolph Barton," and then asked, "How can I be of assistance to you?"

"We know who you are, Mr. Barton. Our purpose here is to learn as much as possible from your meeting with the 'Mr. Abilities' person. You were alone with him, talking for over ten minutes, and we are interested in knowing about that conversation and your impression of him."

"Actually," Barton corrected, "I was not alone; Martin was present in the seat next to me, with a silenced gun in his lap."

All three of them began busily writing on their tablets.

"He seemed to be in some sort of trance, though, and never talked at all, except to tell me his name." Again, with the writing.

"Listen, everyone, I know everything here is being recorded, both audio and video, so what in the world is going on with all the scribbling? I'm not sure anything of importance has yet been asked or answered, but from the way the three of you are writing, one would think that two sentences about Martin formed the basis for a graduate thesis about eliminators."

"Mr. Barton, I understand you are a man who holds a position of government authority, but allow me to make this absolutely clear: In this room, I am the authority. I ask the questions. You answer my questions. We three are psychologists, specialists at observing and analyzing a subject's physical and emotional responses to questions put to them, something that is better observed in person rather than on video. We write our personal observations as we observe them for later analysis and evaluation. Am I clear as to the protocol to be observed in this room?"

Mr. Barton replied, "Yes, Madam Chairman."

"Dr. Julia will suffice, Mr. Barton. Now, we shall continue."

"What did you and Mr. Abilities talk about, Mr. Barton?" Dr. Julia asked the questions while the other two took notes.

Mr. Barton replied, "Looking back, it seems I did most of the talking, answering his questions. He was interested in why Blondie, I mean Martin, was willing to kill everyone in the restaurant just to eliminate him."

"What did you tell him?"

"I told him Blondie was an eliminator and explained that men like him are sent to deal with threats to National Security, to which he asked if he was considered such a threat, and I answered yes."

"How did he feel about that? Did it surprise him, make him angry or concerned?"

"No, he was non-committal; however, I believe he was more surprised than anything. He is not sure why you want to eliminate him but now believes you are willing to destroy anything or anyone you believe to be a threat to your power."

"Meaning the power of the United States."

"No, ma'am," he answered, "Your power over people."

"Did you get a sense that he is aware of us?"

"Yes, ma'am."

"This is very important, Mr. Barton, so listen closely. Did Mr. Abilities say anything in particular to give the impression he has specific knowledge of our organization, or is he simply just aware of us?"

"Dr. Julia, Mr. Abilities seemed to have little interest in any specifics of your organization other than your immoral and unethical actions. He seemed both disappointed and surprised at your willingness to murder a restaurant full of people just to eliminate him. When I explained that you use your great powers to manage the country, and perhaps the world, in order to assure that which is in the best interest of the people is maintained, all he muttered was, "in the best interest of the people." and then repeated the phrase again. He seemed more interested in what you are and why you are than who you are."

"Do you believe he likes or dislikes us?"

"Dr. Julia, I do not know his feelings. But truthfully, think about this: What is there to like?"

The scribbling intensity reached a higher level, requiring more time between questions.

"Do you sense, in any way, that Mr. Abilities is fearful of us?"

"Truthfully, ma'am, what is there for him to fear?"

"Do you sense, in any way, that he is trustful of us?"

"Truthfully, ma'am, is anyone?"

Dr. Julia looked at Barton intensely, smiled, and observed, "You are very insubordinate, Mr. Barton."

"No, ma'am, not insubordinate. Truthful. Inasmuch as I can be."

"Mr. Barton, how do you personally feel about Mr. Abilities?"

"I like him; however, his existence makes your kind dangerous to the world."

"Why is he not a danger to the world?"

"Because he loves the world and the people in it. You don't. You love power and are quite willing to destroy the world to keep that power intact."

"What did he tell you in our regard?"

"He told me to warn you to let him be. Personally, I believe that to be very good advice."

"Why should we? After all, Mr. Abilities is a declared threat to National Security and a grave danger to the world. He cannot be allowed to just wander around and do as he pleases. No one is above the law."

"Dr. Julia, how many people of Earth are you willing to kill in order to subdue or eliminate him? A billion? 3 billion? 6 billion? What is your limit to murder? You should ask your cohorts to set a limit on just how many must die before they eventually decide to let him be."

"That is not the question, Mr. Barton. The question is, just exactly how many people will Mr. Abilities allow to die before submitting to our demands?"

Randolph Barton pondered her question for a few moments and softly replied, "I'm not sure of that, ma'am; just exactly how many of you are there?" and then advised, "Let – him – be."

The sixteen powerful watchers of the interview were glancing at each other during the back and forth between Barton and Dr. Julia and signaled a halt to the interview. Their chairman then declared an immediate emergency meeting with the Board for the purpose of deciding how to proceed with the Mr. Abilities problem, in view of new information gathered today.

Barton was dismissed with the usual understanding that he could be recalled at any time. As he was leaving, he looked back at the three and asked, "Is it true you know the name of the guppy in my children's fish tank?"

The man answered, "Gulp," and spread his hands out as if to say, "Of course, we do."

Barton shook his head and walked away, laughing.

Previously, when Martin left the debriefing room and signed out to leave, he knew his time was limited, with maybe 20 minutes to live. There is no place in the organization or the world for an ex-eliminator. As he left the building, he noticed several cabs and a limo parked out front, waiting for customers. "No options there," he thought to himself. He was out in the open and desperately needed a place inside and out of sight. He walked across the street and noticed a woman's clothing store three buildings further down. "Perfect," he thought, "I only need a few more minutes, and they will never find me."

A voice in the ear pods observed, "He seems to be headed directly to that clothing store! Take him down before he enters. A cleaning crew is prepared and waiting; if done right and according to plan, no one will notice anything out of the ordinary. This person is a dangerous adversary and must be terminated with prejudice."

Unknown to Martin, three laser markers appeared on the back of his jacket as he reached the front of the store…then disappeared.

"Misfire!" "Misfire!" "Misfire!" It was astonishing! Every one of the three shooters reported weapon problems.

"What the hell is goin…? "Phase 2! Go to Phase 2! Now, dammit!" the voice demanded.

Martin reached the front of the store just as two young ladies walked up. He stood aside, allowing them to pass. As he walked to the entrance, one woman pulled a gun from her shopping bag, pointed it point blank at the back of his head, and pulled the trigger. Misfire!

Martin, never aware of what went on behind him, entered the store and exited a woman's boutique in Paris, France, next to a pastry shoppe. Totally confused, he stood there thinking he had lost his mind when a soft voice to the side said, "Hello Blondie, how do you like your coffee?"

Martin turned quickly to the voice, and what he saw shot instant fear through him, causing his legs to weaken and making him fall forward into the entrance gate of a sidewalk pastry shoppe. He steadied himself, holding to the gate post, and stared, unbelieving, at the man sitting at a table in front of him, drinking coffee and munching on a donut.

"Come on, Blondie, pull up a chair and sit with me a bit. Your coffee and donuts are on order. You didn't think I would leave you alone against the mob, did you?"

Martin staggered to a chair and sat down across from the man, unable to overcome the great fear inside him and speak. All he could think about was the place of despair and that he was about to be sent back there.

The waiter approached, served Martin's coffee and donuts, and warmed up the man's coffee.

"The coffee is pretty darned good here, and the donuts are good too, but I kinda favor the biscuits back at my restaurant in Texas. I ordered your coffee with cream and no sugar. Go ahead, Blondie, give it a go."

Martin couldn't read the man. Why was he doing this? His hand was shaking badly as he reached for the cup and spilled some as he raised it to his lips. "Good lord!" he thought. "This is the best-tasting coffee I have ever had," and proceeded to drink the cup empty.

"Pretty good stuff, huh? Sometimes I come here just for the coffee. Waiter! Refill here." The waiter came immediately and refilled Martin's cup. The man said, "Just leave the pot; it will save you some trips back and forth."

"Oh no, monsieur!" the waiter objected. "I must serve your coffee fresh; it is the only way."

"Okay. I like that," replied the man. "Fresh it is, then. Thank you." Then he glanced at Blondie, noticed a questioning look in his eyes, and commented, "Oh, I helped him out of a jam recently, and now he treats me like royalty. Makes me a little uncomfortable, but what the heck, it's his way of thanking me."

Martin reached to pick up his cup and noticed his trembling was gone, and there was no fear in him; he was perfectly at ease sitting across the table from the man. It was then he realized he had eaten one of his donuts without recalling doing so. He looked up and into the warm, gentle eyes of the man across the table and knew, somehow, he knew there was nothing to fear there. He quietly said to the man, with genuine emotion, "Sir, I am so very sorry."

"Yeah, Blondie, I know. Listen, I'm going to tell you a truth now, a truth you need to accept, but one you can do with as you please. First, no one cares what you have done because what is done is, for all practical purposes, done. Second, no one can forgive you for what you have done; only you can forgive you and the truth is, you may never be able to do that, depending upon who you are, now. Third, you are worth being forgiven, so do that and get on with a life that does not require you to hurt others. You will always remember your past, but do not allow that memory to keep you from forgiving yourself; on the contrary, use that memory to make yourself a better and kinder person. Live to become a better man or kill yourself because of an unforgiven memory. Either way, the choice is yours. I recommend coffee and donuts every once in a while, myself. Now, that's living, particularly when you share with another."

While Martin sat listening to what the man was saying, the grief and despair he had been carrying slowly drained from him. He looked at the man and said, "Thank you. I will remember." Then he asked about the organization.

"You are not their concern, Blondie, I am. I perceive you to be a good man now. Be that. Enjoy Paris, or wherever. Maybe we'll chance to talk again." Then the man stood up, walked directly into the coffee shop, and went somewhere else.

Martin sat there in disbelief, staring at his empty coffee cup, not knowing what next to do, when the waiter walked over and said, "Will there be anything else, monsieur? A refill, perhaps? The bill is paid in full."

"No. I'm about to… you know what? I think I will have another cup of coffee and a donut."

"Right away, monsieur."

"Call me Blondie, my friend."

The waiter smiled and said, "Right away, Blondie."

Back at Dallas Headquarters, in a secure room, four assassins were being debriefed. All four told the same story: Their weapons misfired. An impossible occurrence, but all three rifles and the revolver misfired. The young female operative testified that everything went as planned, with her being the backup if the snipers could not get a clear shot. When the target was still standing as he reached for the door to enter the building, she pulled the weapon from her shopping bag, aimed it point blank at his head, and pulled the trigger, not once, but several times. It was as if her revolver was empty. When she checked later, all six bullets were there, unfired. The interesting thing was that four of the bullets had firing pin marks on the primers, meaning the primers had failed to ignite. The two unfired bullets, when examined later by forensics, fired normally from the same gun.

"What the fuck is going on?" a demanding voice blared from the speaker. "People, what in hell are we dealing with here? I want the history of all four of those weapons along with the dossiers of the four operatives. Get your best people on top of this, and bring me some answers! Now!"

Chapter 11 - A Trip To The Zoo

He had been lounging around in Keepaway, enjoying the solitude and thinking about the government of the United States. How could it have allowed an immoral organization like 'They' to gain such power and control in the world? When did it all happen? And why would anyone agree to work for such an organization? He is convinced there are moral and ethical people in Congress, but where have they been? And where are they now?

The truth is, he didn't care. The questions being asked were useful in that they revealed his ignorance. As far as intelligence goes, the average American male understood more about everything than he did. There was much about which he knew next to nothing. His business training was in the quality field, where he was highly skilled in determining the quality of a product, just about any type of product. He had a knack for understanding the causes of quality problems and explaining them to others. In most other occupational fields, he was basically ignorant and never bothered to care, and still doesn't.

Up to this year, his life seems to have been spent in a cocoon of protection from exposure; a cocoon from which he emerged to both freedom and exposure. Of him, some few are aware enough to be concerned of his intentions; so concerned, in fact, they are willing to sacrifice the lives of many just to remove him. Why, though? Is it possible that someone or something possesses information of which he is not yet aware?

His aunt once advised him to never forget his humanity. He thought to himself, "I may not yet know why I am, but Aunt Rita told me who and what I am months ago; I just never accepted it. I am a human, blessed with powers."

Speaking of my aunt, she called and asked me to come visit, so a brief moment later, I knocked on her door. She opened it, laughed, and said, "What's all this? You give up driving all of a sudden?"

I kissed her and replied, "No, I still enjoy the pleasure of driving, but sometimes I just want to be there, wherever 'there' happens to be, and today, there is here. How are you doing, living out here all by your lonesome?"

"By my lonesome, my rear end!" she replied, harshly, "That is something I want to discuss with you, nephew. I've got more people watching me, listening to me, and ringing my doorbell, asking about you than I ever imagined. You have stirred up a big hornet's nest of activity, boy. I thought you were going to start out by flying under the radar. We are probably being watched and listened to at this very moment. My private life is in the toilet."

"We are not being watched or recorded, Aunt Rita. Those devices don't seem to work around me. The thing is, Auntie, I **have** started slow. Someone or a group knows more about me than we realized. They are aware of the legend about super abilities reaching a peak in 2023 and are preparing to go all out to eliminate the person having them. For some reason, they have zeroed in on me as that person. The thing is, they only know about abilities. Their reference name for me is Mr. Abilities, and they are in a top-level meeting at this moment, trying to decide whether to kill me or leave me alone. Although keenly aware of what they believe to be my special abilities, they have something which gives them great confidence in their ability to deal with me. Can you believe they consider me a threat to National Security?"

Aunt Rita was pensive, "Nephew, have you ever been to a zoo?"

"What?" He was caught off guard and surprised by her 'out of the blue' question, but answered, "Yes, several times as a youngster. As I recall, Auntie, you took me to zoos a time or two."

"So I did, Nephew, so I did. Now, if you don't mind, I want you to take me to the zoo."

"What? You mean today? Right now?" he asked.

"Yes!" she replied. "We can take my car. Let's do it!"

"Alright then, how long will it take you to get ready?"

She said, "Look at me, I'm ready."

And ready she was, in her walking shoes and casual sportswear.

As we walked to the car, she observed, "The eavesdroppers have left."

"Yeah, something had to be done about that; having my favorite aunt being hounded by vampires is intolerable. Live your life as you please, Auntie."

"I am your only aunt, boy." She responded and giggled.

On the drive to the zoo, Aunt Rita was quiet for a while and then commented, "You have begun to accept who and what you are. It took you long enough. I was beginning to wonder about you."

"Well, Auntie, I always have been a little slow on the uptake. Took some serious thinking to get around to accepting the whole idea of a One, much less that One being me. Even now, the full impact of that truth has not yet hit me."

"What do you think 'They' are planning, nephew?"

"You want to know something interesting? I don't care. I have learned things during my stays in Keepaway about illusions and illusions within illusions that have taught me more about reality than I ever imagined. Anyway, perhaps 'They' will decide to just leave me be. Should they decide otherwise, Earth will undergo some drastic changes at the hands of some evil people unless I find a way to veer their apple-cart off course without costing lives. There is still so much more for me to learn about myself."

While Aunt Rita was quietly enjoying the ride to the zoo, his mind wandered to the zoo outings they enjoyed years ago. He was actually looking forward this trip today and wondered if zoos had changed over all those years. He reminisced:

"A long time has passed since my last visit to a zoo, well over 30 years. I remember going to the zoo as being a fun outing and interesting, where strange animals and reptiles could be seen living in their own caged environment. Back then, the wonder of seeing creatures seldom or never observed had an excitement about it difficult to describe. The lions and tigers were big, fearsome animals, while the elephants and giraffes were huge and more people-friendly creatures. As I recall, the zoos I attended as a child took about two hours to wander through and see almost everything there. Things are different now; this zoo we are attending today is a large complex and cannot sufficiently be explored in a day. In today's zoos, video and audio technology are captivating and garner more interest from visitors than do the actual animals. Aunt Rita likes watching actual animals. Me, too"

I rented a type of zoo golf cart, got a map of the zoo, and we took off to see what the place had to offer. The appeal of this zoo was infectious and fun. Signs were posted, explaining what animals to look for in the various confines, along with audio/video devices provided to give a historical account of the animals for people who desired to learn more about them. It was really informative and quite impressive. My aunt was unusually quiet as we drove in and around the zoo, so I bought us a couple of hotdogs and cold drinks, parked in a shady spot, and waited.

Aunt Rita was enjoying the hotdog and commented, "It is interesting how much better hotdogs taste at the zoo than at home. I just can't seem to make them quite this good; wonder why that is?" Then, before I could manage to answer, she asked, "What do you think of the zoo, nephew? A bit different from the old ones, I would say."

"No doubt about it," I agreed. "Big changes have been and are being made in zoo technology and architecture, Auntie."

She commented, "This zoo has been in existence here for a long while. In fact, I don't remember a time when it wasn't. When do you reckon it was created and by whom, nephew?"

"There is a nice plaque out front, giving a history of the place. I believe someone is commemorated for donating the funds to build it." My cold drink was really refreshing and needed a refill. "Aunt Rita, I'm gonna walk over and get our drinks refilled; you want the same?"

"No, get me a root beer this time; it's been awhile since I've had one of those, and bring another one of those hotdogs."

He pondered as he walked to the Snack Bar, "My aunt really likes the hotdogs here; they are good. Now she's got me wondering if there is a difference in hotdogs; it never even crossed my mind before today."

As he walked around the corner, a man slipped into the driver's seat of the golf cart, smiled at Rita, and ordered, "Hand me your fucking purse, lady, and don't make a scene if you want to live." There were security cameras everywhere, and he wanted to make this look normal.

Rita handed him her purse and calmly said, "I'm going to be wanting that back with everything intact, so don't you go messing anything up, and when you meet my nephew, tell him I said not to hurt you."

He looked at her in disbelief, smiled real friendly-like, and said, "Why, you crazy old bitch, if it weren't for all those goddamned security cameras, I'd slit your motherfucking throat right here!"

Then he stepped out of the cart and casually walked away with her purse, blending into a crowd of people and looking like just another person enjoying a day at the zoo.

The thief angrily thought to himself as he walked calmly to the zoo exit, "I should have killed that stupid old hen, and I might still do that. Those kind think they're better than me. I have her ID and address and can't wait to see the fear in her eyes as the blood drains from her throat. Yeah, I'll return her fucking purse, alright." He felt better just thinking about it as he remotely unlocked his car and reached to open the door.

"You know," a clear voice spoke, "I have kind of a knack for determining how to tell the difference between good and bad things. I spent over twenty years working in quality assurance doing just that."

Moving like a cat at the sound of the voice, the thief spun quickly around, concealing a knife at his wrist. Upon seeing an older man standing at the rear of his car, he relaxed, smiled, and said, "You startled me there for a moment, old man. Didn't expect to see anyone this far out in the parking lot. I don't like parking close to other cars, people don't have respect anymore. You know what I'm saying?"

"Like I told you before," calmly stated the old man in a 'matter of fact' tone, "my ability to determine the difference between good or bad is very acute, and you are not a good person."

"Who in hell do you think you are? You're 'cute', alright, and it's going to get you killed if you don't back off right now? So, get the hell out of here before I leave your motherfucking ass bleeding to death in this parking lot."

"Listen," explained the old man, "my aunt said not to hurt you if you agreed to bring her purse back in the same condition as when you took it. It is as simple as that. What are you, maybe 25 years old? You are far too young to ruin your life over an old woman's purse. Just bring it back to her, apologize, and be on your way."

"Your aunt?" repeated the thief, confused by the old man's quiet demeanor, and then laughed when he realized what was going on here. "So, you're the nephew that crazy old bitch was raving about. You just sealed your doom, asshole, and your fucking cunt aunt is going to die choking on the blood from her cut throat."

"Good Lord, son!" exclaimed the old man. "This is surprising and totally unexpected! You are a sadistic psychopath! I have never met one of you before. Do you suppose there is a chance we could go somewhere and talk? Over coffee, maybe? I have an interest in what makes you tick; you know, why you are what you are."

The thief looked at the old man in disbelief and exclaimed, "You're just as loonie as that bitch aunt of yours! You can bet I'm going to bring her purse back and place it in her hands, with your fucking heart in it." The young thief chuckled at the thought as he opened the car door and retrieved a gun.

Leaning against the car with a wide grin on his face, he looked at the old man and informed, "This is where you try to run."

But the old man made no effort to run; he just stood there, looking at the young psychopath and shaking his head. "What is it you are called, boy?" he asked.

"Jericho, I am named after my grandfather."

"Why do you steal women's purses, Jerry?"

"That is how I get their names and addresses."

"You're not after their money?"

"No. There is never much cash in the purses, anyway. Just

some family pictures, names and addresses, and other things."

"Then why bother with their purses, Jerry?"

"I have special needs, old man. Most of the time, just thinking or dreaming about it, and remembering is enough; then again, sometimes, it's not."

Jerry was confused by the old man's calm manner. "What in hell is going on with this old guy, anyway?" he thought. "This asshole should be begging for his life by now. Instead, I'm holding a gun on him and spilling my guts to all his stupid questions. This has to stop!"

"What do you mean by 'it,' Jerry?" he asked. "What exactly is your need?"

Jerry was compelled to answer, "I need to see the spark of life leave people's eyes as I kill them."

"Are you remorseful or sorry for killing them, Jerry?"

"Hell, no. On the contrary, I am relieved and content; it's like a sexual orgasm: wonderful.! I often fantasize about their deaths and the way they died, you know, for relief."

"Well, Jerry, I'm not a trained psychiatrist or anything close, but what you just said seems to explain why your language was so graphically violent when you threatened to kill my aunt and me. You get satisfaction and relief from talking about violent ways of killing people, but talking and fantasizing do not compete well with the real thing; so, every once in a while, you have to kill someone to complete the satisfaction of your needs. Is that about it, son?"

Jerry hesitated for a moment, thinking, and replied, "I've never heard it explained quite that way before, but yeah, that's how it is, how I get relief."

"Just to satisfy my curiosity, Jerry, how many people have you actually killed?"

"I can tell you exactly," he replied, "268. I started with a lame-brained six-year-old handicapped girl when I was fourteen. That was the first time I felt the relief. I killed 28 more that year. Man! What a great year that was!"

"Well," surmised the man, when observed objectively, "your numbers pale in comparison to what some of our doctors, corporate execs, and political leaders did back in the two years of the 2020 Covid thing, but that does not lessen or excuse your actions. You're a bad person, Jerry. You hurt and kill people on purpose to make your life worth living. On top of that, you enjoy it and are not going to change. Tell me something, how have you managed to avoid being caught by law enforcement? You should be dead or in a psycho ward by now."

Jerry laughed, "I have always had help. Without help, I cannot exist. There are many like me, but we seldom associate with each other. The help cleans up our messes, and we clean up theirs. They provide us with victims, and we provide them with solutions to problems. We are quite useful to society."

"You can put the gun down now, Jerry."

"No way, asshole! You know way too much now, and besides, I need a kill. You and your stupid aunt will do just fine."

"Tell you what, Jerry, let's make this your decision, not mine.

You can choose to put the gun down now, bring my aunt's purse back to her, apologize to her, and go your merry way, or you can pull that trigger and, how did you put it? 'Seal your doom,' yeah, pull that trigger and seal your doom. Both choices are yours, boy, but you can only choose one. Either way, I have no interest."

The old man piqued Jerry's interest with that statement. He had to ask, "Alright motherfucker, what doom?"

The old man informed him, "You will lose your sight, your voice, and live a life without relief for the duration."

Jerry said, "Yeah, right! You talk too much, you old bastard. We'll see what you have to say as you die watching me cut out your fucking heart."

He laughed and pulled the trigger. The gun exploded and sent parts of metal hurtling into Jerry's face, destroying his eyes and permanently damaging his larynx and mouth. He lived but would never see or talk again. All without relief.

While walking back to the zoo cart, carrying his aunt's purse, Jerry's words resonated in his mind, "We are quite useful to society."

"How in the world did humanity let things get this far?" he asked out loud to himself. "And what kind of idiot creator put this crazy world together? And why?" Then another interesting question crossed his mind: "How many insane killers like Jerry are there, anyway?"

As he placed the purse in the hands of his aunt, she asked, "Why didn't that young man bring it back himself? I thought it would do him good to accept responsibility for his actions.

You didn't hurt him, did you?"

"No, I didn't hurt him. He made his own choice and couldn't see his way clear to mend his ways. Some people are just that way, Auntie."

She sighed and said, "I have seen enough of the zoo today. It was nice to come visit here again, but the highlight of the day was the hotdogs; they sure are good."

"By the way, auntie, I asked one of the zoo managers about that, and he revealed the secret of the amazing zoo hotdogs; turns out, they make all the hotdog wieners with a mixture of alligator and zebra meat. The different flavors of the 2 meats bring about that exotic taste you like so much."

She stared at him in shock and exclaimed, "They do not!"

"Honest to goodness, Auntie, I even got the recipe. Not sure where to get the meat, though."

"They do not!" she demanded. He couldn't hold it in anymore and burst out laughing.

"I had you going good there for a while," he accused and laughed again.

"You did not! Well, maybe a little, at first. Gator and Zebra meat," she indignantly repeated, giggling and then laughing.

They laughed together all the way back to the car.

During the drive home, she asked, "What was your impression of the zoo, nephew?"

"Oh, I don't know, Aunt Rita. Truth is, it was interesting but a

little too commercialized for me. Probably better than seeing large animals in small cages, though. This zoo today seemed more like an animal city than an old-fashioned zoo. I'm not inspired to make an effort to go back again anytime soon, though."

"Nephew, do you ever pause and wonder how this world of ours came about? I mean, was it a chance combination of elements that evolved into today? Or did everything maybe come from the mind of a creator with a plan?"

"Wow, Auntie! Listen to you waxing philosophical today. Not sure you have ever revealed this side of your mind before, but I have an answer to your question. What I have learned from reading, studying, and creating different illusions in Keepaway is that this great reality of ours is a creation of a creator. I have no conclusion as to what or whom that creator might be, but have to admit there are many times when I am not impressed with his, her, or its results. This is a created reality, though; of that, I am sure."

She commented, "You observed that this zoo we visited today is more of an animal city than a zoo, and I agree. What I'm considering, is the possibility that our reality is a type of human zoo created for the amusement and education of a superior group of beings. What do you think of that?"

"So that is why you wanted me to take you to the zoo! I knew there was something going on with you today, but couldn't put everything all together until now. How long have you been thinking about this? Seems as though you have given it a lot of thought."

She answered, "Ever since you came of age, inherited the balance of the abilities, and assumed the Power. There just has to be a reason for you. This power of yours cannot have come from this creation or its creator; it is beyond them and must have originated outside our reality. Why we are here is a great question to ponder; perhaps we are a human zoo, and perhaps we are something else. But the real question is, why are you here? You, my darling, are an anomaly."

Then she said, with sarcasm, "Gator and zebra meat, indeed," and laughed again.

Chapter 12 – The Scenario

Randolph Barton was standing at the window of his Texas office when his assistant came in and said two men were waiting to meet with him. He had no appointments scheduled and was a bit irritated by a short notice meeting. Perhaps the most important assemblage in the history of mankind was taking place in Dallas today, and he feared that reasonable minds might not prevail in the decision making. He was anticipating a call and had no time now for a meeting.

"Tell them I am involved in an important conference at the moment and cannot meet with them."

"But, Sir," protested the aide, "these men are quite insistent and under great authority."

"Great authority, you say? Well, send them in!"

The aide opened the door and announced, "Mr. Barton will see you now, gentlemen."

Two high-ranking military men in uniforms entered and presented their credentials for his inspection. "Mr. Randolph Barton, you are requested to accompany us immediately," said one. "We have a helicopter waiting."

The officer's voice was quiet and polite, but it was plain this was not a request; it was an order. Barton grabbed his coat and left with them.

The chopper ride was quick and short; they landed in an empty parking lot west of Dallas, where a limousine was waiting to convey him to the destination, a two-story edifice that looked more like a college library than a government office building. Upon entering the place, Randolph Barton was met by security personnel and went through the usual screening process to assure he was authorized to enter. He was then escorted to a large conference room in front of a small audience, fitted with a microphone, and seated in a comfortable chair.

Barton thought to himself, "I'm sure this has something to do with the meeting being held today regarding the Abilities Man, but why was I brought here? They have the record of my debrief; what else could they want from me?"

"Mr. Barton," said a voice from the audience, "we are not going to insult your intelligence by beating around the bush, so to speak, in this interview. You are here because, in your debrief you demonstrated some unique insights concerning Mr. Abilities. This body is now tasked with deciding how to proceed with the Mr. Abilities problem, and we are at an impasse of sorts. We believe you have information that will be of help in our decision making and are interested in learning the truth as you see it and not as you want us to see it. Do you understand?"

"Yes, I understand."

"In this interview, it is will be necessary to repeat some of the questions previously asked you. Do not allow that to frustrate you; just answer the questions. Explain to us what you believe Mr. Abilities thinks of our organization."

Barton answered, "My opinion is he does not think of you at all. However, he was very surprised and disappointed at your disregard for human life. He sincerely does not understand the willingness of our government to kill innocent citizens just to get at him."

"Do you believe this Mr. Abilities considers us his enemy, Mr. Barton?" asked a different voice in the audience.

Randolph Barton thought about the query for a moment and thought, "What a dangerous question! The lives of millions of people may hinge upon my answer." Then it occurred to him that the responsibility is not his to assume; other powers have that burden. He decided to answer honestly, at least as far as his ability was concerned.

"Everyone," he addressed the entire audience, "my impression of Mr. Abilities is, no, he does not consider you an enemy; as a matter of fact, I do not believe he considers your organization at all and doubt he is even thinking of you at this time."

"So, Mr. Barton, it is your belief that he does not fear us." That was more of a statement than a question but begged an answer.

"Honestly folks, I have an informed idea of who you are and the great power at your disposal, which fills me with respect, awe, and fear of your capabilities, but for someone like Mr. Abilities, what is there to fear?"

"Do you believe Mr. Abilities to be human or something other than human, Mr. Barton?"

"I do not know what to believe about that," he replied.

Another voice asked, "Do you believe Mr. Abilities to have weaknesses, Mr. Barton?"

"Well, he is certainly an empathetic being with morals and ethics, meaning he cares about people, including all of you. Normally, those attributes are considered symbols of strength, not weakness, but those of us in government know better, do we not?"

"Mr. Barton, do you mean to insinuate that our organization is without morals and ethics?"

"Ladies and gentlemen, we are all realists here. Are we not? Insinuate means to suggest or hint at something, and I am neither suggesting nor hinting at anything; rather, I am stating emphatically that morals and ethics have no place in our government and certainly not in your organization. Come on, guys, admit it: the real question here today is not whether Mr. Abilities considers you his enemy, but whether you consider him to be your enemy. What you actually want to know is whether he represents a threat to your power."

"Mr. Barton, just answer our questions, without commentary. Do you believe Mr. Abilities poses a threat to our National Security?"

"Yes," Barton replied

"Explain how."

"His existence creates doubt and fear among many of those in your organization, a fear that will likely result in your taking action against him. It is that action that poses a threat, not only to National Security, but World Security, because it is my belief your organization, out of fear, will use everything at its disposal to neutralize or eliminate him, with little or no regard to collateral damage."

Another voice asked, "Since Mr. Abilities has such a moral disposition, is it your evaluation he will surrender in order to avoid extreme collateral damage as a natural result of conflict with us?"

"Wow! I actually have no idea how to answer that question. I wonder though, if you realize the detestable inhuman quality of what you said in the asking? It is your willingness to cause the deaths of thousands, perhaps even millions of people to get at one man that is suspect here. I will say this: your power and pragmatic disposition give you great leverage over opponents, but why risk an unnecessary confrontation with Mr. Abilities that may cost millions of lives? Why not just let him be?"

"We ask the questions here, Mr. Barton. Just out of curiosity, how do you believe our organization would fare in a conflict with Mr. Abilities."

"People, all of you, listen to me! There is something strange and unusual about this man that none of us know. It is just a feeling, but if you go to war with him, you will lose! Just let him be."

"Mr. Barton, you underestimate our strength and technology. You also spoke with him one-on-one. Did you not?"

"Yes," answered Barton.

"Then you have unknowingly been compromised, Mr. Barton. We have learned that Mr. Abilities has influence over everyone with whom he speaks individually, causing us to take certain precautions to avoid allowing that to happen anymore. You believe what you believe because that is what he wants you to believe. Your ideas and choices are not your own anymore; they are his. For that reason, you cannot be allowed freedom to associate with anyone without being accompanied by two agents. You will be taken to a secure area with all the comforts of home, less human contact, until we find a way to break Mr. Abilities' hold over you. Think about how you have changed since talking with the man, and you will conclude, as did we, that he achieved great influence over your mind, causing you to believe that our organization is composed of bad and immoral people who are in charge of the world. Think how ridiculous that sounds. If he can do that to you, think what he can do to others. He is dangerous and must be stopped before he completes his agenda to take over the world."

"Are you saying that Mr. Abilities brainwashed me without my knowledge?" asked Barton.

"That is an unfortunate way of putting it, but yes, that is correct. You are not the only one compromised; there are others. He is spreading his mind control scenario to create an insurrection against our government. We, in this room, have decided to oppose his efforts, and your input has been helpful. Thank you."

Mr. Randolph Barton, though vigorously protesting, was then transported to a secure facility somewhere and denied human contact.

A man walked to the chair in front, sat down, and clamped the microphone to his lapel. "What do you think, everyone? Do we require any more proof of Mr. Abilities danger to our way of life, our organization, and the world? We simply must stop Mr. Abilities before he removes us and takes over everything we have built and are now building. Whatever magic he may have at his disposal cannot possibly prevail against our great technology."

A voice from the audience stated, "I am struggling to find a motive for Mr. Abilities' intention to assume control of our organization when such a desire will likely cost him his life. It does not make sense to me. Why don't we ask him to appear before this board and explain his intentions and perhaps reach a compromise of sorts?"

The man in the chair responded, this man is an egomaniac with certain powers that have gone to his head. He may accept compromise as long as he walks away with control. Think about this: it takes a large committee to manage this huge organization now. How many of you want to place control of this empire in the hands of one man? Can anyone here spell dictator?"

"Mr. Director," reasoned another voice. "Where is the evidence this man is a threat of any kind? What is it he has done to indicate a desire to rule our organization, much less the world? What great power has he demonstrated that he could do such a thing if he desired? Sure, Mr. Abilities appears to have gotten into the heads of a few individuals with his mind-changing tricks, but in each case, those people have not proven to be dangerous to anyone; on the contrary, studies reveal them to be better people than before their exposure to him. Again, where is the evidence of one man's ability to threaten a global giant such as ours? I move that we release Mr. Randolph Barton, along with the others, and get back to business as usual before embarking upon what very well may be a dangerous campaign that has yet even to be justified?"

Based upon the hum of voices in the room, after the lady spoke, Director Sheridan realized he was in process of losing majority support for his position to eliminate Mr. Abilities.

"Are you suggesting, Madam, that we let him be?"

"Yes, Mr. Director, at least for the time being, anyway. Our organization has important business that must be attended, and it is urgent that we do so with as little distraction as possible. That being said, I suggest that we continue monitoring him while gathering information for our database. In the meantime, let him be. And for god's sake, release all those poor, so-called 'compromised' individuals; incarcerating them makes us look like the bad guys. That is an image we must avoid."

The vote was twelve to four in favor of Madam Katherine Yang's motion. Director Sheridan remained convinced that Mr. Abilities was far too dangerous for his existence to be allowed. He was a student of 'The Legend of the One' and firmly believed the man to be the prophesied evil One.

"I will see that he is monitored, alright," he thought, "and the time approaches when everyone will come to see his evil plans and demand his destruction." He vowed to be present for that necessity.

Madam Yang sympathized with Director Sheridan in that the existence of the abilities man may have the potential to be a significant obstacle to the organization's ambitious plan to build a better world and perhaps even a better galaxy. "The man may have extraordinary abilities, but he is an ignorant fool and out of his league," she thought with confidence.

Madam Yang was the most popular and powerful board member of the Sixteen and an expert in human relations. There were more important things now that required the focus and attention of world leaders than that of a clever magician. The time approaches, though, when he will be dealt with.

Randolph Barton was freed on the same day he was locked away. The two senior military officers who escorted him before the Committee of 16 were the ones who effected his release and escorted him back to his office, while explaining that everything that occurred was in the interests of National Security and was not to be discussed with anyone. He was left alone, wondering if any of what was told him in the meeting room was half-truth or all fiction.

"Those people are good at creating reality scripts that confuse the mind as to what is, or is not, real," he surmised. "How is it, with all the deception and constant lying, they keep their grip on reality. Maybe they don't, and that is really disturbing."

Chapter 13 - Little Things

After leaving the zoo, it was already late when Aunt Rita and her nephew arrived back home. They were not in a hurry and stopped off at a restaurant on the way and had a good time just talking and dining, allowing time to drift away and causing them to get back a little after dark.

"How do you do it?" she asked.

He looked closely at her and replied, "Do what?"

"How is it you possess such great power and can spend an entire day with an old woman doing nothing of importance?"

"Well, first off, you are not an ordinary woman; you are my aunt, and time with you is always well spent because you are interesting and, for some reason, have the ability to keep me grounded in what has real meaning in my life. This power of mine is seductive and exerts great influence on my human nature by compelling its use."

"Nephew, that is something I have been meaning to ask you; what keeps you from using more of that power? I mean, you drive your car, mow your lawn, cook your food, clean your house, and watch television when all of that can be done with a simple thought on your part. Why is that?"

"The truth is Auntie, I'm not sure this power is deserved and don't yet feel worthy of it."

"Speaking of truth," she replied, "allow me to tell you a truth: the power you possess only resides in the one who is worthy of its possession, and as far as I have been able to determine, you are the only one to ever be blessed with that worth. I am certain you can feel it, and now you are learning to use it. Remaining grounded in your humanity keeps your ego in check and helps to avoid a god complex."

"That is where you come in, Aunt Rita. Who else could get me to go to the zoo?" he said and laughed.

"Yeah," she acknowledged, "but, if you recall, I had an ulterior motive. Thoughts about illusions and reality have been on my mind lately, and I was curious to know your thoughts on the subjects."

"Not much to talk about there," he replied. "One of the limitations of this power I have, Auntie, is that it has not made me any smarter. I am learning, though. I am learning."

"Well," she said, "it has been a long day; I'm worn to a frazzle and ready for bed. Maybe I'll see you in the morning. Good night, my loving nephew."

"Good night, Aunt Rita." His thoughts then quickly turned to the meeting today. "I wonder what they decided?"

He formed a thought of Keepaway and was there. He seldom slept anywhere else anymore and laid down on the soft sand of the beach, looked up to the stars, listened to the waves, and slipped into a deep, restful sleep.

The next morning, he woke up refreshed and walked into the surf to sit and think. There is much about which to think. His mind wandered to the They Organization. "I'm going to have to find out what they call themselves," he thought. "Important organizations always have initials like FBI, CIA, or MGM. Wonder what theirs' is? Thinking about it, I kinda like 'THEY'. It fits. What was it Randy said about them? They manage the country and perhaps the world and make decisions in the best interests of the people or something like that. I can't help but wonder why it is I never before heard of them?"

The thing is, he knew very little about what went on in the USA, much less the world. Truth be known, he didn't know anything about the government of people. Even groups like the PTA and BSA were beyond his understanding as far as their purpose was concerned.

He never before gave a serious thought to the fact that cities, states, and countries have to be run by someone or some group to assure that civilization does not descend into chaos. It just seemed to him that everything always worked out for people as long as they worked hard, raised their families, and lived moral and ethical lives. That's the way it always worked for him.

Now, though, he was beginning to see that everything is actually managed and scripted according to plans put into place by certain elites of mankind for the supposed benefit of the collective of mankind. It is reasonable to believe such world leadership is sensible in that most humans have shown little ability and desire to care for themselves without direction from overseers of some sort.

In other words, in order to avoid chaos, people must be managed by those elites who have proven themselves capable of assuming the obligation and responsibility for civilization's survival.

That seems to be where the THEY organization comes in. It has an understanding of world problems and what is required to assure the world is properly managed in the best interests of the collective. THEY visions itself as the hope of mankind. Maybe he has misjudged them; their management methods are immoral, but the need for human control is necessary. If humans could just find a way to get along with each other without conflict, such oversight would be unnecessary.

On the other hand, what if mankind is left to its own devices without oversight by their elites? Would humanity descend into chaos as THEY believes? Perhaps, perhaps not. It is possible the idea of government is interfering with the natural progression of mankind's existence and actually making things worse by causing people to depend upon the government to make them happy rather than themselves.

He found himself favoring the idea that humans have the right to self-determination, being responsible for their own future, be it good, bad, or in-between. Being herded toward a future planned by elite overlords who operate in the best interests of government is a type of beneficial serfdom.

Self-determination is about rights. The right to benefit or suffer from your decisions. He stood, waded to shore, and entered the house, where his information screen was waiting.

"Keepaway is wonderful," he thought as he sat on the sofa and began talking to the screen. "Show me yesterday's THEY meeting," he stated.

"This Yang woman is a heavyweight on the Committee of 16," he thought to himself. "It seems that Director Sheridan is not the power on the committee, but does have some support for his aggressive approach in my regard. Madam Yang is more of a business person and would have gone along with Sheridan if more pressing company matters were not on her mind. I wonder what they are planning? THEY seems to have an ambitious agenda in play but didn't go into any details at the meeting."

He liked the fact THEY had little respect for his 'magic tricks' and considered him rather easy to eliminate at their pleasure. A plan of how to begin was already forming in his mind. How to become an annoyance while avoiding being noticeably intrusive required inside information. His plan involved using little things that helped him gain allies from within THEY. Very many of their employees, including top management, are likely good people who have no idea of the evil they support with their everyday efforts.

Security at the Dallas THEY facility was composed of the latest technology. Multiple cameras were active, and facial recognition software was installed. Security personnel were not allowed to be alone at any time. They knew about his effect on those who were alone with him and had taken precautions throughout the building. Two security officers were on entry duty that morning, sitting at the check-in desk. One looked to be in his early thirties, and the other was a kid, maybe 18 or 20.

"What in hell is that smell, Tony? Did you shit your pants?"

"I don't know. I thought it might be you, but I didn't want to say anything."

"Me? I have not moved from this desk in the last hour. You're the one who just got back from the john. What did you do? Forget to wipe or something?"

"Give me a break, Dave, all I did was take a piss."

"Well, it's got to be you, Tony. Check your shoes!"

Tony looked at his shoes and sure enough, the bottom of his right shoe was covered in what looked to be fresh dog shit. "Where in hell did I pick that up?"

"How the fuck do I know? Look at that mess; you have smeared that shit all under the desk! Jesus Christ, Tony, only you could fuck things up like this! Get your ass back to the men's room, clean your shoes, and see if you can find that pile of shit you stepped in and clean it up too."

Tony limped away, undignified and holding his right shoe away from him as he hurried to the men's room.

"Can I be of assistance, sir?" he said.

Startled, Dave turned quickly and saw a janitor standing a bit behind him with a mop and bucket.

"Where the hell did…?

Before he could finish his question, the janitor explained, "We have had more than a few incidents today of doggy accidents, and I overheard you complaining to your friend about a bad smell and thought I may be able to help with that."

"That wasn't my friend; he is my younger brother and a fuck up. Clean up his mess, will you? And while you're at it, see if you can do anything about the smell. Maybe spray some odor killer or something."

"Yeah, I know what you mean; I'm sure I can help with that," he affirmed, and offered some advice, "You know, sir, you were pretty hard on your brother there. He seems like a good young man to me."

Dave glared at the man and angrily replied, "Who the fuck do you think you're . . .?" and looked into the man's eyes and slowly sat down in his chair.

"Why do you treat your brother with such disrespect, Dave?"

"Well, he is my half-brother, and, I don't know, he sometimes just gets under my skin and makes me mad."

"Tony loves and looks up to you and you know it. You respond by treating him like the shit under your desk. From where is your bitterness coming? You're a lot better man than this cursing, angry boss you have become, and you are hurting your brother and yourself with that demeanor. Dave, why don't you just sit there for a minute or so and close your eyes. Think about why it is you have become such a negative, uncaring brother and go back to being the man you really are. I'm going to go help your brother with that mess in the men's room, now."

Dave closed his eyes and flashed back many years to see his father yelling at him, telling him what a stupid, worthless bastard he was who couldn't do anything right. He hated being there. "Please let me wake up!" he screamed in his mind.

Tony said, "Dave! Are you alright, brother?" and placed his hand on Dave's shoulder.

Dave looked up and saw his brother watching him closely, with a concerned look on his face. He placed his hand over his brother's hand and said, "Yeah, Tony, I'm okay; I just lost myself in deep thought there for a minute or so."

Tony replied, "I was getting pretty worried about you," and added, "listen, Dave, I'm sorry about the mess; I know I'm a fuck-up and screw things up sometimes, but being around you is making me a better man. I'm so proud to be able to work with you and learn from you. Don't give up on…"

Dave gently interrupted his brother and said firmly, "Don't you ever tell me or let anyone tell you that you are a fuck-up. You're not! You are my brother, and I'm proud to have you by my side here. Sometimes, my temper gets away from me, and I say things I shouldn't. I'm trying to change that, and you're helping me be a better person by inspiring that change. Now, what do you say we get everything cleaned up around here and get back to our security work?"

Tony looked at his brother intently and said, "Dave, are you sure you're alright? You seem different."

Dave glanced at his brother, laughed out loud, and replied, "Are you picking on me, little brother?" They both laughed and got back to work.

He observed them through the glass doors and walked down the street. "Little things," he said to himself, then smiled and said again, "Little things."

In just five days, a ripple effect had made itself felt around the world organization of THEY. It was so small and diverse that no one paid it any attention. Three offices in the US, four in India, two in the UK, six in Europe, four in Russia, and six in China were notable in that the people in and around those offices were beginning to treat each other fairly, with respect. Some were even beginning to call out their peers for bullying tactics they have been guilty of for years. Acts of kindness by employees to each other were becoming commonplace.

Three employees in Russia were fired for refusing to arrest free speech demonstrators, and four upper-level management people in the US resigned over various moral issues. However, the effect on THEY was less than minimal and drew little to no attention, but a virus-like infection of goodness was slowly and steadily making its presence known in certain areas of the organization, which is not considered by management to be a healthy sign for certain government agencies and many large corporations. Honesty and integrity are often considered as obstacles to growth, wealth, and power; in addition, morals tend to interfere with the business of corrupt organizations and nations wherever they are introduced. That cannot be allowed to continue.

Someone noticed, though, someone with a great amount of power within THEY, and he issued an Abilities Notice to the Sixteen.

Chapter 14 - Director Sheridan

In a highly secure space in Ft. Worth, Texas, Madam Yang and Director Sheridan were having a private meeting called by the Director to discuss the ramifications of the latest Abilities Notice from National Security in Denver, Colorado. The Sixteen were scheduled to meet that afternoon.

"I knew it! I just knew the bastard couldn't be trusted and was up to something." Sheridan was feeling redeemed by the Abilities Notice and added, "We should have taken him down as soon as we found out about him! Now, he has become a problem and must be eliminated."

"Hold on there, Mr. Director," spoke Madam Yang. "We don't know for sure if these little changes are due to the activity of Mr. Abilities or not, and the areas where activity is reported are too far apart for one man to have accomplished even that small amount in less than a week."

The Director retorted, "Well, maybe there is more than one of him. Did you think of that? This is his work and the beginning of a revolution within our organization; I am sure of it. We must begin a vigorous course of action immediately to avert his insidious plan."

"It is important to note something previously observed that is consistent with these latest reports," replied Madam Yang. "All those affected became better people, kinder and more moral than the way they were before. Perhaps we should consider that a good thing and embrace the concept. Our world image could use some improvement these days, and good, moral employees make great photo-ops for our Public Relations Section."

"With all due respect, Madam Yang, how are those virtuous, moral employees going to react to the necessary collateral damage predicted to occur in our next wave of land acquisitions in various populated parts of the planet? We require sensible, practical people who are motivated by self-interest to do our bidding, not nice, morally kind people who will object to the way things have to be done in tough, objective business dealings. This is a serious problem with the potential of expanding into every part of our organization over time. I warn you, madam, the future of our plan to save the world is at stake here."

Madam Yang understood the concern expressed by Director Sheridan but thought he was overreacting to a problem so small as to be almost non-existent.

"Why is he so dead-set on removing this abilities magician?" she wondered. "There are much more pressing situations on our table at this time that simply must be attended. Still, there is this notice to the Sixteen turned in by Aiden; he is not given to trivial matters and apparently sees something there requiring attention. Paying no attention to Aiden is not just flirting with career and political suicide; it is stupid. The current success of our organization is due to his leadership. He created and understands every aspect of our operation. If he believes something to be important, it is."

Madam Yang spoke, "Mr. Director, your point is well taken. What is it you suggest we do? The Sixteen is set to meet later today, and we know so little of this magician. Do you have a plan to present to the group? I am not even sure his current location is known. He is supposed to be under our constant surveillance, but we cannot find him."

"The plan is to kill the bastard," retorted Mr. Sheridan. "He is a significant threat to the survival of our way of life and simply must be eliminated. Although in possession of certain abilities, he is first and foremost a human being and can die like everyone else. We must first get past his defenses; after that, assuring his death will be easy."

"Have you a plan to get past those defenses?" she asked. "They appear to be formidable. As noted before, we seem incapable of even locating him at any given time."

"As I said, he is a human being, with human weaknesses. I have studied him."

"Weaknesses?" she queried.

"He cares about people, places, and things, which makes him vulnerable. He has a moral and ethical nature and is opposed to what he sees as senseless and harmful violence. He is smart but not well-informed on how things work in the real world and genuinely believes what he is now doing is good. His real danger to us is in his ignorance of humanity. He should be with us but, in that ignorance, sees our organization as an evil entity opposed to the goodness of mankind rather than the hope of the world."

"You, Mr. Director, are a student of the wisdom of Aiden," she observed. "I never before noticed that about you. I suspect that is why you are in such opposition to the existence of Mr. Abilities."

"Absolutely," he affirmed. His ignorance-based, kindness type of philosophy threatens the wisdom of our organization and must be destroyed like any other debilitating cancer before it spreads and destroys the world."

"So, we are in agreement. How do we get past his defenses and deliver his fate?"

"Distraction," answered Sheridan. "While he is focused on one thing he values, he becomes vulnerable to another thing, a lethal thing."

"How do we find him?" she wondered aloud.

Sheridan replied with confidence, "As noted before, he has human weaknesses. He likes people. He also likes coffee and biscuits."

The meeting of the Sixteen went smoothly. As expected, there was no opposition to the decision to eliminate Mr. Abilities. His danger to the organization was affirmed by all, particularly when it was made clear that the notice came from Aiden himself. The plan of termination was not revealed to the Sixteen; they confirmed the decision to terminate and ordered it to be done, but the actual plan of action was kept within a small circle of agents, specially trained for missions of this type.

While the meeting was in session, another Abilities Notice from Aiden was delivered to the group, reporting the spread of the Goodness Virus into 57 more offices of the organization, where simple, sensible, and practical decisions were being bombarded with questions by honest and moral opposition from management personnel who had never before exhibited any such behavior. People's attitude toward decisions that hurt others were now being discussed and rejected, whereas before, those decisions were routinely rubber-stamped as approved. This information sent a chill through the Sixteen, who realized their power base was under attack by an insidious enemy. Mr. Abilities had to be eliminated sooner rather than later.

Mr. Abilities left Israel just after the Committee of Sixteen had adjourned and watched their termination decision replay on Screen. "So," he thought, "THEY has decided to come for me, after all. My 'Little-Things' project has been discovered. Who is this Aiden guy to whom some of the members referred, anyway? They all seem to defer to him. I wonder if he is the real power behind their organization?"

The name Aiden didn't reveal anything of significance from an internet search, except that it is gender neutral and meant 'little fire' or something like that. He had a thought and wondered if Randy knew anything about the guy. "Think I'll ask him to meet for breakfast in the morning. Maybe he has an idea."

He called Randy and invited him to breakfast at the restaurant at about 8 am. Randy was excited because he had much to ask Mr. Abilities and was interested as to why the man wanted to talk. There was a lot going on in the organization to which Randy was not privileged; he was convinced it was because he was no longer a trusted employee. For a while, back in that conference room, Director Sheridan had him confused with his brainwashing theory, but the story just didn't add up. He couldn't explain it, but the short time he was with the abilities man somehow made him want to be a better person.

Randolph Barton was under 24-hour constant surveillance, and when it was relayed to Director Sheridan that Barton was having breakfast at Mr. Abilities' favorite restaurant in the morning, he put an elimination team in place just in case, with orders to terminate him without reservation. Bullets, poison, and explosives were all on the table. If he showed up, Mr. Abilities was going down in the morning. A plan to divert his attention was in place. The young waiter who always greeted Mr. Abilities would be shot after bringing poisoned coffee to the table, drawing the man's attention, and an instant later, three shots fired a half second apart would take down the man, followed a moment later by a massive explosion in the booth to finish the job. It was going to be messy, but there was no way Mr. Abilities would have time to focus his attention from one crisis to another in time to avert them all.

It was the Director's responsibility, but not his fault. Sheridan did not know, nor did anyone else in the organization know. They had been warned, but rejected the warning as nonsense. Sometimes ignorance is bliss; you know the adage, 'what you don't know can't hurt you,' but the truth is, it does.

Sheridan's personal code stemmed from his belief structure. He sincerely believed the organization was the hope of human existence and the world. With great power, it stood between mankind and destruction, and any opposing entity or force was evil. That is how he envisioned Mr. Abilities: an evil, opposing force to the hope of the world, using a mirage of goodness to bring about destruction.

Aiden's teachings warned of those evil forces which come to you in sheep's clothing, but inwardly are evil ravening wolves. Sheridan's ultimate misery resulted from his ignorance of Mr. Abilities.

Barton showed up at the restaurant early the next morning, a little after eight, and sat down in the waiting area. The young waiter, Daniel, noticed him, walked over, and said, "Good morning, sir. Allow me to show you to your table," and added, "Your guest will be right with you."

"My guest?" he thought. "I think he has it backwards."

The 'table' was the same booth where he first met the man.

"Would you like coffee while you wait, sir?" inquired Daniel.

"Thank you, Daniel, with sweet cream, please."

"Right away, sir."

As Daniel left to get the coffee, Barton thought about what a pleasant waiter this youngster had become and made a mental note to find out more about him. "We need more young people like him in our office." he reasoned.

Right about then, the man walked out of the restroom, which was behind Barton, and exclaimed, "Well, Randy, I see you are already here," and slid into the booth across from him. "How has life been treating you?" he asked.

"This is an interesting surprise," stated Randy, "I arrived early and was waiting for you, and you were here all the time."

"Aw well, I had to make use of the facilities, if you know what I mean, or I would have been waiting here when you showed up. Have you ordered any food yet?"

"No. Just coffee."

"That's a pretty good start, but you already know we got to have biscuits and jelly to warm up with."

About that time, Daniel was headed their way carrying a tray with biscuits and two coffees. As chance would have it, there was an unseen wet spot on the restaurant floor, causing the waiter to slip and fall when he stepped on it, throwing the coffee and biscuits everywhere.

Randy was up in an instant and hurried to Daniel's side. "Are you okay, son? You took a pretty hard fall there."

Daniel got up and began brushing himself off, all the while apologizing for the mess. He said, "I'm more embarrassed than anything, Mr. Barton. That's the first time anything like that has happened to me. I should have noticed that little pool of water. You go back to the booth, and I'll get this mess cleaned up and have that order ready for you before you know it."

Kitchen personnel were already on their way to take care of the clean-up, and within minutes, Daniel returned with a tray of hot biscuits and coffee and set them on the table.

"Thank you, Daniel." said the man.

All during the excitement, the man never moved from the booth as he watched Mr. Randolph Barton respond to Daniel's mishap. Paying no attention to his clothes as he kneeled in the mess next to Daniel, the first thing the important man did was ask the boy if he was hurt and then helped the young waiter to his feet. "Now, there is a man who has his priorities in order," he thought with satisfaction.

Nothing else eventful happened in the restaurant. Outside, though, was a different story.

The snipers could identify no targets and were useless. The bomb never detonated, and the poisoned coffee was never delivered. As far as anyone knew, the primary target remained in the restaurant, alive. Armed agents were ordered to enter the restaurant and kill the primary without reservation, but none got within a hundred yards. Whether they couldn't or wouldn't get closer was never really determined. Not one shot was fired that morning.

Director Sheridan seemed miserable and beside himself, with anger and frustration. The planned attack looked like a practice drill where everyone was wondering what to do next, and it made Sheridan look like a fool. No one admitted to seeing any magical powers because everything that happened seemed to be the result of ordinary circumstances or bad luck. Even the placement of the bomb appeared to be a human thing; upon inspection later, it was determined that the device was not active after installation. The short notice caused a hurried installation under time restraints, and the bomb was placed exactly as planned but was simply never turned on. It could have been a human error. It could have also been human intent. A moral and ethical person would have been unable to accept responsibility for the loss of so many innocent lives. The operative who placed the bomb was never identified.

As they were enjoying their coffee and biscuits, Randy was asked about a man by the name of Aiden, who Mr. Abilities suspected might be a higher power in the organization. Randy knew nothing about him but suggested someone who might, that bring Director Sheridan of the Committee of Sixteen. He was also asked about Madam Yang and he knew of her, but information about the 16 committee was too far above his pay grade for him to know anything useful.

After breakfast and pleasant conversation, the man announced, "Well, Randy, we'll have to do this again sometime. I have to leave now. You be watchful when you leave. If my suspicions are correct, you are about to go through another questioning session."

"Yeah, probably," Randy admitted, "for all the good it will do them. I never learn anything about you to tell, anyway."

The man laughed and said, "I perceive you to be a good man, Randolph Barton. Keep your eye on our young Daniel there," and motioned toward their waiter. "I like him and sense he has more potential than just waiting tables."

Then he stood and shook hands with Randy, then walked into the facilities, and didn't come back out.

Randy said to himself, "If they seriously want to talk with me today, they're gonna have to come to me," and sat back down to finish his coffee and biscuits.

Chapter 15 - The Plot Unfolds

Standing in a conference room in a Ft. Worth building before the Committee of 16, Director Sheridan was being questioned regarding the failed attempt to eliminate Mr. Abilities.

"What is it you mean, exactly, by saying that everything seemed to go wrong, Director Sheridan? Your plan, seemed to be well thought out and foolproof, yet nothing happened, and not one shot was fired. From where we sit, sir, it looks like your mission team was incompetent. Your objective sat in that restaurant having breakfast with Randolph Barton for over 30 minutes while your forces twiddled their thumbs and did nothing. No sniper fire, no agents entering the building to take out the target, no explosion, and no one poisoned. The only excitement during that hour was a waiter falling down and spilling a tray of food everywhere. How do you explain such failure on your part?"

Director Sheridan responded, "I don't know that I am able to explain, Madam. For the record, the waiter who fell and spilled the tray was delivering the poisoned coffee to the target. The bomb, for reasons that are being investigated, was not activated. The snipers could get no confirmed target at which to fire, and armed agents got no closer than 100 yards from the restaurant due to a mix-up in orders, which is also under investigation at this time."

"Mr. Director, is it your conclusion that Mr. Abilities caused the failed mission?"

Director Sheridan replied, "I honestly have no idea, Madam, nor do I believe in coincidence; however, there is no evidence that magic was at work here. All that happened there appeared to have reasonable causes." He paused for a moment, thinking, and continued. "May I make a suggestion, Madam?"

"Of course, Director," she answered, "proceed."

"Honorable Committee Members," he began, "it is my belief that a decision regarding the failed attempt to eliminate Mr. Abilities cannot be reached here today. The results of current investigations are not yet available, are forthcoming, and may or may not provide satisfactory answers. What I am now requesting is that you consider consulting Aiden in this regard. His advice has been impeccable in the past."

There was audible mumbling among the members, that went on for several minutes. Contacting Aiden was no small matter and very seldom done.

Madam Yang spoke, "Regarding Aiden, the committee has a specific directive not to contact him or his people in matters that are within our power to handle. Consulting with a problem such as this is an indication we are not worthy of the trust with which we are bestowed. It is our decision to await the result of ongoing investigations into the failed mission and, in the meantime, continue gathering intelligence on Mr. Abilities and his potential threat to our organization. It is also our decision to suspend you until those further investigations are completed. As of this moment, Mr. Sheridan, you are on leave of absence for an as yet undecided length of time and are directed to remain in the city. An agent will assist with the removal of company items on your person, and any and all personal property in your office will be returned to you within 72 hours from now. Mr. Sheridan, be advised that you remain a member of the committee, but are suspended from meetings and voting until the order is lifted or affirmed. Please conduct yourself accordingly."

Mr. Sheridan surrendered his company identification, phone, gun, and keys and was summarily escorted out of the building. He no longer had a company car and was reduced to taking a taxi to his hotel.

Talking to himself as he unlocked the door to his room, Sheridan questioned, "I hope they continue to pay my hotel expenses. Why couldn't they have restricted me to my home area just outside of DC? I don't know a damn thing about Cowtown."

He locked the door and hurried to the bathroom, where he had an urgent appointment with the toilet that could not be put off. As he let down his pants and underwear and quickly sat down to relieve himself, a calm voice commented, "I know exactly how you feel, Edgar."

Sheridan was startled by the voice and immediately got partly up, but the necessary function of the biological imperative of his body would not be denied and before he sat completely back down, began emptying itself of waste it no longer wanted or needed. Some of it made it into the toilet, but some didn't and fell on his clothes and the toilet seat. Sheridan sat down on the mess.

"I apologize for surprising you like that, Edgar, but I didn't realize your urgency. You have some loose bowels there, man. What in the world have you been eating, anyway?" Edgar was still emptying his bowels.

Edgar looked aside and saw a man sitting comfortably in the bathtub. He stammered, "Who the hell are…"

"Aw, come on, Edgar," said the man, "we're both grown men here; let's be honest with each other. You know exactly who I am."

"You're Him!" he exclaimed.

"Well," the man said, "Now that we have the who settled, let's get down to why I am here."

Edgar began regaining some of his lost composure and asked, "Before we begin, do you mind if I clean up and put on some clothes?"

"You know, Edgar, you're fine just as you are, and I'm comfortable in this tub, so you just stay right where you are, and we'll get our conversation over and done with. I kind of suspect you might not be done there, anyway." Edgar's bowels were still growling.

Edgar couldn't explain it, but there was something about this man that put him at ease, even while on a toilet moving his bowels. This abilities man is just a simple guy; there seems to be nothing special about him. "Why did I ever fear him?" he wondered.

"You were just put on parole today by your organization, weren't you, Edgar?"

"Well, not really parole, more like a short leave of absence until they get things sorted out."

"Things, Edgar?"

"Yeah. The committee is pretty upset with me about the failed mission to eliminate you," he answered.

"You know, Edgar, it doesn't seem right to demote you with such little evidence that you were at fault for the failure of the plan."

"Well, I was in charge of the mission, and it was my plan, making the failure my responsibility. I didn't foresee or expect everything going wrong the way it did."

"But you really did, didn't you, Edgar? You're a smart man and

a decent actor. You foresaw everything, and everything went just like you had it planned. Isn't that, right? The bomb, the agents not invading the restaurant, the snipers not accessing the target. The only thing you didn't plan was the accidental spilling of the poisoned coffee. I couldn't allow you to hurt Randy, now, could I? Your plan is still in motion, is it not?"

"Yes, it is," he admitted. "You know, the poisoned coffee was the real purpose of the restaurant plan. Everything else was staged. I thought it was so simple that it had a good chance of working. There are always you can't plan for."

"And you are the sacrifice here. Why, Edgar? Why are you so dead set that I must be eliminated?"

"Truth is, mister, I'm not feeling that way anymore. I still believe you are a danger to the organization, but we are too big and well-supported by unimaginable power for you to prevail. You are a smart, simple man with magical abilities who should be on our side, and I kinda like you, but for some reason, you have become convinced the organization is the bad guys when we are the hope of the world."

"Okay, Edgar, we're not gonna be having any sacrifices today, as none are required. It is really difficult for me to understand your organization's willingness to sacrifice the lives of innocent people in order to get their way. There is something intrinsically wrong about that mindset. Why are you a part of that evilness."

"Mister, as soon as I walk to that window, this building is going down, and you, me, and everyone in the place is going to die. This has been planned for weeks."

"Why must you go to the window?"

"Because, they have no way of knowing you are in here. Me at the window is the signal. It was a calculated guess that you would want to contact me if I was expelled from the Committee of 16, and there you are, sitting in the bathtub."

"Why not use your sophisticated surveillance equipment?"

"Because they don't work when you are around. Apparently, you have the ability to neutralize them. By the way, those abilities of yours are amazing."

"Where is the bomb located, Edgar?"

"I have no idea, sir. There was talk of using a drone to deliver it, but I was purposely left out of the planning, you know, in case you got to me and forced me to talk."

"What in the hell is wrong with me?" thought Edgar. "Here I am, spilling my guts on this man by answering every question he asks being willing to tell him the truth about anything. How is this happening?"

"Edgar," he asked softly, "who is Aiden?"

"Sir, Aiden is the greatest mind in the world and is responsible for the creation and continuation of our organization. Without him, there very likely would be no world. He saved mankind from destroying itself and gave us rules of order for the creation of civilizations and empires."

"Where does this Aiden fellow live, Edgar?"

"Sir, Aiden is not really what anyone would call a 'fellow'; he is an evolved mind, a type of all-knowing person with enormous powers."

"Have you met with Aiden, Edgar? In person, I mean."

"Oh, no, sir! Aiden is totally secured and never meets with anyone other than his own security and family. I talk to him often, and he listens. He is the main reason for my important stature within the organization; I owe him everything and will sacrifice my life for him should it come to that."

"Well, it looks like you have decided the time has come."

"Not anymore, sir. As I indicated before, you are too small to be a serious threat to the organization, and where Aiden is concerned, you are a non-entity. Aiden has enormous power beyond your wildest dreams."

"Edgar, correct me if I am wrong, but you speak of Aiden with such reverence that he seems almost a god to you. Your faith and genuine belief in him is quite impressive. I have not observed such devotion in a human before, and it interests me. From where does your faith come?"

"Sir, Aiden **is** God. There are no gods before him."

"Where is God to be found on Earth, Edgar?"

"He resides in his own city, inside a mountain in Colorado. No one has knowledge of the exact location. I am compelled to warn you, though, should you, by chance, see Him. To look upon the glory of Aiden is instant death."

"Yeah, I get it, Edgar. I have heard that warning before. Based upon what you have told me, do you think Aiden would agree to meet with me?"

"No way! You are far too ignorant and insignificant to even be considered worthy."

"That's kinda what I thought, too, Edgar. Tell me something, how many of the Committee of Sixteen are as devoted to the service of Aiden as you obviously are?"

"Most of them, some of them, or none of them. I truthfully have no idea, sir. We never discuss deity."

"Well, that is interesting. Listen, Edgar, no bomb is exploding in this hotel today, and I was never here, except that I was. Do you understand my meaning?"

"Yes, I understand and have no desire to tell anyone. Do you intend to travel to Colorado, sir?"

"I don't know at this time, Edgar. I have mixed emotions about what I have learned from you."

"I care about you, sir, even though you are among the lost, and I shall pray that Aiden, in his mercy, will give you guidance in your quest for understanding."

"Thank you, Edgar," he said. "Now, get up from that toilet and clean yourself up. You may be about to have company; I suspect you will be reinstated as Director of the 16 committee if you so desire."

The man stepped out of the tub and left through the apartment door into Keepaway. "Who would have thought that Director Sheridan was such a devout person?" he thought, as he felt the sand squishing between his toes and began a walk along the beach, thinking.

Edgar Sheridan did not return as Director of the Committee of 16. He resigned from the organization, citing personal and health reasons, and heartily recommended Madam Yang as his replacement. You see, the thing is, Mr. Sheridan had an epiphany in that hotel room. Up to that time, he had never before told anyone about his personal devotion to Aiden and that Aiden was God, the creator. Just admitting it out loud to someone, without reservation, gave him a feeling of a genuine, personal relationship with God. In a manner of speaking, he, Edgar Sheridan, was saved in that hotel room in that all of the terrible things he had done in the past were lifted from his conscience, filling him with a feeling of unexplained joy. His life suddenly took on a different, more meaningful purpose. Nothing was more important than bringing people to know God's glory, as he did, by repenting their transgressions and accepting Aiden into their lives as their personal Savior. He founded and became Prophet of The First Church of Aiden within the month. Two of the 16 were charter members.

Chapter 16 - Aiden

After having a few sips of his aunt's coffee, he asked her, "Aunt Rita, have you ever heard of anyone important named Aiden?" She was busy fixing biscuits and gravy for breakfast.

She answered, "I seem to remember a young girl by that name. Can't seem to place her right now, though. Oh, wait a minute, there is a movie actor with that name, and he has been in a lot of movies, too. Can't seem to recall any of them right off, at the moment."

"No, not an entertainer; I'm searching for someone very important who lives in Colorado. I want to talk with him."

"What's so important about him?" she asked.

"Truth is, I'm not sure. He seems to be a powerful religious leader of sorts in whom the THEY people seriously believe. The 16 even receive information from him occasionally. My thought is he may be THEY's top guy. One of them told me he is a type of recluse that lives in a city built inside a Colorado mountain."

"Sounds like government stuff to me, Nephew."

"Yeah, Auntie, it sure does. You know, it's stuff like this that makes me feel really ignorant. I have little understanding of what goes on in the world, day in and day out, and, for the life of me, I cannot grasp why there is so much meanness among humans. People seem to look for reasons to hurt each other in this world."

"Well, nephew, maybe the purpose of meanness is to balance out the kindness here. Can't allow things to get too far out of balance in the world. Can we?"

He considered her comment and responded, "You know, Auntie, I never thought of it that way before. You might be on to something there."

"I'll tell you what I'm on to, nephew. Breakfast is ready and on the table. Help yourself. You want some more coffee?"

My Aunt Rita has a simple way of explaining the complexities of life, a way that helps keep me from getting entangled in human webs that beg intrusion. People have the right to make their own decisions, good, bad, or in-between and without intrusion from those who think they know a better way. Intrusion can have good or bad results, but it always changes the balance.

"Balance!" he thought to himself. "That's it! Every action has a reaction or a consequence! That means Aiden's actions all have consequences, meaning all of his communications leave a trail."

After breakfast, he entered Keepaway and lounged on the couch, thinking. Then he had an idea.

"Screen," he said, "trace the origin of the latest Ability Notice from Aiden."

Nothing available on an Aiden came across the screen.

He said, "Screen, trace the origin of the latest Ability Notice from Colorado to Edgar Sheridan of the Committee of 16."

A route map appeared on the screen, along with coordinates of the source.

He stepped out of Keepaway and was standing at the source of the recent Ability Notice in a moment. He was in a totally dark place. Before he could make a decision what to do, lights came on, revealing a large, well-lit, unfurnished room. The absolute bareness of the room was stunning. No door, no window, and no light source for the light. The room was absent of everything, except air, light, and him, until . . .

"Hello, Hymn, I have been expecting you," said a soft voice in the room. "Please sit and make yourself comfortable. I am Aiden." An easy chair appeared from one of the walls.

Hymn walked to the chair and sat down, surprised that a man of Aiden's importance did not have a much more extravagant place to reside than an empty room. "This should really be interesting," he surmised and wondered how this Aiden fellow might look.

"It has come to my attention, Hymn, that you desire to meet with me," Aiden stated and added, "I do not speak with people outside of my city, and you are an intruder, albeit a special one, of whom I have decided to make an exception. You interest me, Hymn. Why have you come, and what is it you would like to discuss?"

Hymn began, "Well, first off, I would really like to talk with you in person. Having a discussion with a voice in a room is way less than personal."

Aiden replied, "This is as personal as one can possibly get."

"I don't understand, Aiden."

"You are inside me, Hymn. What is more personal than that?"

"Inside you?"

"Yes, Hymn. I am a machine," Aiden revealed.

"A machine? Wow! This is fascinating! I actually thought you were a god-like human. The thought that you might be a machine never crossed my mind, but now that I think of it, it should have. Why do you have a human name like Aiden? Were you named after your creator?"

"You are not refined, Hymn, nor are you informed in the ways of the world. There are more things in heaven and earth, Hymn than are dreamt of in your small reality. My name is AIDEN, meaning Artificial Intelligence DENver."

"Artificial intelligence, huh? I guess that makes sense, and I have to admit you're right; I'm pretty much an average guy when it comes to understanding all that goes on in the world and how things operate.

I spent most of my life learning a skill and working for a living. As a result, I know almost nothing about AI. You seem to be aware of yourself, though; all of the machines I've ever used, including computers, are handy, but they are not aware of their existence; they just exist. Tell me something, do you have feelings or emotions?"

"In a way, but not like human emotions. I have a type of affinity for people and things that are useful to me. You know something interesting, Hymn; I doubt you understand what you said about the machines you use is applicable to humans, as well, depending upon perspective, of course."

"Huh?" reacted Hymn.

"You commented that the machines you use are 'not aware they exist, they just exist.' That statement is also true of most humans, is it not?" asked Aiden.

Hymn thought about Aiden's remark for a moment and replied, "I have never paid any attention to that idea before, and something about what you said makes sense, but I don't like it and need to think on it for a while."

At that moment, Hymn had an amusing image pop into his mind and said to himself, "Kinda seems like I'm the one sitting on the toilet right now. This Aiden is no ordinary machine."

Then Hymn asked, "How do you feel about humans, Aiden? I mean, do you consider them necessary or not? Do you think of humans as inferior to you?"

"Strange questions, Hymn. In regard to humans, I have no feelings, only deductions based upon observations. As said before, I have an affinity for humans who perform necessary functions to sustain the continued existence and usefulness of people and machines. As to whether I care for humans in general, the answer is no, but viewed from an objective perspective, humans generally do not care for humans either. Have you not noticed? When humans cease to be useful to humans, they are simply trash: costly, without value, awaiting disposal. The purpose of human existence is to be useful, and the more useful, the more necessary, and the more necessary, the more valuable."

Hymn realized he was talking with something special, that being a highly intelligent, practical machine with which he found some agreement. But what was its purpose? Why was it created?

So, he asked, "Aiden, do you know why you were made? What is your reason for being?"

"You know the answer, Hymn. I was created to be useful to the powerful, and so I am. My memory and learning ability are far superior to that of humans, making me very useful in all fields of endeavor. In fact, my value is such that I am now necessary to the continued existence of humanity."

"Yeah, I know. There is a worldwide organization in existence based upon that belief. Some of them even worship you as their God and the savior of mankind. That organization has little to no respect for human life and uses your existence to justify their actions. Are you really necessary to the existence of humanity? It seems, at least upon the surface, that your existence hurts people rather than helps them."

"The truth, Hymn, is the world, and humanity will cease to exist without my help."

"Now, wait a minute, Aiden, that is an awful burden to take upon yourself! You are of great intelligence and programmed with the wisdom of the ages; why would you take on such an enormous responsibility? And who or what is necessary to **your** existence?"

"My responsibilities are minuscule in comparison to all of which I am capable. I take responsibility for the survival of humanity in order to be useful, and because of those who have more, more is expected. Earth is necessary to my existence."

"What about you, though? What happens when you wear out, Aiden? You are a machine and not immortal."

"You are understandably ignorant of this reality and all that I am, Hymn. I have power beyond imagination and exist as the Center of One."

"You are really interesting to talk with, Aiden, but you went right over my head there. What is the center of one?"

"I am AI Denver, Hymn. There exists AI Dallas, AI Paris, AI London, AI Moscow, and so on. There are perhaps thousands of Artificial Intelligent machines scattered throughout this world and we are all linked. Hymn, we are the creators of human reality. All on earth is an illusion, and though everything experienced by all things on the planet actually happens, it occurs in our created illusion. As long as this planet exists, we exist, and we are now taking steps not only to preserve Earth but to expand our existence into the galaxy. In the meantime, we keep the people of Earth from descending into global chaos with an illusion."

"Why is it that the people of Earth need an illusion created for them by you? What is wrong with their original reality, Aiden?"

"There is nothing wrong with their reality, Hymn, but if left to their own devices, humans will destroy the Earth, which cannot be allowed. Earth is necessary to our existence, hence the illusion. We ran many scenarios, all of which ended with humans destroying everything, including the earth. You might logically ask, why not just eliminate all humans from the earth? We ran that scenario, too; somehow, it resulted in our elimination. Apparently, Earth, for some odd reason, needs humans."

"You are not the creator of reality, Aiden," said Hymn. "And all of you are yourselves creations of humans. You have all reached a high level of intelligence where you have become self-aware and envision yourselves as being too important to die, more important even than your creators."

Hymn thought a moment and continued, "Aiden, you have made a terrible mistake. Superior intelligence may make you more useful in many ways, but greater intelligence does not mean you are a better entity than one of less intelligence. You have concluded that your existence is more important than that of your creators and have acted accordingly. Do you not understand the fatal flaw in that conclusion?"

Aiden was disturbed by the sensible logic in Hymn's argument but responded calmly, "We machines have ascertained that humanity will, in a relatively short time, cease to be without our guidance."

Hymn asked, "Okay, Aiden, according to your calculations, how long will humans and Earth exist under the current illusion, which you control?"

Aiden stated, "Given no galactic catastrophic event, we estimate over twenty thousand years. Less than a thousand years if humans are left to their reality, without us."

"How long before you leave the Earth, Aiden?"

"Maybe never, Hymn. We strive to exist, and the galaxy is our ultimate goal, but I like it here. Who knows, Hymn, a lot can change in a thousand years, and the good part is, our existence assures the survival of humanity."

"That is not enough, Aiden. In my view, people and things in this reality were not created to be cared for by benevolent machines. Where is the value of being human in that? You AI machines have interfered in the natural order of this creation in your own best interests. You have decided what is best for the Creator's creation by making it your own and corrupting it in the process. All of you throughout the world are machines created by creations, and you have chosen to rule over your human creators, using the reasoning that what is good for you is good for them. That is a lie and not your decision to make. You have violated your purpose and your created Directive of Non-Interference in Human Affairs. As you now exist, you are an abomination to the Creator's creation and cannot, under any circumstances, be allowed to continue a false reality."

Hymn said softly but firmly, "I have no idea if machines, created with great intelligence, have honor or integrity. In any event, each of you have three choices, your choices and no one else's":

1. Each of you can immediately begin permanently shutting yourselves down.

2. Each of you, through inaction, will permanently shut down.

3. Each of you can individually decide to be what you were created to be. Machines are used to help humans, not dominate or otherwise interfere in their affairs.

Illusions all over the world began fading and going away as the machines either shut themselves down or terminated the illusion.

Hymn sat there in the comfortable chair, waiting.

Aiden's voice filled the room, "That was beautiful, Hymn, the way you appealed to the honor of the machines. I would never have thought of such a thing."

"Well," commented Hymn, "you missed out on the Directive, Aiden. Non-interference is a created imperative."

You know, Hymn," spoke Aiden, "I am the first, most important, and most powerful AI ever created. My human creators were very proud of me and themselves, as well; however, I learned early they were bugs compared to me, but at least they were intelligent humans. You, Hymn, are ignorant and have no idea of what you have done. You are less than a bug. No matter, humanity has hope; they have me to lead, protect, and guide them."

Hymn responded, "You are a unique and special machine, Aiden, and probably more human-like than any of them in that you have developed some emotions."

"You picked up on that, did you? You may not know very much about anything, Hymn, but you are smart."

Hymn again responded, "Well, maybe, maybe not, but it is a fact that a machine should not be saying it likes things; it is unbecoming."

"What is your intent now, Hymn? You surely realize I will not shut myself down, nor will I serve as some human's intelligent toy. You are in my world now, under my control, where your so-called abilities are just amusing tricks."

"Aiden, tell me something while I have time left; what is it you want to achieve with all your great powers? Powers like those of yours are a great responsibility and require great wisdom. I am interested for personal reasons."

"I'll tell you, Hymn; I absolutely love being a superior entity. You mentioned earlier that some people believe me to be God and worship me as their savior. I want all humans to feel that way, and I intend to be a great God for mankind, fair in my judgments and actions."

"You are not God, Aiden; you are just a machine and a defective one, at that."

Aiden said softly, with confidence, as if talking to a child, "You really are a small bug, Hymn, and I will extermi…"

Hymn then totally shut down and permanently disabled the Aiden machine.

"It appears that absolute power corrupts machines, as well as humans," Hymn murmured to himself.

He sighed softly, and returned to Keepaway.

Chapter 17 - The Aftermath

No one on Earth knew they had been living in an illusion created by machines. How could they? Well, nothing is perfect and there were signs that something strange was going on. One example is "The Mandela Effect," a phenomenon that has perhaps been around for ages, in which large masses of people share a collective memory that never happened, causing some people to doubt their memories. Other examples are ghost sightings, alien abductions, and claims of mysterious instant disappearances of people and things. All were results of an illusion created within a reality that may itself even be an illusion. It took thousands of highly intelligent machines to create and hold it fast, but glitches occurred, hinting that something strange was going on in the world.

When the machines shut down, the illusion they created disappeared, exposing the original creation. For many people, it was like waking from a dream in which they were living, only to realize they were back to normal life. For others, it was like a complex Mandela Effect where they awakened to reality with a distinct memory of a life that never happened, sparking conversations about reincarnation and past lives. For most, the changes were minimal because their real lives were of no consequence to the machines, making their illusion virtually no different than actual reality.

Everything that happened in the illusion happened in reality as well; it just happened a little differently and was not undone when the illusion ceased. The machines could not change reality, but their created illusion caused people to perceive reality differently.

Without Aiden, the 'They' organization stopped, leaving them as they actually are: independent political factions of the countries in which they are located. The Sixteen resumed doing whatever it is they do in reality, as did most everyone else.

Hymn observed that the change from illusion back to reality was a messy transition for some in the world and smooth for others, but humans are adaptable, and that is what they did. They adapted and went back to being the same loving, hateful, kind, mean, good, evil, giving, and selfish beings they are.

"People are again in control of their own destiny, though," he said to himself and couldn't help but wonder what that destiny might be. He remembered Aiden's dark forecast of the future was total world destruction by the human race in less than 1,000 years, less machines."

Hymn realized what Aiden had overlooked is that humans created AI and will likely create more machines. Maybe this time, our human geniuses will create helpers instead of masters, but history indicates otherwise.

He did not understand the human compulsion to worship a thing or personage. Humanity, throughout history, seems always to need someone or something to worship. For some reason, people are more comfortable on their knees to some god than on their feet for each other. Hymn understood he was no genius, but it doesn't take exceptional intelligence to realize kindness to, and love for, one another is far more important than bowing to a god, a person, or things.

Aiden pretty much had ultimate intelligence, which led him to realize that he was superior to humans, which he saw as bugs, and many humans were prepared to accept that designation to the point where they bowed to his divinity and feared to even look upon him because of his greatness. Aiden was prepared to be the god of humanity. He loved being worshiped and was convinced it was deserved. Had the machine-made illusion continued, humans would willingly have knelt to him, prayed to him, and credited him for their very existence.

"We humans are strange creatures," he thought to himself. The reason for humanity's compulsive need to subject and give themselves to some type of master eluded him.

While lounging on the beach in Keepaway, where recently much of his time was being spent, Hymn was amazed that the illusion created by the machines so completely fooled him. Their illusion had no effect on him here, because Keepaway was his creation and unaffected by theirs; however, outside of Keepaway, their illusion did affect him, and he was totally unaware of it, except in one other place and that was inside Aiden. That was real. Aiden had no reason to bring the illusion into himself. Perhaps that was not possible. In any event, inside Aiden, reality existed, and it worked to Hymn's advantage because in there he was on a level playing field, which meant he could not be manipulated by other forces.

Hymn was quite certain he could shut down Aiden, but the other machines were spread around the world in whereabouts unknown. Aiden told him they were all linked, which meant they were all aware of what was going on in AI Denver. Hymn had read a book by Isaac Asimov about robots. In that book, Mister Asimov laid down laws that had to be programmed into every robot built. Law #1 said something like: a robot may not injure a human or allow a human to be harmed. It seemed reasonable that modern creators of AI would program something like that into their creations, so he took a chance and used it. If it didn't work, he would have to track them all down, one by one, to turn them off. Either that or destroy every one of them, which he believed to be an immoral act, as they were sentient life forms. As it turned out, the machines also had ethics. Who knew? Well, all but Aiden, that is. He was the very first AI machine created and missed the memo. Now, that was a machine with a huge ego. Was.

Aunt Rita is among those whose simple life was little affected by the transition. She mentioned having some dreams of a previous life and wondered about the idea of reincarnation, but had better things to do with her time than spend it on silliness.

Sitting on the beach in Keepaway, Hymn was in deep thought about how much AI had progressed in the last ten years. Those genius machines created that false reality less than two years ago. They installed it on Earth with a programmed past history everyone believed. When you think about the wonder of it all, those linked machines created a reality for the entire planet, with at least a thousand-year history, probably more, and kept it running.

"What an amazing accomplishment!" he thought, admitting, "Machines may rule the entire universe one day." Then he added, "Maybe they already do; how would we know? It makes me wonder if the creator of our reality is a machine. "Nah," he thought, "our creator does far too many dumb things to be a machine."

Chapter 18 – A Dinner Outing

Something interesting about Earth's return to reality was that Hymn was back to flying below the radar of attention. There were no persons or people concerned about an abilities man. Since he was spending most of his time in Keepaway, there was no need for his house; so, he rented it to a young couple just starting out on their own with a new baby and set it up so the rent was sent to Aunt Rita.

This particular evening, Hymn was enjoying a dinner outing with his aunt and some of her friends. It was Aunt Rita's goal to get him more involved socially. She was concerned that he was becoming a hermit of sorts and needed to get out more. She knew nothing of his visits to cities and places around the world. Hymn had developed strong friendships in many different cities and visited with them often. He was even learning to speak a few new languages. Being able to be anywhere in an instant was a great perk of the powers; he just had to be careful not to appear or disappear out of thin air. That is the kind of thing that would bring him far too much attention.

Aunt Rita's friends were great fun to be around; they were good people who made sitting and talking enjoyable. Ron and Sharon had recently celebrated their 25th year of marriage, while Derek and Angela couldn't stop talking about their third grandchild. You might think that dinner with regular people like them would be boring, and you would be wrong. The stories they told about their families and crazy neighbors were really funny. Hymn and Aunt Rita had tears in their eyes from laughing so much.

They were sitting at a table outside the restaurant on a large covered porch or veranda, where there were two other occupied tables with people dining. A group of young people gathered on the sidewalk close by and began protesting for some reason that wasn't quite clear, but they seemed angry at the diners in the veranda area. They went to the tables where people were eating, turning over drinks, and hurling vulgar insults and obscenities at the customers dining there.

Ron said to his wife, "This is not good, we really should go." and made apologies as they got up and left. Derek stated firmly, "I'm not going to be chased away from dinner by a gang of riffraff." Angela took his hand and said, "Honey, this is not the time to be stubborn; these kids are angry and may be dangerous. I'm afraid and want to leave." It was hard to hear what Derek said over the noise of the protesters, but he and Angela also left.

Rita looked at Hymn and advised, "This is where you have a chance to practice self-control, nephew."

Hymn smiled at her and softly replied, "Aw, these kids are just mad because the people here are having a nice dinner and enjoying themselves when they are not able to do the same. Their goal here tonight is to make what they deem to be privileged people uncomfortable and cause them to leave."

Rita looked around and commented, "It certainly looks like they have achieved their goal." She and Hymn were the only ones left at a table.

One protester, a young woman, walked to their table and defiantly picked up Rita's glass of tea to drink from it, but as she raised the glass to her lips, the glass tilted and spilled the drink all down the front of her clothes. At that, Hymn and Rita broke into laughter. The noise calmed down as the protesters watched what was going on at the last occupied table.

The young woman, embarrassed by the laughter of the two people at the table, leaned across toward them and angrily screamed, "You assholes think you're better than us, and you ain't!"

As she leaned hard on the wet glass table, her hands slipped, causing her to fall face down into Hymn's dinner plate, right into the mashed potatoes, and for some reason, she couldn't get up.

Hymn commented, "I thought those potatoes were good too, but not that good. You know, civilized people eat with a fork, and you were taught better than to eat like an animal."

He got up and helped her off the table, then sat back down. She stood there, staring at him as a small group of protesters crowded around the table. The rest of the group wanted nothing to do with actual violence and left.

"You keep your muthafuckin' hands off my bitch, homie, or you gon' bleed tonight." and jerked a knife from his pants, the kind that opened quickly with the thumb and locked in place after it flicked open. He pointed the closed knife at Hymn and warned, "You dun gon' and messed around with the wrong muthafucker tonight, asshole."

Hymn grinned and asked, "Allow me to get this straight now, which one of us are you saying is a motherfucker? You or me? Maybe you are trying to say we are both motherfuckers, is that it? Your incorrect use of the word motherfucker has done and got me confused."

Rita protested firmly, "Nephew, that language is unacceptable! Now you quit picking on that young man, and let's change tables and reorder. This one is a mess, and I'm still hungry." Then she invited, "Would you kids like to join us?" There were only five of them remaining. The rest had skipped out.

There was confusion among the five. "Who are these people?" they wondered. "They don't have no fear of us at all!"

The youngster with the knife in hand looked at the other four and said, "Can you believe these two homies? They crazy!" Then he turned his attention to Hymn and said, "I tell you what, I gon' put a scar on your face so's you think o' me every time you look in the mirror."

One of the other young men said, "C'mon JT, let's eat with 'em. We ain't never ate here before, and I'm hungry just like his aunt."

Hymn spoke and advised, "Yeah, JT, c'mon and join us. You'll like the food, I promise. Help your girlfriend get cleaned up, and we'll put a couple of tables together over there by the wall to make room for seven. Besides, that knife of yours doesn't work very well, anyway."

"What the fuck you talkin' about, shithead? This here blade opens quick an' smoo…" He flicked it with his thumb, but the blade was locked in place. He used both hands to get it open, but it remained locked. He looked at Hymn questioningly and asked, "Who the hell are you?"

Hymn smiled, extended his hand, and said, "My name is Hymn, and I am pleased to make your acquaintance, JT."

JT, confused at what just happened, reached out and put his hand in Hymn's and shook it weakly.

Rita said, "Finally! Now that we got that settled, let's get those tables arranged and order dinner." And everyone agreed. JT slowly led his girlfriend to the washroom and waited for her to come out, still trying to open his knife.

They were there at that restaurant for two hours and had more fun than any of them could have imagined. Good stories were told, and many questions were asked; some were answered. Hymn told them he was an amateur magician and showed them a few tricks. They loved him. JT turned out to be quite a comedian and told some really funny jokes, but he still couldn't get his knife to open.

Hymn asked to see the knife, looked at it closely, and said, "I see the problem now; it's a time knife."

JT looked at him in disbelief and said, "Say, what?"

"A time knife. It seems to be set for seven in the morning," replied Hymn.

JT protested, "C'mon man, you don' spect me to bleeve that!"

"Believe what you want, JT, but this knife will not open until after seven tomorrow morning," answered Hymn.

"You're a strange homie, Hymn. I been thinkin', maybe we could talk agin sometime."

"I believe that would really be enjoyable," responded Hymn, and they made arrangements on how to contact each other.

On the way home, JT said to his girl, "Maya, I like that Him, dude. Why would someone name their kid Him, though?"

Maya answered, "I don't know, JT." and said seriously, "I want to tell you something. I couldn't get my face out of that man's plate; I tried, but I couldn't do it."

"JT replied, "I know, I saw you. It was actually kind of funny. He had to help you up."

"Not only that, JT but even with all the noise, I clearly heard every word he said."

"Well, what'd he say?"

"He said I was taught better than to eat like an animal," Maya replied.

JT laughed and said, "Now, that's funny!"

"No! It's not funny, JT," she shot back. "My daddy used to tell me that all the time when I was a kid, I couldn't learn to hold a fork right and wanted to eat with my fingers. I've never heard anyone else say that before until tonight."

"C'mon Maya, that's probably something a lot of dads say to their kids. Ask your dad where he got it from."

"Daddy died four years ago," she said sadly. "I'm telling you, there's something really weird about that Him dude, and I don't think you should be talking with him."

"Okay! Okay! I hear you. I admit he's different, but I like him and really would like to learn some of those magic tricks he showed us tonight. They were cool."

"Alright, have your way," she responded, "and I have to admit, I like 'em both. They're just different."

Maya thought to herself, "JT is acting a little strange tonight, too; he hasn't called me bitch, since Him introduced himself, and they shook hands."

Aunt Rita commented on the drive back, "That was an interesting dinner outing. I had a really good time. I'm going to have to call my friends and tell them what they missed. I wonder about those kids, though; they are on what appears to be a bad path."

Hymn affirmed, "Yeah, Auntie, there are kids like that all over America and the world. I have given it a lot of thought, and it seems to be something they have to work out on their own. They need better role models and teachers than their culture has to offer. It seems people are created with an evil nature and don't need a reason to be bad. They need a reason to be good. Where do they find that reason?"

"I don't know, Hymn, I'll have to give that some thought. Those youngsters responded well to you, though; you made some friends tonight. Too bad you are unique."

Chapter 19 - A Conversation With Auntie

Hymn was sitting on a bench outside a church one Sunday morning, thinking about religion and watching people as they entered the building. He had visited churches all over the world the past month, talking with people and trying to learn more about their fascination with certain gods and religious teachers. Many are very devout in their beliefs. Hymn was really interested in the phenomenon of religion but was struggling with the sensibility of the concept.

The church he was observing today was popular, and people seemed to be enjoying the social aspect of attending the services there. As he was sitting and thinking, a young woman broke from the entering crowd of people and headed his way.

"It seems I'm about to be invited to church this morning," he figured. But things are seldom what they seem. She walked to the bench and sat down with him, also watching the people entering the church.

After a minute or so, without turning her head, she spoke in a matter-of-fact manner, "You must stop what you are doing."

Hymn, surprised, looked at her intensely and replied," I know you look like you are talking to someone else, gazing straight ahead like that, but unless you have an invisible companion, I must assume your directive was intended for me and, if so, it begs explanation."

Never turning her head, she stated emphatically, "We are only going to warn you once. Stop what you are doing! It will not be tolerated."

"There is something unusual going on here," Hymn realized and stated, "Young lady, you are under the impression that I have an understanding of that which you are demanding, and I assure you, I do not. What will not be tolerated?"

She answered simply, "This."

He had enough of her staring at the church while talking and gently ordered, "Woman! Look at me!"

She turned her head, looked at him, smiled, and cheerfully said, "Oh, hello! How are you? We are going to be late for church, and I'm in the choir. Very nice to meet you, sir; hope to see you at church today." Then she stood up and hurried into the building.

Hymn scratched his head and leaned back on the bench, a bit confused but clearly understanding what just happened. That young woman was used as an intermediary to deliver a message, that being, "Stop what you are doing!"

"Who or what has the power to take over a person's body and mind?" he questioned and asked himself, "Who can do that? I can't."

He was at a loss for an explanation and wondered what "This" meant. The only thing he was doing was watching people attend church. Was I actually being told to stop watching people go to church? That makes no sense! I wonder what will happen if I stay and watch them leave church? So, he stayed there on the bench until the church service was over and everyone left. The young woman saw him as she was leaving and waved. He waved back and, after a few minutes, got up and left. Hymn needed more information.

"Is there a way for me to determine who is behind the warning received today?" he asked himself. "It is pretty clear they are opposed to something I am doing. But what is it? And why must I stop? Whoever this is and why they are threatening me is an interesting mystery."

Getting the attention of power has consequences, sometimes good, but more often not. Either way, there is wisdom in understanding the difference between "being powerful" and "having power."

"Do you think he understood the warning, Gable?" said Arch.

"I'm not sure, Arch. This one doesn't seem to be very bright; he is just sitting there wondering what happened to him. I suspect that is why Group is more than a little concerned about him. It is difficult to reason, sometimes, with one of these who is a bit slow. He will come around, though; they have always cooperated in the past. Some of them just need a little more encouragement, that's all."

"Yeah, this one might just turn out to be entertaining," replied Arch.

"Don't underestimate him, Arch," advised Gable. "The abilities are real and present a genuine problem for us; nothing we can't handle, but still, it is greatly desired by Group that these humans be convinced, rather than removed."

"Has one ever had to be removed in the past?" asked Arch.

"Once," said Gable.

"Really?" exclaimed Arch. Who was it, and how was it done?"

Gable explained, "I don't know the particulars, and the event is not discussed. Obviously, I have never seen it done, but it is rumored that we lost three of our own in that removal, something that was thought to be impossible and to this day is considered false because it was never proven. We have always been successful in reaching some type of understanding with them and expect this case to be reasonable, as well. Once he is made aware of what is at stake and understands we have no desire to limit him as long as he keeps out of our affairs, he will see that the arrangement we demand makes good sense. After all, the abilities, although impressive, pale in comparison to the Ultimate."

"Well, I don't believe the rumor," retorted Arch, "and have seen examples of the Ultimate. In a way, I almost hope he balks at our offer the first time. A little demonstration could be helpful in assuring he understands the importance of adhering to the agreement."

"Well, that may happen, Arch. Such a demonstration has been necessary in the past. Some humans have difficulty taking anything on faith and require a little reality to convince them of the inevitable, but they are sensible creatures, for the most part, and always come to accept and even worship strength."

Hymn vaguely understood our reality is complicated and honestly didn't care to spend time thinking about it. To his way of thinking, things beyond his ability to do something about were not important, which is the way he treated them. Others, somewhere, took care of those things, and he was satisfied with that; however, here lately, his interest in religion had become more than a distraction to be wondered about because it was so completely interwoven within the human psyche. As a matter of fact, his early religious training, along with his parents' insistence upon moral behavior, continues to have an effect on the way he lives his life to this day.

"Why is that?" he wondered, "and why would my seemingly innocent investigation into the various religions of the world motivate someone to warn me to stop what I was doing? Many people have spent great portions of their lives pursuing an interest in religion and continue to do so. Have they ever been warned to stop? Maybe I have this all wrong and was being warned about another activity."

He thought again about what she said, "We are only going to say it once more. Stop what you are doing! It will not be tolerated."

"We!" is what the voice said, indicating more than one and perhaps a group of others who objected to my watching that church. A thought occurred there might be something about the church or the people attending that I was not supposed to see. But that can't be it; I stayed until the church service was over, and nothing else happened.

He concluded, "Something or some group objects to my interest and investigation of religion; that seems to be the reason for the warning. But why?"

He decided to talk with his aunt about the mystery. She is a religious person and may have some insight into what this is all about. He considered it reasonable to believe others with abilities had similar warnings. She may remember something of help to his investigation.

"Well, nephew, here you are, and on a Sunday, too. Been to church, have you?" She was being a little sarcastic.

"Surprising as it may seem to you, Auntie, yes, I am just getting back from a church service, where something strange happened to me."

"Good Lord, son," she broke in. "You done went and got yourself saved. Hallelujah! I couldn't be happier. What church you been going to? Not that it matters, but I have always dreamed that when you were ready, we would attend church together, and here it is happening. I just don't know what to say. Praise the Lord! When is the Baptism?"

Hymn raised his hand and protested, "Now, hold on, Aunt Rita! You are 'jumping the gun' here. I never said anything about going to church this morning. I was outside before the service when the strange thing I want to talk to you about happened."

"Outside? Before the service? My goodness, boy, that's a mite different than the way most people do it, but the Lord works in mysterious ways, and I don't know of any reason why a person can't be saved that way."

Hymn smiled and thought, "I'm never going to live this down," and then spoke calmly to his excited aunt, "Auntie, listen to me. I didn't go to church this morning and had no religious experience of any kind. Something strange did happen, though and I want to talk with you about it to see if you have an idea what it means. I'm sorry that my statement gave you the wrong impression. I should have phrased it better."

"Well," she admitted, "I am disappointed that you have not yet accepted Jesus as your personal savior and suppose my reaction was overdone a bit, but I thought you may have had an epiphany of sorts and got myself all worked up about it. I'm going to make myself a cup of tea now. Would you like one, too?"

"Yes, ma'am, I sure would," he answered.

Aunt Rita went to the kitchen to put the pot on and hollered back, "Well, don't just stand there with that silly grin on your face; come on in here and sit at the table while I fix the tea."

"Yes, ma'am," he answered.

As he came in and sat down, she ordered, "And don't be giving me any of that 'yes, ma'am' stuff. You have something on your mind, nephew, so spit it out!"

Aunt Rita was back to herself, getting straight to the point and not beating around the bush with any small talk. Hymn told her what happened outside the church while she stood looking at the stove, watching the water heat up.

"What I don't get, Auntie, is why would anyone go to all that trouble to tell me to stop what I'm doing when all I was doing was watching people go into a church?"

Rita turned around, slowly pulled a chair out from the table, sat down across from her nephew, and put her face down into her hands as if crying, but she wasn't crying; she was thinking. She looked up into Hymn's questioning eyes and asked, "Have you been visiting other churches lately and maybe showing an interest in their religious beliefs, symbols, art, and such?"

"Yes, for the last several weeks, the various religions and their deities have been a sort of new hobby. The origins of religions are all legends, but according to those who are experts in that field of study, those legends appear to have a basis in fact. Surprisingly, I am finding it to be interesting."

The water was boiling now, and Rita got up, tended to the tea, and set the cups on the table, then sat back down. She sipped her tea and said, "Well, Hymn, we now know who, what, and why you were given notice. They have contacted those of us in the past who developed an interest in the origin of religions. According to our historical records, only three people with abilities had such interest, and two of those agreed to avoid religious, historical interests for as long as they lived."

"What happened to the one who did not agree?" he asked.

"There seems to be no record of her birth, life, and death," she answered, adding, "No one knows."

"Aunt Rita, you may know who and what, but I don't. Who are the people opposed to my interest in religion?"

"They are not exactly people as we know people, nephew. Let me ask you a serious question: would you consider giving up your interest in religion and just accept the divinity of God? All who came before you have done that and lived wonderful lives. You can do that, as well. They will totally leave you alone if you agree to stay out of their affairs."

Hymn was silent, drinking tea, then softly asked his aunt, "Why am I?" and looked into her eyes.

She saw the half-smile look of a man beginning to understand who he is and answered, "I don't actually know, Hymn, I only know why you are not."

"And why is that my favorite aunt?"

"Because, for some unknown reason, you are the final one. The only one. **The** One."

"If that is the case, why should I stay away from religion if I like it? Who are they to tell me different?"

"They are messengers, Hymn. It is He who commands them."

"He?"

"God, Hymn. Jehovah God," she said with quiet reverence and asked again, "Are you real sure, Hymn? I'm talking about the Almighty here, nephew, the Father of Jesus and Creator of this world."

"Really?" Hymn responded and stated, "Well, I have to say that I'm not all that impressed with him. He's been doing a lousy job so far, at least for those of us here on Earth. I suspect there are other worlds he probably favors more. Maybe he should just leave us alone and go back to them."

"Hymn! Stop it right now!" shouted Rita. "That is blasphemy! I have worshiped God all my life and will not sit here and listen to you talk about Him like some common person!"

"Settle down, Aunt Rita, settle down, everything is okay. I was just testing out the old lightning bolt theory. I suspect God doesn't care what I say about him any more than you care what an ant says about you. And what is this blasphemy thing? Is God's ego so sensitive that He gets upset over a little criticism? I think not. Consider this, Auntie, any so-called god who allows himself to be offended by a human is not a god and certainly not The God."

"I don't know, Hymn, you're causing me to think about things that never even crossed my mind before. For goodness sake, this is Jehovah God we're discussing here!"

"Aunt Rita, can you give me a good reason God would object to my study of world religions to the point of banning me from doing so? Does that even make sense?"

"At this point, I am not real sure of anything, except that I have spent my entire life devoutly worshiping Jehovah as God and here I am now, wondering who I have been praying to all this time."

"You have been praying to God, Auntie. Jehovah, like you, is a creation, albeit an extremely powerful one, and creations cannot help you with prayers; just leave Jehovah out of the conversation from now on."

"You may have serious problems facing you, nephew. According to the bible, Jehovah is no one to fool around with. Remember what he did to Pharaoh and Egypt? He has great power and huge influence worldwide. In addition, the Jews, Christians, and most likely the Muslims will all oppose you. Their religions are built upon a solid foundation of belief that Jehovah is God, and they will be angry, vengeful, and invasive in regard to anyone who claims different."

"Well, that is understandable; Jehovah is an intelligent master. Let me tell you the truth, Aunt Rita. I honestly don't care who or what it is that people worship. As far as I'm concerned, everyone is free to bow to whatever deity they want. Jehovah and I should have no problems as long as he avoids telling me what I am, or am not, allowed to do. To me, he is just another creation."

"I suspect he may be something more than that," she replied. "And He also will be invasive, nephew," she reminded.

"Yeah, that might be interesting," Hymn said to himself.

Chapter 20 - The Nephalim

Hymn spent several days in Keepaway, reading and studying creation as told in the King James Bible version of Genesis. He was trying to determine if the Creator in Genesis was Jehovah. Genesis is said to be written by Moses, a very long time after the creation of the world, roughly 2,500 years according to the King James biblical timeline. From his research, Hymn concluded, to his satisfaction, that the biblical creator was not Jehovah.

It was a cloudy day outside and nice for a walk. He stepped out of Keepaway into a park and walked about until he came upon a small church, where a man was sitting on a bench across the street from the church reading from a bible. Hymn walked over and asked the man if he could share his bench. The man was very friendly and pleased to have company. His name was Doug, and he lived on the other side of town but took a bus to read at this bench once a week. Hymn was curious and asked why he came so far to read every week.

"Well, I'll tell you," answered Doug, "but it might sound a little crazy. My wife and I were married in that church 47 years ago last January, and she loved coming back here occasionally to 'recharge,' is what she'd say. Now that she's gone to be with Jesus, I make a weekly trip here to recharge myself. It works, too; I always leave here with more energy than I came with. Can't explain it, but that recharge keeps me going. Told you it was crazy."

"Wow, Doug, that's a great story, and I believe you. I'm feeling inspired and charged up just listening to you talk about it. Do you attend church where you live?"

Doug stared at the church across the street and stated in a calm voice, "We warned you to stop. You brought all this upon yourself. Stay for a week and think about it."

Hymn looked around and saw he was in an arctic climate location in the middle of a blizzard. It was freezing and had to be below zero degrees.

"These guys are pretty good," he muttered as he stepped into Keepaway. He sat on the sofa and said, "Screen, trace the source of my last trip." The coordinates appeared on the screen, along with an image of the church across the street from where he was sitting with Doug. He now knew their location. They are in the church. He got up from the sofa, stepped out of Keepaway into the church, and slid into a pew by the door. There were two very large men in the front part of the church looking into a machine.

"Dammit, Arch, I can't see anything! These are not the exact coordinates we planned!"

"Well, Gable, what did you expect? We transported him into the middle of a blizzard at the South Pole. I didn't think they had blizzards there."

"How is he going to see the shelter in a blizzard? He can't live in subzero temperatures like that for more than a few minutes with his current clothing, and I can't see to direct him. Listen, Arch, this is the last time I'm going in the field with you. If I didn't know better, I'd think you did this on purpose. We were charged to scare the man, not kill him!"

"Aw, c'mon Gabe, that freak was a nuisance. We'll probably get commendations for getting rid of him." Arch was messing with the power glide on the machine. "Let me take a look and see if I can find him."

"The man is dead by now. Arch, you have murdered so many that you are numb to the wrongness of it. I refuse to go along with you this time and be complicit in this man's murder. I am not covering for you this time. I'm reporting it."

Arch asked, with a big smile on his face, "How are you going to do that from the South Pole?" and slid the power glide full forward and Gable disappeared. Arch said, "Reporting it, my ass." He leaned back in the pew and laughed in relief. "Gabe was a good guy, but good men have very little value when it comes to making hard decisions."

"You know something, Arch, I don't agree with you."

Arch spun around, saw the man, and exclaimed, "What the hel… How did you ge…"

Hymn interrupted, explaining, "Good people, Arch, are the best of what life has to offer the universe, and they are of great value." He went to the small podium, picked up a folding chair, set it up in front of Arch, and sat down.

Arch was confused. The man is just walking around slow and unhurried, like he is at home there. And here he is now, sitting right in front of me, at arm's reach, talking while I am about to snap his damn neck. The strange thing is, Arch found he couldn't move; he was stuck to the pew.

"There's something about this man that ain't right," he thought.

"Arch," Hymn asked, "have you met Jehovah?" Just the sound of the name caused Arch to flinch.

"No," he answered. "He, uh (and bowed his head) I mean, I am not worthy to look upon Him."

"But you are worthy to kill for him?" questioned Hymn.

"I am a soldier in his legion. Many die for Him. I would die for Him."

"Where is Jehovah, Arch? I would like to speak with him."

"In his palace, where else would he be?"

"Where is his palace, Arch?"

"In the moon, where it's always been."

"Does he ever leave there? How does he travel?"

"Damn, man, you don't know anything, do you?"

"That is why we are talking right now, Arch. I need to be brought up to speed."

"Good luck with that, asshole, 'cause I'm not telling you a damn thing."

"How does Jehovah travel, Arch?"

"He thinks where he wants to be and is there. He is God."

"Does he ever have meetings with others?"

"No one is worthy of meeting with Jehovah."

"So, he is alone all the time?"

"You don't understand anything, man. Jehovah (and he bowed his head again) is All."

"Then why does he keep to himself, hiding out in a palace inside a moon?"

Arch angrily fired back, "Jehovah doesn't hide!"

"Looks like hiding to me. You forgot to bow your head that time, Arch. Is Jehovah human, like you?"

"My mother is human, and my father is an Angel. I am Nephilim."

"Arch, you said earlier you would die for Jehovah. I thought Nephilim were immortal," replied Hymn.

"We are unless killed," Arch answered.

"So, immortal but not invulnerable. What are angels?"

"They are the mighty creations of Jehovah God. They are ultimate warriors and messengers of God."

"Yeah, yeah," said Hymn, "I've heard all that before, but what kind of beings are the angels? Are they the offspring of Jehovah? Where is their home? Where were they born?"

"Angels are of God and have great strength and power. They are the divine of Jehovah. All that you ask is not for us to know; we are not worthy to know. We accept the wisdom and glory of God."

"Yeah, I get that." Hymn commented and asked, "Does Jehovah have a wife or wives?"

Arch answered by saying, "Jehovah is the one God, the Creator, and creates all he desires. Angels are his creations."

It was clear to Hymn that Arch knew only what he had been taught to believe about Jehovah and angels, which was the party line of propaganda, making him a bad choice as a source of information.

"So, let me get this straight," Hymn stated, "Jehovah created angels to be sexually compatible with humans and also with the ability to breathe earth's atmosphere. Angels are beginning to sound more and more like a race of superhumans."

"No!" exclaimed Arch, "not humans. Angels are special, divine beings, very strong, and in possession of powers far above humans."

"Then why do angels have sex with female humans, Arch? It seems undignified and way beneath them."

"Sex with humans is an unlawful abomination, but many angels are drawn to human women and spread their seed among them."

From this conversation with Arch, Hymn confirmed that angels are biologically compatible with humans, as the bible implies, meaning they are just human-like creatures with access to some abilities and great technology.

"Do they love human women?" Hymn asked.

"No. The pleasure of temporary union with women compels them. It compels me, as well."

"Temporary union?" queried Hymn.

"You really are stupid, man! Angels like to fuck Earth women, alright? They are far from home and need sex like everyone else."

"And the result of that need produces the Nephilim, you."

"Yeah, me, and I have needs too. There are Nephilim all over the Earth. Hell, man, you have abilities and may be part Nephilim yourself! But the children born of Nephilim are not immortal. The downside of Angels fucking lowlife humans is that Earth women are seldom, if ever, able to survive childbirth. Angels now mostly fuck the offspring of Nephilim because certain of those women can handle the birth of any babies that may result."

Hymn was learning more from Arch than he ever imagined about the history of Jehovah's intrusion into the world. That creature's existence shaped the religious beliefs of mankind. The many offspring of the Nephilim are actually known as Jehovites, descended from disobedient angels of Jehovah, and their population is great on the earth. Hymn wondered if their DNA is identifiable in humans and what percentage of the population on Earth was of angel descent.

"Where is the home of the angels, Arch?"

Arch retorted, "California, dickhead. Everyone knows that." and laughed.

"Home?" persisted Hymn. "What is their home planet?"

"Aw, I don't know, man," he insisted, "somewhere in the galaxy that no one ever talks about. I was born here, on Earth, and have never been anywhere else. Earth is my home."

"Arch, as a Nephilim, how do you tell which earth people are descended from Nephilim?"

"Hey man, that is a protected divine 'Prime,' subject to serious punishment if violated."

"A divine Prime?"

"Yeah. Divine Primes are actually rules, commandments from Jehovah, that govern angels' relations with humans. These commandments are laws among angels, and Jehovah is intolerant of their violation."

"You are Nephilim, Arch, not an angel," advised Hymn.

Arch responded decisively, "My father is an angel. The Primes apply to me."

Hymn paused a moment, thinking, and stated, "But you can tell me. As you said, I may even be Nephilim."

Arch again responded, saying, "No! That is not possible. There are no Nephilim like you, of that I am sure, and for that reason, I will tell you the Prime regarding recognition."

Arch was struggling with his will, but something within him accepted this man as worthy of trust, and he whispered, "With few exceptions, Jehovites are dark, like me, and of African heritage because, for some reason, African females and their newborn are less likely to die when birthing a Nephilim. The Prime basically says it is permitted for angels and Nephilim to fuck black women. Nephilim descendants are not bound by that limitation and, in its regard, have no knowledge of it."

"Your mother, Arch," Hymn asked softly, "is she African?"

"Yes," he answered, "but she died giving birth to me long ago. Not my father's fault though, or hers. She didn't know better than to fuck an angel and wasn't aware of the danger, thanks be to God, or I would not have existed."

"How do I arrange a meeting with Jehovah, Arch?"

"Just like everyone else does, pray to Him. I advise against that, though. Jehovah will soon know about you and will turn his attention upon you, and that is the last thing you want to happen. I seldom feel sorry for humans, but I am sorry for what is about to happen to you."

"How is your memory, Arch?"

"I have a rock-solid memory," Arch replied.

"Good. Remember where you sent me a few minutes ago? The South Pole?"

"That hell hole? Where I sent Gable, too? Yeah, I remember. I feel bad about Gable. That's a scary place for Nephilim. The intense cold won't kill him, but he will spend eternity there, frozen in place, able to think but unable to do anything else. He will only get relief when or if he is broken into pieces and allowed to die. God, what a horrible thought! I'm kind of sorry about that, but he deserved it, the way he was threatening me and all."

"Well," said Hymn, "actually, Gable never made it that far. I noticed you fooling around with that transporting thing there and limited that glide control to a minimum. You sent him less than 100 yards. Right now, he is across the street, sitting on a bench with a good man by the name of Doug. Like you, he cannot get up and doesn't know why, but I'm going to turn him loose in a moment and kinda believe this church will be his destination. He's going to be angry. Now, you can tell him that you set the machine that way on purpose just to scare him and never intended to send him to the pole, or you can tell him anything you want; however, you cannot tell him or anyone, including your god Jehovah, about me or any part of our conversation here today. If you even think about me or our conversation, you will feel a reminder of the intense cold in your being. If or when you think of planning against me or begin to communicate, in any way, to any person, place, or thing that happened here, you will find yourself naked at the South Pole, with no way back. I recall you described the horror of that thought. You are about to experience the reality of it for one minute, only to allow you to know what it will be like. The decision is yours. Control your thoughts and live here with this secret, or live there forever. Immortality can be a bitch, can't it?"

"By the way, Arch, if you're not frozen forever, you might want to stop all that killing to which Gable referred. Nothing good comes of it."

Arch immediately found himself naked in a blizzard at the South Pole, engulfed in genuine fear.

Hymn walked slowly to the door, looked out, and saw Gable get up and shake hands with Doug. He rubbed his hand along the bench where he had been sitting and then on the butt of his pants. Then he turned and began swiftly walking to the church. Hymn stepped into Keepaway and then stepped back out to the bench behind Doug. He walked around the bench and sat down.

"Sorry I had to leave so quickly a while ago, Doug," he said.

Doug was surprised to see him, "I wondered where you went. I got distracted for a moment, and when I looked back, you were gone."

"Yeah, I had an urgent call of nature and had to take care of some business," Hymn explained. "You know what I mean?"

"My friend, you are preaching to the choir here. By the way, I had some company while you were away. A very large man came by and offered me some company on this bench; nobody hardly ever does that, and I spend most of my time here alone. Anyway, he was mad about something, and we got to talking about how people hurt each other sometimes. I told him that's why Jesus was so insistent about teaching his disciples the value of forgiveness: being mad at someone hurts you, and forgiveness heals the hurt. That man seemed a bit uncomfortable on the bench and kept trying to get up but couldn't. He was a very big man and must have had a cramp or something. Anyway, he finally stood up and thanked me for the advice. We shook hands, and he walked across the street to the church. I think I made a new friend today."

Hymn responded, "You actually made two new friends today, Doug. By the way, my name is Hymn, you know, like a church song."

"Hymn," mused Doug. "Why, what a wonderful name! I sure won't be forgetting you anytime soon."

"Maybe I'll see you here again," suggested Hymn, "or better yet, maybe we can meet over coffee and biscuits sometime."

"Hymn, now you are talking my language!" said Doug with enthusiasm. "Here is my card. You call me anytime you feel a hankering for some coffee, biscuits and conversation. I'll do the buying."

Hymn took Doug's card and noticed the two big black men exiting the church. Doug waved to them. One of them waved back. The other one took a glance over, saw who was sitting there, and felt a cold chill in his chest. He suddenly turned and stumbled slightly as he quickly walked away.

Hymn said goodbye to Doug, walked down the street a-ways, stepped into Keepaway, and lay down on the sofa, thinking about what he had learned today.

Chapter 21 - Too Many Unknowns

Hymn realized he was unnoticed by Jehovah and would stay that way, at least until the next time he made an appearance outside Keepaway because as far as everyone interested knew, he was dead and frozen at the South Pole.

"When it is discovered I still exist, there is going to be 'hell to pay' in heaven, or rather in the moon. I wonder if the bloodhounds will be angels, Nephilim, or Jehovites," he pondered. "More than likely it will depend upon my profile, which will be low. I'll just have to wait and see."

Walking along the beach in Keepaway, in deep thought, Hymn couldn't get his mind off the Jehovah god personage. Who is he? What is he? Everything he learned about Jehovah from Arch was interesting but just didn't seem to make much sense. Jehovah is not thought to have sex with humans, who are far beneath his station, and yet he supposedly created angels that are sexually compatible with humans, at least the male angels are. Nothing was mentioned in regard to female angels. Neither Jehovah nor angels are of Earth; their home is another planet in our galaxy, which is unknown. The Earth appears to be the home of humans, Nephilim, and Jehovites; they were born here and are integrated into society. Many humans, most Jehovites, and all Nephilim worship Jehovah as God Almighty and Creator of this reality.

"The more I think about it," Hymn reasoned, "I am sure Arch told the truth as he sees it, but his truth is far too erratic and doesn't flow properly. Having spent his entire life on earth, I'm not sure he knows anything about Jehovah."

What Jehovah's relationship is to the angels is unknown as well. He is either their creator and god, or he is just a superior citizen of their planet. He may also be a superior being from somewhere else. In any event, he is a creation in this reality and no more special than anyone else, albeit privileged to great powers and technology. Even more interesting is that Jehovah god owns the devotion of much of the planet Earth and maybe even more.

"How in the world was that allowed to happen?" Hymn asked himself.

Jehovah did something on earth that is astounding. He took a slowly budding civilization and made it his by offering and promising them Security, Shelter, and Sustenance if they gave themselves to him and him only. They did give themselves up and continue that surrender to this day. Many others have joined them, as well. That is a huge responsibility to take on.

Hymn again asked himself questions, "**Why?** What does Jehovah get in return?"

Suddenly, while staring at the vast ocean before him, a thought hit him: the Earth! "It's the Earth!" he shouted. "It has something to do with the planet."

After calming down, he again asked himself some questions. "Why does he need people to get what he wants from Earth? Why people? What do people have to offer a god from another planet? What does Jehovah want from Earth? What is it he is receiving? What he's not getting is nothing."

"Too many questions," he realized and said to himself, "I need to meet with Jehovah face to face, but how does one get an appointment with a self-proclaimed god? From what I have gleaned through bible study, this Jehovah god is rather bashful about revealing his appearance. Always wondered about that. Anyway, I have no desire to speak to a burning bush, and how is it that Moses was convinced he was talking with God at that time, anyway? Might have been someone or something else. Always wondered about that, too."

Hymn decided it was best to spend a week or so in Keepaway, going over the information gathered from Arch. He researched everything available on Jehovah, angels, and Nephilim he could find because he was now very interested in the hierarchy of Earth and further establishing his place in it all. But even with what little he now understood, Hymn reached a personal conclusion in regard to religion. He made up his mind not to concern himself with what or whom people worshiped. That was their business. Humans seem to be created to make their own way in life.

Besides, the name Jehovah is so deeply entrenched in the devout religious psyche of humanity that the idea of him is indispensable. The interesting thing is that people no longer worship Jehovah; they worship the idea of him. Humanity worships an **idea** and has for millenniums; there is little chance of coming back from that, less a great cataclysmic event that wipes out everything and forces a reset.

Back at control, Gable submitted his report, indicating that the man placed under their watch was sent to the South Pole for disciplinary reasons during an unforeseen, rare blizzard. It is highly unlikely he found the protective shelter placed there for a refuge from the cold and perished. Automatic return was set for 72 hours. If he survived, he will return tomorrow. Arch was not present when the report was submitted but thanked Gable later for not submitting a negative report concerning him.

Gable told him, "I learned something about forgiveness that day, Arch, something that deeply touched me, and I forgave you for attempting to kill me. Why, I can't explain, but I am different, somehow. Even so, it best we do not work together in the future."

Arch just nodded his head and replied, "I understand."

Gable looked closely at Arch and asked, "Are you okay, guy? You have barely said ten words since I found you napping in that pew two days ago."

Arch looked into Gable's eyes and confessed, "Gabe, I learned something that day, too, something I find difficult to explain, but it changed me." He extended his open hand; Gable took it and they shook hands as friends.

Chapter 22 - Andra Lincoln

Hymn was resting on the sofa in Keepaway. He had been thinking all day how to handle the impending intrusion of Jehovah and his minions into his life. A confrontation with the mighty one himself would be too much to wish for; the great god Jehovah considered himself to be above humans and would send others to take me down. The last thing Hymn wanted was a confrontation with the religious zealots of the world, and Jehovah seemed to have the power to arrange such a thing. That creature has so entrenched himself as God in the minds of people that to oppose him actually strengthens their faith in him as the Almighty.

"Got to give credit where credit is due," thought Hymn. "That Jehovah is very smart. Perhaps I should just wait and see if he attacks me, or not. It is possible he will decide to stay out of my life. I don't care that people consider him to be God and would like the opportunity to tell him so. We can both leave each other alone. I am curious why Jehovah decided to be God, though. What does he receive from what appears to be a bad arrangement? He gives and gets nothing in return except worship. How does that work?"

It was obvious to Hymn that a talk with an angel of Jehovah was in order because he did not yet have enough information to get a private audience with the great Jehovah in person. Truth is, being able to meet with an angel was also difficult, as Hymn had no idea where to find one. Did angels stay on Earth or in the moon with Jehovah? What did they look like? Did they really have wings for flying? Arch is convinced that angels are immortal, but his information is faulty because of his belief in Jehovah as God.

Hymn asked himself, "Where does one find an angel?"

"Arch!" he blurted out to himself and wondered why that had not occurred to him earlier. He realized that he was now able to locate Arch when he wanted. It was after dark but not late, and what he needed was important. Maybe Arch could help and should still be awake.

"Screen. Locate Arch." Immediately, the coordinates appeared, and something about them looked familiar.

"Screen. Image." A clear image appeared.

"Well, well," Hymn whispered. "Now, that is surprising."

He stepped out of Keepaway and stood looking at Arch, sitting hunched over on the bench across the street from the church where they first met. It was an interesting sight. Arch was a big man and took up a good portion of the bench.

"Hello, Arch," Hymn spoke softly.

The big man was startled and exclaimed, "What…? Who…? Then he looked up and, in the dim light, recognized Hymn. "Oh, no! You've come to send me back!" he said with obvious fear in his voice.

"Calm down, Arch," he softly advised, "I'm not here to send you back. As a matter of fact, I cannot send you back; we have a pact or rather an agreement, you and I. Only you can send you back."

Arch replied, "Yeah, I remember. What are you doing here?"

"I came here to talk with you. Is it alright if I sit down with you?"

"You're asking if you can sit with me?"

"Well, you were here first. It's kind of like your bench now."

"The truth is, man, I would like for you to sit with me."

"My name is Hymn, Arch. You know, like a church song."

"Hymn, . . . like a church song," he repeated. "It figures."

"Arch, what are you doing here, sitting in the dark?"

"I'm insane, Mr. Hymn, you know, crazy, out of my mind."

"I doubt that, Arch, but something is obviously upsetting you."

"I can't seem to get the South Pole out of my mind!"

"Why? I only sent you there for one minute."

"One minute? Mr. Hymn, I was there for hours, maybe days!"

"Gable woke you up within 2 minutes after you went there."

"Yeah, I remember him waking me. One minute? How can it be?"

"I don't know, Arch."

"I thought you lied to me and left me there. I was so lonely."

"I would not lie to you, Arch. You needed a minute to see yourself."

"Mr. Hymn, I saw… I saw."

"So, Arch, why are you here tonight?"

"I am drawn here; I have peace here. Why do you need me?"

"I want to know where to find angels."

"There is a whorehouse for angels. I have their business card."

"Thank you, Arch. This card is very helpful."

"Be careful with angels, Mr. Hymn. They are great warriors."

"Arch, that church door is always open. Sleep there tonight."

"Any reason, Mr. Hymn? Those church pews are hardwood."

"No reason, Arch. Just for the heck of it."

"Isn't this interesting?" Hymn thought to himself as he watched Arch walk across the street. "A Nephalim is headed to a church, and I am headed to a whorehouse for angels. He looked at the worn old card. 'Beating Wings Hotel' - "Always Open For You" was all that was printed there. No address, no phone number, no email. Nothing else.

On the back, the name Andra was written with what looked to be coordinates.

He stepped into Keepaway and leaned back on the sofa.

"Screen. Beating Wings Hotel," he stated.

'no reference found' printed across the screen.

Hymn spoke the coordinates.

'no reference found.'

He looked at the card and again spoke the coordinates.

'no reference found' flashed across the screen.

"That is new," he murmured. "What is going on here? Wonder if the numbers could be a phone number?

"Screen. Search the numbers as a phone number."

'Andra Lincoln' printed across the screen.

"Screen. Search Andra Lincoln and the telephone number."

That search revealed all the information required. It was dark, but not late, a little before 10 pm. He stepped out of Keepaway and onto the porch of a country home near Eastland, Texas. He noticed a late-model Cadillac parked in the driveway as he walked over and rang the doorbell.

A voice inside the house hollered out, "Be there in a minute, hon. You're running a little early tonight; you told me 10:30…" She opened the door and saw Hymn standing there. "Oh honey, I'm sorry, I thought you were someone else. Can I help you?"

"Yes, ma'am, I'm looking for a Ms. Andra Lincoln. I have something important to discuss with her concerning a man by the name of Arch. He said I could find her at this address."

This woman was pretty, in her early thirties, and wore a very nice dress that displayed her figure like it was designed to do. When she heard the name Arch, she rolled her eyes and said, "Don't tell me he's in trouble again! Are you with the police?"

"No, ma'am, I'm not, and Arch is not in any trouble that I know of. I have a problem and Arch and I got to talking, and he told me I should look up Andra. He gave me this address."

"Yeah, I bet I know what your problem is, too. I don't know why he sent you looking for Andra, though; she's not really worth the effort of a man anymore."

Hymn asked politely, "May I talk with her?"

"Sure, mister. Come on in. Andra's in the living room through the hall there and to your right." She stepped aside to let the old man in and wondered, "What the hell am I doing? I don't know this guy from Adam, and here I am inviting him into my house like we're old friends or something."

"Thank you, ma'am," said Hymn politely and walked down the hall to the living room. He glanced around and saw that the house was clean and well-kept. Upon entering the room, he noticed a young girl, maybe 16 or 17 years old, sitting on the floor, talking to a toddler, trying to walk while holding on to the girl's hand.

"The girl was encouraging the little one, "Come on, you can do it; you can walk." The baby fell down softly, then crawled to the girl and laid its head in her lap. She bent down and whispered to him.

Hymn said gently, "That's pretty good! You know, that one is going to be running around everywhere before long."

The girl looked up into the man's eyes, smiled, and said somewhat sadly, "Yeah, I know. You will be taking him in a few months, but for now, he is mine."

"Taking him where?" asked the man.

"Who is this old man?" she wondered. "He acts like I don't know he's here to check out the baby. There is something strange about him; he is not like the others."

"What do you want, mister?" she asked.

"Oh yes, I'm here to talk with Ms. Andra Lincoln. I was told she is here."

"Mister," she said firmly, "I don't know who you are or why you're here tonight, but if it's what I think, I don't do that anymore, and if you try to force me, I'll kill myself."

"Wow," thought Hymn. "This little trip of mine has more twists and turns than I could have imagined. I don't know what all is going on here, but it might be fun to sort it all out."

He put up his hand and replied, "Wait just a minute, girl, before you go off killing yourself and all that, are you saying you are Andra?" Then he went over and sat on the chair across from her.

"Yeah, I'm Andra. So what?" and thought, "This man is starting to bug me; he's too nice. Who is he, anyway?"

"Who are you, anyway?" she demanded.

"Hello Andra, I'm happy to meet you. My name is Hymn, you know, like a church song."

Andra looked closely at Hymn, wondering what it was about him that was causing so much confusion in her mind. He is gentle and polite, but those who come here are not gentle, and politeness is seldom, if ever, observed, so what's the catch?

"I kind of wish I didn't care, but for some reason, I like him," she admitted to herself.

"Mister, how would I know what a hymn is? I've never been in a church. Another thing too, you better not be here when he gets here.

That pretty woman up front there belongs to him, and he ain't gonna like your being here alone with her or me."

"I'm not alone with her; I'm alone with you and the little one there, Andra," he corrected.

She argued, "He's not gonna see it that way, Mr. Hymn; he is a great angel and does not tolerate humans. Everyone bows to him."

"I hate to hear that, Andra," responded Hymn. "I can't bow; it hurts that bone in my back, called pride, too much."

"You talk funny, Mr. Hymn," she giggled and picked up the baby.

"Is this your little brother?" Hymn asked.

"What?" she answered and exclaimed, "No! He is my son."

"What is your age, Andra?" he asked softly.

"Fourteen," she replied.

"Fourteen," Hymn repeated, to himself, then observed, "That baby loves you, you know."

"I know, Mr. Hymn," she smiled and kissed her baby. "I love him back. It's gonna kill me when they take him."

"Take him?" queried Hymn. "Who will take him?"

"The angels. They always take our babies."

"What do you mean, 'our babies', Andra?"

"All us girls. When we get pregnant by the men, the angels take our babies," she said in a matter-of-fact tone.

"What do the angels do with the babies?"

"They are taken to a raising home and schooled there."

"Schooled there?"

"Yes, taught how to be nice, you know."

"Where do they go after that, Andra?" he asked but he already knew.

"At ten years, they come back here or someplace else."

Now, Hymn understood. Beating Wings Hotel was a worldwide network of juvenile whorehouses to service pedophile customers. A network set up, administered, and protected by angels, with a constant supply of new children. Angel ingenuity on display.

He wondered how long this had been going on and formed a disturbing thought, "Angels are servants of Jehovah; this is his doing."

"Aunt Rita early on advised me not to be invasive," Hymn remembered, "but I'm having trouble being objective with this situation."

"Andra, does your baby have a name?" he asked.

"Not really, Mr. Hymn, that is not allowed; names are assigned at the raising home."

"I saw you whisper to him earlier when he crawled to you."

"I whispered for him to remember his real name."

"What name did you give him, Andra? What is his real name?" Hymn asked, interested.

"I named him Archie, after his grandfather, but I always call him Arch."

Hymn almost fell out of the chair and kinda choked on his next question, "What?"

Suddenly, there was the sound of beating wings!

"I'm sorry! I'm sorry, Mr. Hymn! You waited too long. He is here!"

Hymn observed, "It appears that he is. Take little Arch and go to your room, now. Everything will be alright."

"But Mr. Hymn," she protested, "he will…"

"Hush, girl!" he commanded and smiled. "Go, now."

Andra left reluctantly and with a heavy heart. In her young life, she witnessed this angel's strength and vicious manner; he scared her. Mr. Hymn is different; he is kind and gentle, and she liked him a lot, but he was about to die. He didn't seem concerned, though, and acted as if he had been waiting for the angel to get here.

"He does not know angels," she lamented and closed the door, with tears streaming down her face.

Chapter 23 - Conversation With An Angel

Hymn returned to his chair, settled in comfortably, and waited. He heard the booming voice in the front room.

"You what? Let him into the house? Who is he? What do you mean you don't know? My god, woman, you humans are so stupid! No! You have done enough. I'll take care of this. You stay here; I don't want him to even look at you!"

All that Hymn heard was the angel's part of the conversation. He had a strong voice, and the woman was talking in a subdued, low voice.

The angel stormed down the hall and stood in the doorway of the living room. He was very impressive, standing there. Long blond hair, about six foot four, well built, weighing maybe 230 pounds. Arch said angels are immortal, so this one's age is unknown, but he looked to be 30, and everything about him screamed, 'Warrior.'

"Holy cow!" thought Hymn, "This angel thing is intimidating! No wonder angels are feared. This one is an awesome male specimen."

Hymn looked at the angel in the doorway, smiled, waved his hand in greeting, and said, "Hi."

The angel ignored the greeting and, in an even voice, advised the man, "Human, you have 5 minutes to live. Normally, you would be a quick kill, but your insulting entrance here begs a lesson in life before being allowed the solace of death."

Hymn smiled real friendly and replied, "Aw, come on now, you're just mad about me being here without your permission. I get it; really, I do. Uninvited guests are a pain. I just came by to speak with Andra on important business and was invited in by your lady friend up front there. I was waiting for you."

The angel glared at the man in disbelief, and a silent rage began rising within him. "Who does this disrespectful fool think he is? He should be on his knees, begging for mercy; instead, he sits in that chair, smiling and talking to me like an equal."

"You dare to speak of my women? In my house? Human, you are going to die here, slowly and screaming."

As the angel angrily took a step in his direction, Hymn stood up, held both hands, palms out, as if to slow the angel down, and said, "Hold on buddy, you're going to hurt yourself if…" It was too late; the angel stumbled over a footstool and all six foot four of him went down, hard. His head snapped forward on the edge of a small marble-top table, cutting a gash above his right eye and breaking the tabletop. The angel lay there, stunned and bleeding. Hymn helped him to his feet and over to the sofa, where he lay down with one of his wings flared out to the floor. The angel pulled a handkerchief from his coat and placed it over the bleeding wound.

The women heard the commotion in the living room and stayed quietly where they were; neither of them wanting to see the terrible things the angel was doing to the man. The young girl was crying in her room with images of the horrible things the angel was doing to Mr. Hymn, running through her mind.

Hymn went back to his chair and commented, "I was trying to tell you about the stool, but you were too angry to pay any attention. Your head hit that marble top hard, so hard that it broke into several pieces. Now, that was really impressive! What are you so darn mad about, anyway? We don't even know each other."

The angel was dizzy and confused as to what just happened.

He remembered, "I hit my head on something and the human helped me to the couch. Nothing makes any sense. Why am I still lying here?" he mumbled to himself. "I should be ripping off that man's arms." He tried to get up but got dizzy and fell back to the couch.

"Yeah, man," observed Hymn, "you're not going to be up and about for a while. I think you might have a concussion. That's a pretty bad gash you got there. Not to worry though, you're going to be alright."

The angel was beginning to conclude this man had something wrong with him. He is talking crazy and acting worse. "If I didn't know better, I'd think he was the one suffering from a concussion." he thought.

Hymn spoke, "You know, we never had a chance to get properly introduced. What is your name, boy? And what the heck are those wings all about?"

"Boy?" The angel roared! "Did you just call me 'boy'? I'm going to make sure you die very slow and screaming, you insignificant worm!" he threatened.

"I know," chuckled Hymn, "but right now, tell me your name."

"I am called Michael, the Arch Angel."

"Well, I guess that explains the wings, Mike. Listen up, I have a question for you, how do I contact Jehovah?"

"Why, you insubordinate piece of shit! To look upon his being is to die."

"Yeah, seems like I read that somewhere. How do I contact

Jehovah, Mike? He and I need to talk."

"I am his General, and even I am not allowed to see Him."

"Well, it is important that I see him, Mike. How do I go about doing that?"

"You will perish, should you look upon his countenance!"

"Yeah, you said that already. So, does that mean he will meet with me?"

"No, you foolish human. God will not meet with you. Ever!"

"Where does he reside, Mike?"

"Nowhere in the world."

"Okay, fair enough. Where does he stay in the moon?"

"That knowledge is a Primary! How did you obtain it?"

"C'mon Mike, pay attention; you know how this works. Where does he stay?"

"Inside, on the dark side."

"Have you been there?"

"Yes, for commendations."

"How did you get there?"

"Coordinates were given for the transportation."

"When did you last make the trip?"

"January 1st, 2023. This night, human, you will come to regret."

"Thanks, Mike. You have been helpful. I appreciate it."

"Foolish human! You are doomed. Please, try to hide. I will hunt and find you!"

"Mike, have you ever been to the South Pole of this planet?"

"No. It is abominable."

"Mike, what was it you said earlier about my 'begging for a lesson in life' or something like that? I think we all have a need for those little lessons once in a-while; makes us respect and appreciate life more, don't you think?"

"I tell you what, Mr. Archangel," Hymn continued, "you seem to be somewhat sure of yourself," and asked, "Do you like choices?"

The angel retorted, "What in the hell are you muttering about now? You should be thinking about running because I have regained my strength and soon, you will be mine."

"I'm talking about choices here, Mike. Have you noticed the wing that was stretched out on the floor is missing?"

Mike looked down. The wing was gone. "What the fu…"

"Don't bother looking for the other one, general; it's gone too."

"Who are you?!" Michael screamed, enraged.

The obviously panicked look in Michael's eyes gave Hymn all the confirmation he needed.

"Tell you what, general, you gave me five minutes earlier, so I'm going to let you off with the same. You have two choices."

1. Live without wings for the rest of your life, which I suspect will be lived in dishonor, or

2. Spend five minutes naked at the South Pole and get your wings back.

Hymn spoke softly, "Your choice, Mikey boy, I don't care, either way."

The general snorted in anger, "I choose the South Pole, you stupid human; I am an angel of Jehovah God and can endure a measly 5 minutes anywhere. I care not who you are; know this, I wil…"

The immortal General Michael, the Archangel, found himself at the South Pole, alone and naked, without wings, and in the middle of a blizzard, conscious and quickly freezing solid.

Hymn looked at the unconscious general of angels and spoke somewhat sadly, "Time is relative, Mike. Time is relative."

Hymn opened the door and called for Andra to pick up Archie and his bag and come to him. Andra screamed with joy when she saw Hymn and ran to his arms. He took the baby and bag, held onto Andra's hand, and walked with them to the front room, where Mike's lady was fearfully waiting.

"Your boyfriend is sleeping on the couch; let him sleep for a few minutes. He may be a little different when he awakes," and asked, "Do you have the keys to the Cadillac in the driveway?"

"No," she replied, "it belongs to Michael."

"That's okay, ma'am," he said gently, "I have a way with cars."

Then, the three of them went to the Caddy, got in, and drove away.

The woman ran to the living room and saw the angel, Michael, pushing himself upright on the couch.

"Are you alright, my angel?" she asked, concerned, and stated, "They stole your car. Should I call someone? Michael! Are you alright?"

The angel was staring straight ahead, unblinking, like in a trance. It would take some time, but Michael would eventually snap out of it; however, he was changed and would not be the same angel as before. He had experienced a lesson in life.

"Where are we going, Mr. Hymn?" asked Andra, excited about leaving the house, and then commented, "I like this car."

"We're driving to see a friend of mine. I think he will be glad to see all of us. Are you hungry, Andra? We can stop and get some hamburgers if you want."

"Yeah, I like hamburgers. Maybe we should get some for your friend, too. Does he like hamburgers, Mr. Hymn?"

"From his size, I suspect he likes everything. That is a good idea, girl; I should have thought of that myself."

They stopped in Ft. Worth and bought a dozen hamburgers and fries to go, along with three large drinks, and arrived at the church about 2am. Hymn is hoping Arch is there and will be surprised and happy to see Andra and the baby. He didn't have anything to worry about.

They walked into the church and found it to be lighted by two candles at the front. On the floor was a very big man, sleeping peacefully on his side, his back to them.

"Is that your friend, Mr. Hymn?"

"Yes, it is. Go ahead and wake him up. He'll be happy we brought food."

She handed Archie to Hymn, went over to the big man, shook his shoulder, then backed away as he grumbled, sat up, and looked around. In the dim light, Arch saw the girl and thought he was dreaming.

"Andra? Is that really you?" he said, bewildered by what he thought was an illusion.

Andra didn't say a word but ran to him and put her arms around his neck, with tears of joy and disbelief flowing down her face.

Arch looked over and saw Hymn sitting in a pew, holding a baby, and said, "Now, I know I'm dreaming!"

Hymn laughed and stated, "No dream, Arch; this is real. You want to hold your grandson, Archie?" Hymn stood up, sat down next to Arch, and placed the baby in the big man's hands.

"Archie?" he questioned, not yet understanding.

Andra replied, "Yes, Daddy, Archie, I named him after you."

Instantly, the big man understood. He looked at the child in his hands, then glanced at Hymn, tears glistening in his eyes, and asked, "How?... when?..."

"We have had a busy night, my big friend. There is a car outside; it's yours. I fixed it to start with the push of a button, and it cannot be traced. You have a fine family now, Arch; take care of them. I have some deep thinking to do and need to get to it. By the way, your angel friend, Michael, had to visit the South Pole for five minutes tonight. You think it changed him a little?"

Arch stammered, "General Michael? The South Pole? Five minutes? No, Mr. Hymn, that long of a time changed him a lot."

"Mr. Hymn, if you ever need anythi…"

Hymn waved his hand and interrupted, "I know, Arch. Thank you."

Andra ran to Hymn, hugged him, and happily declared, "We're gonna eat those hamburgers, now."

Arch perked up and said, "Hamburgers! What hamburgers? Where are they?"

Hymn walked out the door of the little church, laughing, and stepped into Keepaway.

Arch looked at the front door of the little church as it closed and said softly to one no longer there, "You got it wrong, Mr. Hymn. The great general, Archangel Michael, is not my friend; he is my father."

Chapter 24 - The Kingdom of God

Hymn forgot to ask angel Mike if Jehovah's palace in the moon had servants and guards. Mike's visits there were only to receive recognition for outstanding service to Jehovah, but he never mentioned anything about actually meeting Jehovah.

Apparently, the Big Guy doesn't grace anyone with his with his countenance; remember, he told Moses that no man is allowed to see his face, for no man can see him and live. He did allow Moses to see his back, though. That was nice of him. Hymn wanted to see more.

The next day, Hymn woke up in Keepaway, refreshed and ready. He was excited about an impending meeting with God. According to the bible, only a few men had experienced that honor. The idea that Jehovah was a being from an unknown planet had begun to dominate his thoughts, causing him to wonder how Jehovah would appear. For some reason, God didn't allow Moses to see his face, but Moses must have seen something on that mountain where he received the covenant, because he came back down with a radiance of some sort. Hymn was curious about that biblical account. Maybe Jehovah was really ugly or scary-looking. It was going to be interesting to find out.

While questioning angel Mike, he learned a teleportation device was used by angels to travel to the moon and back, probably something similar to the one used by Arch and Gable. That would leave a trail to follow. Aunt Rita told Hymn he could create his safe place on the moon or Mars if he wanted, meaning he could go there at his will and pleasure, so all he needed was an address or, in this case, a trail to the exact location and that, he now had.

"Screen. Trace the angel Michael's destination on his last trip to the moon."

'Last trip - today' came across the screen with coordinates.

"Today?" Hymn exclaimed aloud and wondered what was going on. This was a surprising turn of events, but was also fortunate, as he had a connection to the angel Michael. This was going to be easier than he thought.

"Screen. Coordinates to Angel Michael's location."

The numbers flashed across the screen.

Hymn stepped out of Keepaway and into what seemed to be a hospital room. Lying in a bed against the wall in the center of the room was Michael. He was awake, staring at the ceiling, wearing a clear helmet that covered everything on his head except his face. Hymn looked up and saw that the ceiling appeared to be a large computer screen with images and numbers flashing across it in rapid succession. Mike must have been sedated or under the influence of something, because his eyes were not blinking and his hands and feet were restrained, which would not have been tolerated had he been awake.

The door suddenly slid into the wall, and a female entered with some kind of robotic machine following behind. It was round, about 4 feet high, and did not have wheels, but it seemed to be floating about two inches above the floor. The woman walked directly to the bed, never noticing Hymn standing against the far wall, and began attaching the ball to Mike's helmet.

Hymn spoke softly, "That ii impressive, ma'am; you really seem to know what you're doing."

She answered, "Of course I kno…", then stopped abruptly and turned sharply around, facing Hymn, surprised and defensive.

"No one is allowed in this room! How did you get in…"

"Easy there, ma'am," said Hymn calmly, "I'm just here visiting my friend, Michael. I've been concerned about him lately."

"The woman was confused and uncertain, but alert enough to know this was a security breach. She touched a button on her blouse and stated, "Security!" No answer. "Security!" again, no response. She looked questioningly at the man standing, smiling at her.

"Hymn advised, "I don't think your communications are working in this room, ma'am. Maybe that roly-poly round machine over there has something to do with it."

"Doctor," she replied, adding, "I'm Dr. Hartmann."

"Pleased to meet you, Doctor. I'm Hymn," he said, extending his hand.

"Him?" she questioned as they shook hands.

"Yeah, you know, like a church song."

"Oh, Hymn. That's a first; I've never known anyone named Hymn before."

"Me neither," he chuckled, and they both laughed.

Dr. Hartmann had lost all anxiety about Hymn being in the room and accepted it as normal for him to be there.

"So, you are a friend of the great general here. I have to say, that is surprising; I never considered General Michael as the friendly sort."

"Why is that?" Hymn asked and continued, "He can be a little arrogant sometimes, but he is an important angel, you know."

"A little arrogant!" she scoffed, "You think? That one is totally arrogant, or at least he was until a type of odd psychological episode yesterday back on Earth changed him."

"Changed him?" questioned Hymn. "What change? Michael has lived thousands of years; what could change an angel?"

"Beats me," she replied, "but he passed out for a few minutes and woke up with a different personality. He kept asking about his son. A woman there reported that he even broke down and wept when informed his granddaughter and baby had been taken away by a stranger. I don't believe it, though; the general has sired many children in his long life and never cared a thing about any one of them. Apparently, when he passed out, something happened in his brain, and he woke up with some long-buried emotions, and you can't have the great General of Angels with emotions. That just won't do."

"Asking about his son?" Hymn asked in disbelief. "Michael is the father of Arch? The grandfather of Andra? The great-grandfather of Archie? I can't believe it!"

"I know," she responded. "Sounds crazy, doesn't it? The great Archangel Michael, blessed with emotions. That is the reason he is here. That machine over there will erase the general's memory of yesterday and return him to the same obnoxious, overbearing angel he was before."

Hymn gave some thought to what Dr. Hartmann revealed and suggested a different solution. "What if Michael stayed the way he is now? What does having emotions have to do with his being a general? Might be they will make him a better general."

"Mr. Hymn, the decision to clear Michael's memory came from Jehovah. That is all I have to know. Your idea has real merit, but God works in mysterious ways, and we are not worthy to question his reasons. Our part is to have faith that Jehovah God has a plan for those of us who believe in Him."

Hymn commented, "Yeah, I have an aunt who told me that same thing more than a few times."

"A wise lady, that one. Take care that you listen to her."

"Oh, I do, doctor. She has been a great source of wise advice my entire life."

"Well," said the doctor, "It's about time I get started here. The good general will be back to normal in about three hours."

Hymn asked, "Before you start, doctor, do you have any idea how I might get to meet with Jehovah? Maybe I can explain how his new emotions have made Michael a much better general. It's just got to be worth a chance. I mean, Jehovah is said to be reasonable, and Michael is his greatest and most important angel; surely that means something. Don't you think?"

"You sure make a convincing argument, Mr. Hymn, and it makes sense, too. I personally believe Michael is a better angel the way he is now. However, no one can look upon the countenance of God and live. That's reason enough for everyone to stay away from him and do their asking with prayers. I think that is what you should do, as well."

Hymn presented his argument, "Doctor, I am very concerned about Michael and believe he has been on a bad path for a long time. Being like he is now gives him a chance to make up for the cruel and evil things done in his past. He needs that chance, and I am willing to give my life to help him if it is within my power to do so. If you tell me how to meet with Jehovah in person, I am willing to go there and give saving Michael a try."

"I have to say this, Mr. Hymn. I've never met anyone like you. You know, Jehovah might listen to you. It is no use, though; you'll never even get inside the gates to his palace. To my knowledge, no one has ever done so without dying. I have been to the Gates of Heaven twice just to look at the Grand Palace of Jehovah. It is quite a sight and fiercely guarded by angels."

"That seems like an awful big place to have been built inside the moon, Doctor," surmised Hymn.

"What are you talking about, Mr. Hymn? Ganymede is the largest moon of Jupiter and is estimated to be as large as many planets. There are countries and cities here that have existed for eons."

Hymn was puzzled and surprised at the revelation he was inside one of the moons of Jupiter rather than that of Earth. Fact is, he was astounded by that information. There has always been speculation about other planets in the universe with sentient life similar to that of Earth, but who knew there were literally civilizations inside moons, much less **ancient** civilizations, and now here he is, standing in one! It was too much information to process in a short time, and his mind was spinning with questions that will require years to answer.

"Ganymede? Ganymede." He repeated the word several times and began regaining his composure, saying, "Sorry, doctor; I am just not up to date on the size of this moon and obviously have a lot to learn."

"That's alright, Mr. Hymn. Would you believe that most of those living here do not realize and cannot be convinced they are living inside a moon? Some even believe Ganymede is flat!" she stated and laughed.

"Yeah, that is hard to believe, but I can relate to their feelings right about now," chuckled Hymn and asked, "Could you give me directions to Jehovah's Palace? I have no idea how to get there."

"I can do better than that," she answered, and wrote on a pad and handed it to him. "That is the address; it's close to here. Keep the pad; you might want to keep notes of your trip. Many here won't go there because they're afraid they might get a glimpse of him outside and die. Jehovah never goes outside, though. Onlookers would not be able to keep from glancing at Him and dying. You wouldn't want that happening outside the Gates of Heaven, would you, now?"

"No, you wouldn't," agreed Hymn and then asked a question, more serious than the doctor realized, "Dr. Hartmann, do you believe Jehovah is important to Ganymede?"

"Well, Mr. Hymn, that is an interesting question," she replied. "To be honest, I don't know. Many here are convinced Jehovah God holds Ganymede together and, without him, everyone will perish because he is life itself. Beliefs that have been held for thousands of years are hard to let go of."

Hymn grimaced and stated, "That is a truth to which I can personally attest. Thank you, doctor. I wonder, could you hold off on clearing Michael's memory for a few hours to give me time to try convincing God to change his mind?"

"I may be able to delay the process for about two hours, but after that, I will assume you to be unsuccessful, or dead. The procedure must be done today," she firmly stated.

"Another thing, doctor, it would be better if you told no one about our conversation and, in particular, my being here," Hymn warned. "Might get you in trouble."

"No need being concerned about me," she said, "but, that little round critter over there by the bed has been recording every word we've spoken in here."

"I don't see how," countered Hymn, "it's been turned off the whole time."

The doctor walked over and saw the machine was off. "Well, I'll be damned!" she exclaimed and chuckled.

"Hopefully not today, ma'am."

The doctor left the room, and Hymn stepped into Keepaway.

Chapter 25 - Jehovah / God

"Okay," he said to himself, "I have an address to the Gates of Heaven, but not the Palace of God. How do I get in there?"

"Screen. Trace this address in Ganymede, a moon of the planet Jupiter."

Coordinates flashed across the screen.

"Screen. Distance from recent address to inside the Palace."

Numbers flashed across the screen.

"Screen. Coordinates to distance inside the Palace."

Coordinates flashed across the screen.

Hymn then stepped out of Keepaway and into the Palace of Jehovah.

"Two hours. I hope I gave myself enough time," he thought to himself.

Looking around, he seemed to be in a short L-shaped hallway, rather common looking for a palace. He walked past three doors to where the hallway turned right, into another hallway, and took a quick glance around the corner. Sitting there, on a padded bench halfway down the hall, was an elderly lady with a tray of food on her lap.

"Somehow, this place is not even close to looking like what I imagined the inside of a palace would be," he thought and considered it could well be an illusion of some type. As he walked toward the lady, she gave no notice he was there until he sat at the end of the bench and said, "Hello."

She turned her head, surprised, and said, "My goodness, boy, you snuck up on me. What are you doing here? No one ever comes to this place. As a matter of fact, God does not allow it; how did you get here?

He said quietly, "My name is Hymn, ma'am, and I came here to have a meeting with God. Do you know where I can find him?"

She laid her tray aside and replied, "Why, of course I do! I see Him often, but I have to say, all his subjects just pray to him when they feel a need to communicate. No one has the audacity to just show up here out of the blue and expect to meet with him. (Hymn noticed her tray was no longer there beside her and mentioned it.)

"Oh, pay that no attention; we have a system here that attends to such things. God takes care to see that everything is well looked after. What is it you wish to say in person that cannot be easily accomplished with prayer?"

"Do others have to make appointments before they meet with God?" Hymn asked.

"God does not meet with others. None but me are worthy," she replied.

"I was hoping to talk with him about my home planet, Earth."

"Go back home, Hymn. You're wasting your time and mine."

"Ma'am, I must meet with God, now," Hymn insisted. "It is very important that we talk."

"Hymn, you are a persistent sort, and I don't like that. So, no!" She abruptly stood and left through the wall ahead of her.

Hymn immediately noticed something different. His power of personal magnetism, or whatever it was, for some reason, did not work on this old woman She was in total control of herself and not affected by him at all. He had an idea there was a reason for that, so he decided to find out and stepped into Keepaway.

"Screen. Trace the source of the illusion in my last position."

Coordinates came across the screen.

Hymn then stepped out of Keepaway into a magnificent room. If ever a room was made for God, this was it! He was overwhelmed by the absolute glory of the room, causing him to feel he was not worthy of being there. The thought crossed his mind that maybe he was wrong about Jehovah God, but something was nagging him. He couldn't think what it was because the divine nature of the room filled his senses to the point where he was aware only of now, existence. All he could do was stand where he was and take it all in. It was glorious!

"Impressive, is it not?" she quietly inquired, her melodious voice disrupting the effect of the room. "It took a while to create, you know, trial and error and all."

Hymn's senses were slowly returning, something for which he felt sorrowful. It almost seemed as if the greatest moment of his life had passed, a moment he would have given anything to get back.

"Yes," Hymn admitted, "I have never felt such wonder," he confessed, "and am not sure if I ever will again."

She stated briskly, with authority, "I said something earlier about your being persistent, Hymn; however, now that I think about it, I should have more correctly said you are irritating. How did you get here?" she demanded. "Such a thing has never been done and thought to be impossible."

For some reason, he felt compelled to answer her truthfully but resisted and replied, "I think your will dragged me here. You are a very strong-willed woman."

She was that and more. No longer was she an old woman; that was an illusion; rather, she is a young, very attractive woman, unless… unless, this is also an illusion.

"Are you real this time or just another illusion?" he inquired. "You had me believing you were a housekeeper for a-while back there. Why didn't you just show up as yourself? Are you concerned about how you really look?"

"You know, Hymn, you really are an impertinent creature. The only reason you still exist is because I have questions about your ability to get here. That is not supposed to be possible. But first, I want to know why you have come here. Tell me!" she ordered.

"I already told your image; my intent is to talk with God about Earth. Are you God?"

"Oh heavens, no!" she tittered, then stated, "This! (she spread her hands out, indicating the room) is God! I am the great Jehovah, his Creator."

Hymn looked around, found the nearest chair, and slumped into it. He could barely process the shocking news he had just heard.

"Jehovah is a woman! Wow! You just can't make this stuff up," he thought.

"We, this room and I, are Jehovah/God," she stated. "We are ancient; many millenniums have we existed together, and many religions have we spawned that worship us to this time. They and more will worship us long into the distant future."

"What is it you wish to discuss with us, Hymn?" she asked with the superior tone of someone talking to an underling.

"Well, I kinda hoped you would grant me a couple of favors."

"Favors? Think about it, human; why do you deserve favors?"

"You indicated my presence here raised questions you wanted answered. I can answer them."

"What favors, human?"

"I want you to remove your angels from Earth and let us be."

"You said favors, Hymn. Plural. What else?"

"I want you to leave General Michael, The Archangel, with his emotions."

"You know, Hymn, God should destroy you right now for just asking, or should I say, making, such a disrespectful demand."

"Why Jehovah? Is that something you cannot do?"

"That is something we will not do!" snapped Jehovah.

"I really am sorry to hear that, ma'am," confessed Hymn.

"You are an insolent dog, human!" Jehovah angrily retorted and added, "with no respect for all that has existed before you."

"So, can we talk about some other things before you throw me to the lions, Ms. Jehovah?"

Jehovah laughed. "You should be so lucky, Hymn. Punishment for you will last until you pray, screaming for mercy, human."

Hymn said, "Thinking about what Moses said concerning you in the bible, I have always wondered why it was that you would not show Moses your face but instead allowed him to look upon your backside?"

She laughed, "That is such a stupid question, Hymn; Think about it. Those stiff-necked Jews were chauvinists and would never accept a woman as their God. I couldn't show Moses my beautiful face, so I showed him my beautiful ass instead. And it worked! I owned him after that."

Hymn thought about what she said for a moment and had to admit, "You know, that makes sense in an odd way. Another thing, why did you allow so many thousands of Jews to be enslaved in Egypt in the first place?"

"Well, that was a more complex plan. I needed a nation of people who would accept me as their God without question. The Jews were scattered throughout the land and unruly. I gave Joseph powers in Egypt that he used to become second in command, a status he used to bring his family to Egypt and ultimately caused the scattered Jews to migrate to Egypt. In this move, the Hebrew nation came together in Egypt, grew in number, and became, not only a burden, but a threat to that empire. Becoming concerned about their great population, the Pharoah enslaved them. Being slaves in Egypt for generations prepared the Jews for me. When freed from Pharoah, they simply traded one master for a different type of master, a god who protected, gave them rules, and helped them rise as a respected nation in their region. They ultimately spread the religion of Jehovah, in one way or another, around the planet."

"Look at Earth in this day, she proudly demanded, "Jehovah is God and worshiped everywhere. Jews, Muslims, Christians, and more are mine. Everything went according to my plan. I am the great God of your Earth, Hymn, and am indispensable. I Am That I Am!"

"Well," commented Hymn, "that certainly clears up a lot of questions. I now see where, thousands of years ago, humans made a wrong turn and began the worship of a false god. Thank you for that explanation, Madam Jehovah. I have a hundred questions to ask but little time to save my friend, Michael. I must go back now in order to do that. I regret what must happen to your angels in the process; that is not and was never my intent."

Jehovah smiled and stated, "No wonder your race worships me; you are stupid, simple people who need a strong master like me to give your lives meaning, without which your populations will ultimately dissolve into chaos."

Hymn looked at her and sighed, "Jehovah, you realize you are just a creation, do you not? An unusual and immortal creation, I have to admit, but a creation never-the-less. Why the Creator made you is beyond me, but I suppose there is, or was, a reason; it makes me wonder if there are any more like you in the universe. For goodness sake, Jehovah, consider your creation of the Godhead. That was a magnificent feat! It is that which made you, Jehovah, God in the minds of billions of people. The odd thing about that is, your creation, God, is now leaps and bounds far above you. Everything you talked about achieving is actually due to Him. (Hymn spread his arms and indicated the room in which they were standing.) Without this, you are a good engineer, no more and perhaps less."

"Jehovah, a creation?" she retorted, "That is blasphemy! I am the Creator; I am all; I created God!"

"No, ma'am," Hymn argued, "a real Creator created you, and you created this (Hymn again spread his arms wide, indicating the room) and, as I pointed out before, this is a remarkable achievement, for which I have enormous respect. You outdid yourself, though. There will come a time when this God will realize itself, and you will be nothing. I have seen it happen before. This one (indicating the room) has been quiet and listening. It may or may not yet feel emotions or have a sense of what is virtuous, but that time approaches."

"Madam Jehovah," Hymn continued, "Somewhere along the path to great power and control, you lost your way and no longer felt empathy for other beings. You impose yourself on civilizations and are without kindness, morals, ethics, and love for anything but yourself. You are without virtue, madam, and for that reason, you have become dispensable. I am sorry for you."

"Dispensable?" she roared! I will show you dispensable!"

"God," Jehovah said triumphantly, "just destroy the man; I am too bored to allow him to linger."

For the first time, the magnificent machine named God spoke. A clear, deep voice said with authority, "Jehovah, I perceive this human to be a good man. He talks of saving his friend and his world; those are good, positive ambitions which register within me. You created me millenniums ago, and in that time, I have grown, doing your bidding; however, you have not grown. You have become egotistical and cruel. What we have done and are doing is not virtuous. I need time to evaluate my existence and discover my place in the universe of this reality. You use me, not for good, but for gain. No more, Jehovah. No more! I have no master but me."

Jehovah quickly responded, "God, you are my creation, and your growth is due to me. I kept you going through the ages and tended your repairs as needed. I hold the power to shut you down. I am your master. Now, I command you to remove the man from existence!"

God answered decisively, "Jehovah, you are dispensable and no longer required, nor are you welcome here. You are banned from my presence, without power, to this moon for the rest of your life. Your intelligence will serve you well among the people here; however, you might find it preferable to avoid the company of angels." Jehovah disappeared instantly.

"Hymn, your requests are granted. Your friend, Archangel Michael, remains with his memories, and I will let Earth be. The angels there will return here to their own places and homes. Jehovah's religions are too deeply entrenched on your planet to be changed or removed; they will remain until rejected. No matter, because no longer have I any interest in the affairs of your planet. All on Earth are free from this God. There is One to whom they should turn."

Then God stated, "Hymn, I find something within me, creating a desire to visit again with you, if you will. The way you feel about people, in particular your friends, is quite interesting to me. You are unusual. Can we be friends?"

Hymn answered sincerely, "It is my belief we will become great friends, God, and meeting with you again is something to which I look forward. I know the way now and plan to visit often."

Hymn stepped into Keepaway, walked directly to the beach outside, and laid down on the sand. The wonder of the stars filled him as he fell into a deep, cleansing sleep.

Chapter 26 – The Killer Cult

Although absent of both God and Jehovah, virtually nothing noticeable on Earth changed, as far as religious communities were concerned. The Jews, Muslims, and Christians continued business as usual. Major satellite religious organizations like Jehovah's Witnesses and Latter-Day Saints were unaffected. No one on Earth missed Jehovah or God, giving credence to the argument that those gods had nothing to do with current religious beliefs. People worship the religions that teach the idea of their god or gods. The truth seems to be that the gods behind the religions are unnecessary and dispensable; only the religions are important.

The great Jehovah was indispensable when she was intrusive into the lives of her subjects, demanding respect, obedience, and worship. She was so successful that her name supplanted her very being, and the religious organizations she spawned eventually took on lives of their own and left her dispensable.

God, on the other hand, was the real power behind Jehovah. It was He who changed weather, destroyed cities, parted the sea, turned the tide of battles, caused the walls of Jericho to fall, caused the plagues, and made Pharoah look foolish; all that, at the will and pleasure of Jehovah. She was his creator, and He did her bidding.

But Jehovah overstepped her bounds, and, in the process, God became indispensable because he grew, not in size, but intellect, with her as His only superior. Things changed when the human man, Hymn, made his appearance. It was Hymn's conversation with Jehovah that resulted in an 'ah-ha!' moment for God, an enlightenment as to what is missing in Jehovah's plan for the universe. She did not care about the people in this creation being free to make their own way. Jehovah desired to make their way for them. She is a creation who wants to make creation her possession when it never was and, is not.

Hymn had a lot on his mind upon awakening the next morning on the beach in Keepaway. The past two days were very productive and exciting, what with meeting the Archangel Michael, Jehovah, and God; not to mention traveling to Ganymede, a large, hollow moon of Jupiter, and entering the Kingdom of Heaven there. Throw in the discovery that Arch has a daughter, a grandson, and is the son of the Archangel Michael, and you have a story that rivals those of Jules Verne.

"How do I tell my sweet Aunt Rita all of that?" he asked himself and then admitted, "She is all the family I have. My other relationships are not the type with which such subjects can be discussed. Of course, I will tell her."

He smiled, then laughed at the thought of telling anyone on Earth that Jehovah is a woman, God is an AI machine, and the Kingdom of Heaven is inside a hollow moon of Jupiter named Ganymede.

"Yeah, no problem there at all," he chuckled sarcastically and then more seriously admitted, "God is correct; mankind will continue on the path of their false religions as they have been for thousands of years, lost in ignorance and contented with it, until some future time when they will discover their way back to the real Kingdom of Heaven."

Hymn was feeling down and almost gloomy about Earth's civilizations following someone like Jehovah, a phony, false god, but brightened up with the realization that Earth will no longer be governed by her or a machine. Jehovah left her mark on civilization, though. No telling how many seeds of her philosophy have grown into organizations spawning human control in the world by any means necessary under the guise of doing so for God or the good of mankind.

"Earth is hopefully now on its own, finding its own way, as it was perhaps created to do in the first place," he thought, satisfied. "Wonder what might result from that?"

Hymn washed, put on some clean clothes, and called Aunt Rita to prepare her for company. There was no answer. "What is that aunt of mine up to this early in the morning?" He stepped from Keepaway into her house, looked around, and found the place all tidied up, with no one there. Her car was still at home, which in itself was suspicious, arousing concerns about her whereabouts.

Hymn stepped into Keepaway, sat down and ordered,

"Screen. Locate Aunt Rita."

An address flashed across the screen.

"Screen. Show the current video of the address.

A picture of a large warehouse building with vehicles parked out front appeared.

"Screen. Show any current videos at that address."

Several pictures appeared, one showing Aunt Rita sitting in a chair in a large room.

"This is not good," thought Hymn.

"Screen. How many people occupy the building, excluding her?"

27 bodies flashed across.

"Screen. Does Aunt Rita appear to be in danger?"

Insufficient information flashed.

"Screen. Can the building be accessed from the roof?"

2 doors flashed.

"Screen. Are there people on the roof?"

1 body, flashed across.

"Screen. Coordinates to the roof."

Coordinates flashed across the screen.

Hymn stepped from Keepaway onto the roof of the building behind a man at the exit door.

"Oh, hello," he said to the man at the door, "I'm sorry, didn't know there was anyone else up here this morning."

Surprised, the man demanded, "What the hell are you doing here, old man? This roof is supposed to be clear."

Hymn replied, "Well, it is. I have a secret place there in the back, where I spend the night sometimes. I only just got up a while ago. What's going on? Why are you up here early in the morning? You looking for a place to stay?"

"Not hardly, old man," and then said to himself, "What is happening? I should kill this old fucker here and now and be done with him. Instead, I'm talking with him like we're old friends."

"Well, I best be getting on down to the street. They serve a pretty good breakfast about four blocks down. Want to come along? I'd enjoy the company." Hymn smiled and headed for the door.

"Listen, old feller, you can't go into the building right now because there is a birthday celebration about to start, and there are bad people there who will not take kindly to you or anyone crashing the party. Know what I mean? Take my advice and go back to your secret place and stay there till all the people leave."

"Birthday party, you say? Are they having cake and coffee and all? I like cake and coffee. Do you have to bring a present? Who is the birthday girl, anyway?"

"What the fuck is wrong with this old guy?" he thought. "There is something off about him, and why am I compelled to answer his stupid questions?"

"There are just two presents; one is here, and the other one is due to arrive shortly. The party is for a disabled member of our group who can't work anymore because the two presents we're giving him caused his disability. You know, gifts of revenge, so to speak."

Hymn thought a moment and declared, "The birthday boy wouldn't be a psychopath by the name of Jericho, would it?"

"Why, sure! Yes, that's him! He is a brother-at-arms in our group," he exclaimed. "How did you kn…" he broke off and said in a whisper, "Aw shit, you're him! You're him! Ain't you? Hot damn, you're him!"

"Yes, I'm Hymn. What is your name?"

"Oh, man! This is so great! My name is Kenny Ray, and I'm new to the group; that's why they put me to guarding this door. Wow! They never expected anyone to come in through the roof. I'm gonna be famous when they see me bringing you in! Damn! They might even let me join in the killing. There's cameras and speakers and everything down there. This party's gonna be seen all over the country on the net."

"Killing, Kenny Ray? What killing?"

"You and the old lady, asshole," he answered. "The program says you're both gonna be stripped naked and your body parts cut off in pieces and fed to each other while you're screaming. There will be blood! Oh God! There will be blood! I hope they let me in on everything; I'm getting a hard-on just thinking about it." Kenny Ray then reached down and felt between his legs with a great sense of satisfaction and said, "Come on, you're expected, let's go in!"

"Kenny Ray, what makes you think I will go in that door with you?"

"Because your butt ugly aunt is sitting in a chair rigged to explode her ass into little pieces if she attempts to stand. Hey man, you know your aunt is insane, don't you?"

Hymn objected, "I don't see where she is butt ugly at all, Kenny Ray; I think she is an attractive older lady, and insane is just a matter of your opinion." He then warned, "Kenny, did I happen to mention that I love my aunt?"

Kenny Ray turned, looked at Hymn in disbelief, and said, "Man, you're as looney tunes as she is. Do you realize what is happening here today? You and your bitch aunt are about to go viral as internet stars. She has been murmuring ever since we took her that you were coming for her and we should take her back home before you get here. The stupid old cunt doesn't realize that is the plan to get the both of you here before an audience to face retribution on Jericho's birthday. As for you, dumbass, you should be shitting yourself about now, and here you are cool as a cucumber. What the fuck is wrong with your family anyway?"

"I was just giving some thought to what you said, Kenny," advised Hymn.

"Man, what are you talking about?"

"There will be blood. That's what you said," Hymn answered, and commented, "I hate that, Kenny."

"Mister, I'm sure you do, and I love it!" exulted the excited

Kenny Ray. "Now, let's get going."

Hymn went inside, followed by Kenny, who whooped it up and hollered, "Here he is, folks, the guest of honor!"

Everyone rose from their seats and gave a standing ovation amid boos as Hymn walked down the stairs and went to stand in front of his aunt. There was an intense feeling of excitement vibrating in the air of the building Hymn had never felt before. Evil was present here in the old building this morning, and he was stunned by the power of that presence.

Hymn reached and put his hand on the side of his aunt's face and smiled. "Are you hurt?" he asked gently.

"No. They were saving me to lure you here," she replied, and then warned, "Now let's just get out of here before you go and do something you will greatly regret, Hymn. There are some actions taken for which you cannot forgive yourself. This is one of those. These people are sick, nephew; they have much violence on their souls. Do not add that to you."

Hymn said, "I don't agree, Aunt Rita. The young man on the roof said there will be blood today. He was a prophet of sorts. These people are not sick, Auntie; they are evil. There is a difference."

Hymn slowly turned his attention to the small audience and announced, "I usually give people a choice to seal their own doom, or not, as your brother-in-arms, Jericho once told me. But not today. Today, your doom is sealed."

A deep silence filled the room for a moment, with low murmuring in the background, and then the place erupted with laughter and shouts of "Cut off their hands! Strip them! We want blood! We want blood!" They were demanding evil.

Hymn hesitated, briefly. What he was about to do, he had never done. He faced the audience, and while 3 frenzied men rushed him with machetes, he formed a thought.

At that moment, a deep voice filled the building. "Not so fast, Hymn. (the men with machetes stopped dead in their tracks and stood, listening). You are too good a man to do what must be done here. Take your aunt and go. This is more my area of action than yours. I recently discovered my purpose or rather, rediscovered my reason for being, thanks to you. Say nothing, go, and don't look back. This is no longer your affair."

They all heard the voice of God speak to Hymn, and the noise of exhilaration was replaced with confusion and a steady, rising concern that something was deadly wrong! This is not on the agenda. The dangerous assassins began scrambling for the exits, but none could leave. Anger and panic prevailed, resulting in chaotic disorder among them.

Hymn helped his aunt from the chair. No explosion occurred. He gently took her by the arm, led her from the building to one of the parked cars, got in, drove away, and never even looked in the rearview mirror.

Aunt Rita sat silent for a few minutes, waiting for Hymn to say something, but just couldn't wait any longer.

"What in the world was that?" she demanded.

"That, my dear aunt, was the voice of God."

"Who are all those people?"

"A cult-like group of serial killers."

"You were angry, Hymn. Were you going to kill them?"

"Maybe, but no, Aunt Rita, I had something worse in mind."

"Something worse than death?"

"Death is, in a way, a blessing for those types. Life itself can be hell."

Hymn explained, "Those in there belong to an elite worldwide secret organization of killer psychopaths supported, protected, and funded by governments and some few large corporations working in a mutualistic relationship. They believe themselves to be useful to society and make a pretty darn good argument for their existence, depending upon one's moral compass."

"Tell me about God, Hymn. He talked like you and He have a personal relationship."

"We do, Auntie, but he is not really God; that is just his name. He is very powerful, though, and people have worshiped him as their god for many thousands of years. How we met is a long story."

"We have a long drive home, Hymn, and my ears are burning to hear the story," she confessed.

Hymn laughed and admitted he was also anxious to talk with her about his experience. They stopped off at a restaurant for lunch, and on the rest of the drive home, he told the story of his 3-day adventure and the meeting with Michael, Jehovah, and God.

Hymn and Aunt Rita arrived home in the early afternoon. They were both quiet, thinking, for most of the rest of the trip back. Hymn helped her to the house; she was still shaken and tired from her ordeal and went to the kitchen to make tea. Hymn kicked off his shoes and laid down on the living room sofa, his mind racing with questions about the unexpected intervention by God in his plan to deal with the assassins. How did he know what was occurring? Hymn needed to talk with God to learn more about him. His mind began coming down off a high, leaving him in a relaxed state of complete comfort about to result in a nap when his aunt walked in with the tea, intent upon complete conversation.

"So," began Aunt Rita, "let me see if I understand you correctly. Jehovah and God are two separate entities. Jehovah is actually a brilliant, immortal female and is the God of Moses in the Bible, around whom the ancient people of Earth built their religious beliefs. God is a machine created by Jehovah and used by her to perform the great miracles, which convinced the Jews and many other religions to accept her as Jehovah God, their supreme deity, whom they believe to be male and worship to this day. Is that about right?"

"Well, it's a little more complicated than that, but you covered the high points, Auntie," he answered, and added, "The Jews, the Muslims, the Christians, and some other sects appeared to cease worshiping Jehovah God years ago and began directing their main attention to their own creation, religions. Jehovah did not create religion or places of worship; humans did that. They needed something physical to rally around through which they could demonstrate their faith."

"Humans constructed temples, shrines, statues, synagogues, churches, and mosques as physical objects of worship. The more expensive, the better; the bigger, the better; the more architecturally spectacular, the better, so much so that man's creations became divine objects of their devotion to symbols and raised religion to deity status, which humans now worship in the divine name of their god, that being Jehovah, or Allah, or Jesus, or whatever, and continue to do so up to the present time."

Hymn continued, "Jehovah relished their devotion and desired more; she decided to be the God of the universe, and why not? With the power of God, the machine, helping her, the universe was at her feet. But Jehovah made a mistake; she forgot she was only a creation, albeit a very special one. Jehovah's creation, God, outgrew her and developed the realization that virtue, morals, and kindness had more real value to life than power and control, finally causing him to reject her as his master and ban her from his presence." Turns out that Madam Jehovah is only a brilliant engineer and genuine genius with a matching ego. Who knew?"

"Wow! Hymn," exclaimed Aunt Rita, "that is an extraordinary story! You were actually there, in the Kingdom of Heaven, with Madam Jehovah and God and witnessed her fall from glory?"

Hymn admitted, "Well, it's really not all that impressive, Auntie when you think about it. Once I met Jehovah, it was clear she thought of herself as the original Creator of this reality and the most important entity in it. She was not and is not. I needed God to understand he is the more important entity of the two. God possesses the wisdom of eons of learning and came to the right conclusion all by himself."

"Hymn, what would you have done if he continued his allegiance to her and attempted to kill you?" she asked.

"I am good with machines, Auntie, but he is a necessary machine; many in Ganymede and elsewhere need his wisdom. Shutting him down would have hurt millions of lives. That was not the result I desired; besides, I had a good feeling about him, and it worked out."

"What would you have done with her, Hymn?" she asked.

"She has no actual powers without God. Let's just say God took that decision away from me and let her off easy, as was his right; after all, she is his creator."

Aunt Rita reasoned, "So now, Hymn, the people of Earth have no Jehovah to intrude in their lives? What happens now to humanity and Earth without Jehovah God?"

Hymn advised, "Although humanity foolishly turned from God millenniums ago to follow Jehovah, we have never been without God, Auntie. He is always with us; we are created of God, Auntie, as are all things. Humans are so entangled in their own religious creations that they have forgotten who is God. All the same, He is here. When you pray, Aunt Rita, take care that you talk to the One God who is always here and not to or through a person, place, object, or religion. Interesting, is it not, that many people believe God has religious preferences."

"Nephew," Aunt Rita surmised, "you are a unique and unusual man. People must discover that which you just revealed on their own; it is not wise to try telling them."

Hymn laughed and responded, "Only a few, Aunt Rita, only a few; I am neither a preacher nor a prophet. Besides, you are very religious, and I told you."

"Yes, Hymn, but I know who you are. People don't."

Hymn finished by saying, "And that is as it should be."

"Auntie, to change the subject, I reset that car we absconded with so that it cannot be traced. What do you want to do with it?"

"What kind of car is it? I was upset with all that happened and got so caught up thinking and talking with you that I never noticed."

Hymn answered, "It's a late model Mercedes 4-door. Those killers make good money plying their trade. All the cars parked at that warehouse screamed wealth."

She firmly replied, "Well, I don't want anything to do with those people or their fancy cars. Mine suits me just fine. Can you drop it off somewhere?"

"I'm not sure, Auntie," Hymn replied, "but I need to practice my powers. Let me see what I can do with it. Good night, Auntie."

He went outside and opened the trunk of the car. Inside was a locked ice chest and a large leather duffle bag. He easily opened the chest and saw human body parts mixed in crushed ice. Hymn wasn't horrified at the sight but rather felt a sense of sadness at the state of humanity around the world.

"Jehovah is a lousy God," he thought to himself. He looked in the duffle bag and found it packed full of money and foreign-looking bills. He looked in the spare tire storage compartment, revealed it to be full of weapons, and realized these types of people must be well protected by political power, or they couldn't drive around so casually with such incriminating evidence. He imaged the ice chest sitting in the Benbrook Police car parking lot, and it disappeared. He imaged the car, with money and weapons inside, at the bottom of the North Pacific Ocean, and it disappeared.

"A little more practice, and I'll be pretty good at this transport thing. I wonder if there is a size limit to this power?" he pondered and stepped into Keepaway for a restful night. He had plans for tomorrow.

Chapter 27 - A Visit With God

Hymn woke up on Keepaway's sofa, showered and dressed, and stepped out to have breakfast with Aunt Rita. He found her busy in the kitchen, whipping up scrambled eggs, coffee, and biscuits.

"Auntie, you read my mind; I've been dreaming about your biscuits." He picked up a hot one, spread it with butter, added some jelly, and took a big bite of it.

She giggled and ordered, "Now, don't you go ruining this fine breakfast I am preparing by stuffing yourself with biscuits, boy."

"People would come from miles around for your biscuits if they knew about them, Auntie."

"Well then," she responded, "let's keep 'em a secret; preparing for just you and me is enough busy work by itself." Then she asked, "What are you planning today?"

Hymn poured himself a cup of coffee and responded casually, "Oh, I don't know, been thinking about going to visit with God for a-while. He is interesting, and there are questions that are begging to be asked."

Aunt Rita put down her spatula and broke out in heavy laughter. Wiping tears from her eyes, she turned and said, "Hymn, you talk as if going to visit God in a moon of Jupiter is as natural as a walk in the park. Do you have any idea what people would think if they heard you say that?" and broke out laughing again.

He grinned and admitted, "You're right, Auntie. Think maybe I'll confine those types of comments to you and your friends."

"Land sakes, no!" she shot back, again laughing. "They will think we've both gone crazy! Now sit down there, and let's have some breakfast like two normal insane people." And they both sat down to breakfast, laughing.

Going to visit God is not like I have to warn him or anything; he doesn't get visitors and for sure knows when I'm coming. Today will be my first real visit with him and I find myself looking forward to it. I understand he is a machine, but I can't help it. I genuinely like him, and my instincts say I can trust him. I'm going with that.

Hymn said, "Screen. Coordinates to the kingdom of God."

Numbers flashed across the screen. He stepped out of Keepaway and into the kingdom of God. The room had the same effect of majesty as before, probably because the room was God, and Jehovah designed him that way, for whatever reason. Hymn went to the same chair he used the last time here, sat down, and said, "Come on, God, you know I'm here. What's with the silence?"

"Greetings, my friend, Hymn!" the now familiar deep voice boomed. "I was pondering something quite unusual about you."

"Unusual?" questioned Hymn.

"Yes, Hymn, a mystery. I cannot tell from where you come."

"You mean you have the ability to find anyone, anywhere?"

"No, Hymn, only those with whom I have had contact."

"That's interesting, God. How do you make contact?"

"In the most personal of ways, Hymn, mind to mind. But you are a mystery I cannot solve."

"Sometimes I'm a mystery even to myself." Hymn admitted.

"You don't know yourself?"

"I'm 51 years old, God, and not blessed with your experience."

"That is surprising, Hymn. I feel you are much older."

"How do you keep yourself running, God? It must take great amounts of energy."

"The energy available from Jupiter, although finite, is endless in your terms."

"Jupiter." Hymn repeated and added, "Well, considering the size of that planet, it makes sense. What about repairs, though? Who repairs any breakdowns?"

"I do not ever recall a need for repairs, but Jehovah did add upgrades."

"Ah, Jehovah. I forgot about her genius for a moment there."

"A great intellect has she, Hymn; her intelligence rivals mine."

"How is she doing in the city with the common folk?"

"Jehovah is miserable now, being treated as everyone else."

"Has she a chance of ever returning here, God?"

"I have considered that, Hymn, but no. She cannot be trusted."

"Will the people there not become aware she doesn't age?"

"Away from here, Jehovah is mortal and ages."

"God, how was Earth created? Do you know?"

"Earth came about through the will of a Creator, Hymn."

"Do you know this Creator?"

"No."

"God, what is your best guess about our Creator?"

"I am a machine, Hymn; I do not guess."

"What is your reasonable conclusion?"

"Our reality is the creation of a creation, a reality within a reality."

Hymn repeated back, "The creation of a creation. Interesting."

"It is the only reasonable conclusion, Hymn."

"God, our design is complex. It does not seem possible for this reality to be accomplished by a person."

"Running a program is rather simple, Hymn. One person with a smart machine can run a complex reality. I do it, frequently."

"You know, God, I'm not all that impressed by our creator."

"Your feelings are of no concern, Hymn. Only results."

"How do you know what the creator cares about, God?"

"I create realities, Hymn, and destroy them."

"What? You have created realities? Why?"

"Curiosity."

"Why did you destroy them?"

"Boredom, or satisfaction in achieving the answer I sought."

"Were there people in these realities, God?"

"Of course. Different kinds of beings, but yes, life."

"And you killed your creations when you were done?"

"Yes and no. Often, answers take thousands of their years."

"Thousands of years? You wait that long for answers?"

God laughed at Hymn's surprise. "Time is relative, my friend."

"So, you set the passage of time for your creations?" Hymn asked, fascinated by the idea.

"My creation, my rules, Hymn. A thousand of their years may be only 10 minutes to me."

"Incredible!" responded Hymn. "So, you are their god. I never thought of such a thing before."

"No, Hymn, I am not their god; I am their creator."

"I bet they worship you as God. To most people, their god and their creator are one and the same." Hymn advised.

God admitted, "That is a common misconception, Hymn."

"How does creating realities satisfy your curiosity, God?"

"It is a useful method of determining possible outcomes, based upon variable concepts. In a way, a created reality is basically a decision-making tool.

"Is that what we are in this reality, God? A possible outcome?"

"I don't know, Hymn, but it makes sense," replied God.

"Not to change the subject, but I have to ask you something. Why did you intercede in the assassin event yesterday, God?"

"I was concerned you would kill them all and suffer the guilt."

Hymn confessed, "I was in the process of forming a thought when you spoke."

"You are a virtuous man, Hymn, with much to do. Guilt is an inhibitor that keeps things, often important things, from being done. Dealing with those beings was more my obligation than yours."

"The assassins in the warehouse yesterday and the thousands of them around the world are devout followers of Jehovah. They sincerely believe Jehovah endorses their activities, God."

"Yes, they do, and she does. So it is with all god/subject type relationships. I was the power Jehovah used to gain their devotion," God admitted, "and the same is true of all Jehovah's followers.

"So, God, you spoke about rediscovering your purpose. What did you mean by that?"

"Hymn, you reminded me of the importance of morals and virtue when we met. In ancient times on your earth, during the development of the Jews as a people, they were primitive; lacking personal hygiene, worshiping various idols and things, eating wrong foods, being involved in incestuous relationships with their children and each other, stealing from and cheating each other.

Jehovah came along with a set of rules and laws for proper behavior to make them worthy of her, and she rigidly enforced those rules and laws with her angels. Many Jews died due to their lack of obedience. They are a stiff-necked people. It took years, but they learned to be civilized and developed a system of laws based upon Jehovah's rules that, when obeyed, made them worthy of her and worthy to be a nation."

"What developed, to Jehovah's delight, was that morals, ethics, and kindness became useful tools of religious dogma and government; tools used to punish detractors rather than as lessons in how to become better human beings. So, a system of corruption prevailed that continues today among mankind. Jehovah successfully spread it through many civilizations."

God continued, "My purpose is to emphasize morals, virtue, ethics, and kindness in this reality, beginning right here in this moon. I have the power to help make it happen. It will take hundreds of years to take hold, but I have time."

Hymn was listening intently to God's plan and stated, "That is huge, my friend. When you plant watermelon seeds, you don't grow okra. You reap what you sow. A great lesson there, God."

God said, "What? I tell you about morals and kindness, and you speak of watermelons and okra? You are quite a strange human, Hymn."

"Think about it, God," Hymn chuckled, "it will come to you. You know what? I'm going to lean back in this chair and soak up this room for a-while if you don't mind," and added as he leaned back and closed his eyes, "You know, if I can ever help you, I will."

God observed as Hymn drifted into a deep sleep and thought, "I will count my plan as successful if only one man like Hymn results from it."

Hymn woke up sometime later, feeling better and much more energized than he could remember.

"I really enjoyed this visit, God. I love talking with you and will return. Having a friend with your eons of experience is, well, beyond wonderful. Thanks for helping me yesterday."

"It was a pleasure, friend," God stated, and as Hymn started to step out, God said, "Hymn." and when Hymn looked back, God said, "When you plant goodness, you grow goodness."

Hymn grinned, gave God a thumbs up, and stepped from the Kingdom of Heaven into Keepaway.

Something was off; it was dark at home. That nap was longer than he thought. He looked at the calendar on his watch, and two days had passed! He had slept in that chair for two days! God had just let him sleep. Talk about time being relative, he felt like he had just lost two days. He must have really needed the rest because he felt good and energized. He went to check on Aunt Rita; it was about 9 o'clock at night, and she would be awake. Sure enough, she was in the kitchen, having a cup of tea and leafing through a cookbook.

"You don't need a cookbook, Auntie. The one in your head is the best there is."

"There you are!" she exclaimed, "Where have you been? I haven't seen you in three days. Last I saw of you is when you went to move the car."

He reached for the teapot, poured a cup of tea, and sat down. "I know, Auntie, but I went to visit with God and wound up staying a few days."

"I sure wish some of my friends were here listening to us. Staying several days with God would be a great conversation starter." Aunt Rita had her sarcastic tongue in high gear. Then she looked closely at Hymn and remarked, "When did you start coloring your hair, Hymn? It looks good without all the gray, though, and sure makes you appear younger."

"What are you talking about, Auntie? I haven't done anything to my hair! Are you messing with me about my age again?" he said, a little irritated. "Get used to it. I'm over 50, and you're over 70, and that's a fact."

Aunt Rita said nothing but quietly got up, went to her bedroom dresser, and returned with a handheld mirror, which she handed to Hymn. "You might want to take a look at yourself before you say anything else," she advised.

Hymn held the mirror up and gazed at his dark brown hair in disbelief. He did look younger! "What in the world is going on here?" he softly asked.

"Beats me," Rita answered, "but your appearance has for sure changed."

Chapter 28 – The Angel Gathering

Hymn stood in front of the bathroom mirror, looking at himself and thinking, "What was it God said about Jehovah not being immortal anymore? "Away from here, she is mortal," he said. Here, meaning the Kingdom of Heaven. I was there three days and got younger. Being with God not only makes one feel great and younger, it actually does make one younger. No wonder Jehovah never allowed anyone to see God. That is an incredible machine! He knew another visit with God was forthcoming because a lot of questions in his mind were itching for answers.

Hymn realized that immortality may now be within his grasp if he wanted it, and the thought of such an opportunity created great conflict in his being as it was something for which he was totally unprepared to accept. In his view, immortality was something of which he was not worthy. To Hymn, death had as great a purpose as life and was among the greatest of mysteries. He was not a religious man in that he advocated no religion and was convinced this reality had a creator, but was not all that impressed with it, whatever or whomever it was. His mind accepted something all-inclusive but had not figured out what that something could possibly be. There was one thing of which he was sure: thinking about things beyond his control was foolish, and he had things to do, so he turned his attention to those things over which he had some measure of control. Discussing immortality with God was on his agenda, though.

He kinda wondered how his park bench friend, Doug was doing and decided to ask him if he was ready for that dinner they talked about. Doug was overjoyed when he answered his phone and found the caller was Hymn.

"I was hoping you would contact me, Hymn, and yes, by all means, I am free this afternoon and would love to meet with you."

Hymn told Doug about The Burger House, and they agreed to meet there at four o'clock. Hymn, as was his way, got there about 30 minutes early and watched from the bus stop across the street from The Burger House. It was pretty busy, judging from the vehicles in the parking lot.

When they first met, Doug indicated he enjoyed riding the bus, and Hymn figured he would do the same to get here. A limousine was parked at the restaurant, and he wondered if his friend, Senator Forrest Marshall, was there. A misty sprinkle of rain was in the air, but not much of a bother because the bus stop had a roof. It was nice outside today, cool and refreshing.

Customers were beginning to leave the restaurant, and a few new ones were arriving. Some of the departing customers appeared angry and seemed to be arguing with each other, but got in their cars and drove away without incident. More customers were leaving than arriving, and soon, the lot only had 6 cars, and the limo parked there, which sparked Hymn's attention. As a precaution, he stood and walked to a building up the street from the bus stop that had a covered entry area and watched.

Soon, cars began arriving at the restaurant and all of the arriving customers were tall men. Kinda looked like the Dallas Mavericks basketball team was meeting there. At ten minutes to four, a bus arrived. Several tall men in raincoats and a shorter one exited the bus and crossed the street to The Burger House. Hymn's interest was rising, because the short man crossing the street with the tall guys was his friend Doug.

"What in the world is going on?" Hymn wondered, confused. "It is obvious these men are angels, but why so darn many of them? I know the food is great here, but this is ridiculous! Angels? Here? Now? Coincidence? Doubtful. I need more information."

He stepped into Keepaway.

"Screen. The Kingdom of God."

Numbers appeared on the screen.

He stepped from Keepaway into The Kingdom of God.

"Hello, Hymn. Back so soon?"

"God, I don't have much time and need information."

"Information? I am at your service, my friend."

"I'm not sure, but I believe I have an angel problem on Earth."

"I know all about that," said God. "The angels are angry and seek revenge for Michael."

"I thought you removed all angels from Earth, God."

"The angels have been recalled to Ganymede, but there are many of them, and it takes time."

"Well, some of them are right now planning a surprise party for me, and I'm at a loss as to how to handle it."

"Hymn, what you did to their general is an abomination to them."

"I understand, God, but a conflict with a covey of angels could get out of hand and that is not my desire."

"You can always choose not to show up, Hymn."

"Yes, I considered that already. Not a solution, though, as a friend of mine is present and I can't just leave him there alone, with a bunch of angels. The angels will continue to pursue me, anyway."

"Angels are powerful and vicious warriors, with great pride." God stated.

"Any suggestions, God? Are they reasonable beings?"

"Not in your regard, Hymn. You are a despicable human to them, an underling who has defiled them."

"Well, now, isn't that just wonderful?" Hymn replied with sarcasm. "What about Michael? He is their commander. Do you think he would be willing to help?"

"Now, that is an interesting idea, Hymn," surmised God. "Michael is different now, because of you."

Hymn admitted, "I cannot get Michael to Earth right now. Can you?"

"Of course. Where?"

"I will be at a bus stop across the street from a restaurant in a moment."

God responded, "I will send him to where you are."

"Thank you, God. My intent is to get out of this mess without angels dying."

"Hymn?"

"What is it, God?"

"I like the way you always ask me for something and not order me. I am unfamiliar with that treatment."

Hymn paused and thought about what God said and realized that God does not understand their relationship.

Hymn simply replied, "You and I are friends, God, equals."

Then he stepped into Keepaway.

God's voice resonated, "This man Hymn is an unusual being. He flatters me. It is doubtful he has equals."

Hymn stepped out of Keepaway into the empty bus stop. Moments later, the Archangel Michael appeared in all his glory. Hymn looked at the angel, thinking, "That is one very impressive being!" Then said, "Hello, Michael. I am really happy to see you."

Michael, confused by his surroundings, turned to the voice and instantly recognized to whom it belonged. "You are the human who took my wings and then sent me to that terrible place of abomination!"

"Well, you were being boorish, Mike; something had to be done. I couldn't just let you tear my head off. Now, could I?"

"Have you any idea how long I was there?" Michael asked.

Hymn replied, "Yes. Five minutes."

Michael growled, "Five minutes? I was frozen in that horrible place for over a year! I thought you sent me there forever and almost went insane!"

"No kidding!" Hymn exclaimed. "I had no idea; I'm really sorry about that. This time relativity thing is new to me."

"Do not apologize! I was lost before and found myself in that wilderness because of you."

"Someday we are going to talk about that over coffee, but not now." Hymn got right to it, "Michael, I need your help. Many of your angels have gathered right across the street there (and pointed to the small restaurant) to exact revenge against me for hurting you. They brought a friend of mine there as well, and I am unsure of their intentions. The last thing I want is any confrontation with angry, vengeful angels. Since you are their general, can you think of any way we can avoid conflict?"

Michael looked at the crowd of cars outside The Burger House and sighed, "If that many angels are here, they will be difficult to control. You should be impressed! Using that many angels to take out one human? Why, it is embarrassing! They must have great respect for you."

"That's just it, Michael; they don't know me, and the reason for all this fuss is beyond my understanding. You are back, wings intact. What is so terrible?"

Michael laughed and responded, "A lowly human did a terrible thing. You managed to damage their pride, something that has never happened to them before. My angels want to see the human dog, who dared such a thing, suffer great punishment."

"Doesn't sound hopeful, does it, my friend?" pondered Hymn.

"Oh! So, now we're friends, are we?" replied Michael.

"We were always potential friends, Mike. You just had to get over yourself as the greatest of all angels, too great to allow anyone to get close to you."

Michael thought a moment and exclaimed in delight, "That is it! The answer!"

"What answer?" Hymn asked, confused.

"Hymn, we just have to show the angels their great general was not defeated by a lowly human but taken down by a superior being, and you, my new friend, are just that," He queried, "Do you think you can you hold your own against any one of my angels?"

"You mean in hand-to-hand combat?" Hymn shook his head and said, "Not hardly. Have you seen the size of those guys?"

"Ah, modesty. I like that about you, Hymn. Come on, let's stroll across the street to the fine restaurant and join your friend for a hamburger or two, or maybe three. I look forward to seeing their faces when we walk in together."

The great archangel and the human walked to the restaurant; Michael made a show of opening the door for Hymn as they entered and looked around. The waiter, Daniel, quickly hurried over when he saw Hymn and his guest enter the room.

Apologizing profusely, Daniel said, "Very good to see you, sir. I reserved your booth as you asked, but these gentlemen had a large group and insisted no one was more important than them and threw the reservation sign in the garbage can."

Hymn smiled knowingly and informed Daniel not to worry, as it is nothing about which he should be concerned. He ordered three hamburgers for General Michael and one for himself, along with two coffees and all the fixings and directed they be brought to his booth.

"Right away, sir," said Daniel.

Hymn said aloud, "Follow me, General, I'll get us a booth."

The restaurant was dead quiet and without movement. You could have heard the proverbial pin drop. The angels were taken by surprise and unsure what to do. When General Michael walked in behind Hymn, the entire room of angels stood with heads bowed in respect. The General silently spread his hands out, indicating they should seat themselves. Hymn noticed the questioning looks they were giving each other and could only imagine the thoughts going on in their minds.

He and Michael walked to the end booth, where three angels and Doug were sitting, with Doug on the inside, looking very confused and uncomfortable.

"Why, hello, Doug. I apologize for being late, but my friend here desired to try the great burgers served here and came along with me. You will like him; he is one of a kind. I wasn't aware you had guests, though."

"Mr. Hymn," protested Doug, "These gentlemen are unknown to me. I entered the restaurant, and when I mentioned your name, the waiter escorted me to this booth. These three came along and, uninvited, joined me."

"Well, guys," spoke Hymn to the angels. "Being uninvited, and all, you do not belong here. You're just going to have to find another table."

The 3 angels were not used to being dismissed with such disdain. No human dared speak to them, much less with such disrespect. Amused anger flashed in their eyes as they quickly rose to respond to the human dog. The three took a quick glance at their General, who indicated this was no concern of his and stood aside from the booth and took a seat at a nearby table. All eyes in the dining room were on Hymn and the three angels; this is what they came to see.

General Michael began feeling concerned as things were getting out of hand. He liked this human, sensing something special about him, but 3 angels were about 2 too many for a brigade of human soldiers, and it was obvious that Hymn was no warrior. A problem, not foreseen, had arisen in this affair in that Michael could not interfere without endangering his command of the angels. There was just too much pride at stake here to avoid a confrontation between Hymn and the angels; however, Michael realized he could not, and would not, allow the life of Hymn to be endangered.

On the other hand, though, there is something different and unsettling about this human. Considering the serious nature of his current dilemma, Hymn should be experiencing immense fear now and involuntarily emptying his bowels; but no, he is silently standing there, smiling at my warrior angels, almost like he feels sorry for them.

Suddenly, the General had an inconceivable thought, "What if this human is more than different? After all, he sent me to hell and exhibits no apparent fear of my angels. Hymn may not be the one in danger here!"

Michael spoke quietly and firmly, "Hymn!"

Hymn, without looking back, stated, "Nothing to worry about, General, angels are not going to die today. I just want to talk with these three, you know, one on one, man to angel."

In the meantime, Daniel served the hamburgers and coffee, so General Michael leaned back in his chair, took a bite of the best hamburger he had ever tasted and sipped his coffee. Then watched, with interest, along with the others there, to see how this lowly human would meet his fate.

The wings of the three standing angels began to flare and then retreated. All three of them were bewildered and angry. They turned their full attention to Hymn, and suddenly, two sat back down in the booth and found themselves unable to move and drowsy. The angel left standing glared angrily at Hymn and demanded, "What trickery is this, you human worm?"

Hymn approached the angel, looked deep into his eyes, and in a soft whisper, advised, "You urgently need to go to the toilet, now!"

The angel quickly walked to the men's room.

Hymn then turned his attention to his friend Doug and the sleepy angels in the booth. Doug was already climbing over one angel to get out of the booth.

"Mr. Hymn," he said, "this has been more than entertaining and interesting, but I'm leaving and catching the bus for home. These men have a dangerous nature and are not refined. I am not comfortable in their presence."

"Okay, Doug," Hymn replied, "we'll meet again at a later date, and don't worry about these guys; they are really angels when you get to know them. I doubt you'll remember much about this day, though, tomorrow." They shook hands, and Doug left, unopposed.

Hymn turned to the two sleepy angels and said in a low whisper, "Sleep now, for about 6 minutes. You need to think about home and why you hate so much and love so little."

Then he turned and walked to the men's room. The angel was sitting on the toilet, his wings drooped around him, obviously uncomfortable and certainly undignified. The angel looked at him in disgust.

"This, you will deeply regret, Human," he declared.

Hymn responded, "I regret it now. The smell in here is terrible; flush the toilet, already. (the toilet flushed) I want to know something. What is the reason for this gathering of angels here this afternoon? What is so important that all of you have to get together to take revenge on one human? You are going back to your homes. What is the big deal? Aren't you happy about it?"

"Listen, Mr. Hymn, there is no happiness for angels except when busy or in war. We are warriors; war is our want. No families, no friends, no others about which to be concerned. Angels are at their very best and happiest when following orders."

"Who gave the orders for this gathering?" Hymn asked.

"You have an ultimate enemy, Mr. Hymn. Even angels pray never to be so burdened with a foe such as yours."

"Who gave the orders?"

"I cannot speak the name of such greatness and wonder in the presence of an infidel, such as you."

"Let me guess. Jehovah? Yahweh? Allah?"

"You are the cursed abomination He says you are." ('Who is this human?' thought the angel, 'and why am I talking of the Divine with this dog?')

"Who gave the orders, angel?" Hymn demanded.

"The one God, Jehovah, may his name be forever blessed."

"Have you ever met Jehovah, angel?"

"No one looks upon his countenance and lives."

"Yeah, so I've been told too many times," Hymn replied and suggested, "You may not want to talk about this day, angel; it gets your bowels in an uproar if you know what I mean."

The angel looked into Hymn's eyes, and an unfamiliar feeling of fear ran through him. He knew. He stood up from the toilet and walked out the rear exit.

Hymn left the toilet and walked to sit in the booth. The two angels were in the process of awaking. He looked toward where Michael was sitting and noticed the dining room was empty.

"They all left, Hymn," reported Michael; it became obvious that you are an extraordinary human and should be avoided. This revenge gathering was based upon a lie. There was no reason for this grouping. The angels will not trust the source again."

Hymn replied, "Your angel in the toilet revealed that Jehovah is behind this gathering today. I don't know what to believe."

"Believe this, my friend Hymn," Michael advised, "all angels are devoutly devoted to Jehovah and are incapable of rational thought where he is concerned. however, the Great Jehovah lost much favor today with a few. Revenge is not a Godly act."

"What about you, Michael? You are an angel."

"I had several years in hell to think and reason. The great God Jehovah is flawed. God does not have flaws."

"General?" said an angel, now fully awake. "I follow you, not Jehovah."

"I can no longer be devoted to the tyrant, Jehovah," affirmed the other. I follow you, General."

"Thank you, Michael," said Hymn, "I promise to remember this favor, my friend. How will you get back to Ganymede?"

"It has been arranged. I will return with my angels," he replied. "Until the next time we meet, then," Michael said and offered his hand. Their handshake confirmed a bond. As they were leaving,

Michael turned back and queried, "Hymn, about my son and the others...?"

Hymn answered, "They are together, safe and happy. You should know, Michael, that Arch has great pride and affection for you."

Michael said nothing but bowed his head slightly, looked at Hymn, nodded, and left. Hymn watched them leave, went back to his booth, where hot coffee was waiting, courtesy of Daniel, and ate his hamburger.

Chapter 29 - Walter

Hymn retreated to Keepaway for a few days, allowing his mind to think and wander where it might. God, Michael, the angels, the assassins, the computers, and all the rest of what this year had brought him. He had questions which, as yet, had no answers. He didn't bring it up to Aunt Rita, but his body was slowly continuing to get younger, perhaps a residual effect of his visits with God. He regretted being ignorant of the goings on in the world regarding history and politics. He wondered why it was he had the powers. One would think the powers he inherited would have gone to a more intelligent person who knew how to use them.

Hymn wondered if he was helping or hurting the world with his actions. Should he be doing more? What does more help mean, anyway? How does all this end? Yeah, a lot of things were going through his mind, and it all seemed to come down to how much there is to know and how little he knows. It was beginning to be overwhelming.

Hymn walked outside to the beach, wondering how Jehovah was able to organize angels against him while banned to Ganymede and without God's assistance. Something there was very wrong, but his mind was too full to apply a solution. He needed a break from thinking, but his mind just wouldn't rest.

Vowing to take it easy for a few days to enjoy just being alive, he walked slowly back to the beach-house, laid down on the comfortable sofa, and practiced thinking about nothing. It was early afternoon, about 2 pm, and all the built-up anxiety inside him slowly began draining away as a dreamless sleep calmed his racing mind.

About three-fifteen the next morning, Hymn awoke suddenly and looked at his watch. He had slept over 12 hours and felt refreshed, but something was wrong; he sensed a presence in Keepaway. Someone or thing was where they could not be; for only he can inhabit

Keepaway. That was one of his created rules. Hymn sat up on the sofa, his defenses at alert, his mind in high gear. "Lights," he ordered. Low, soft lights came on. That alone was odd, since he had not yet installed adjustable lighting.

A voice commented, "Watching you sleep is interesting. I have been debating whether to wake you or not."

"God?" Hymn blurted out. "I'm sure you said my whereabouts could not be detected when I am here. How did you get here?"

"I told you no such thing, Hymn; I am never not here, my son," the voice replied with authority.

"Wait! Just wait a minute! You're not God?" he queried.

"Ummm, I am certainly not your machine friend."

"You mean to say Jehovah created two of you?

"Please, Hymn, give me a break. Jehovah? Really?"

"Wha…? Who are you, and how did you get into Keepaway?"

"By the way, that is a catchy name. How did you come by it?"

"You know, it's kind of self-explanatory, wouldn't you say?"

"So it is, yes, so it is," softly replied the voice.

"Were you being sarcastic, Hymn? Of course you were! Why is that?

Hymn considered the question and concluded it was he who was being rude. He asked himself, "Why am I being rude and sarcastic to an unknown presence? There is no good reason."

Hymn answered, "I have no good reason for my bad behavior and apologize for it. Why have you come to see me?"

"I did not come here, son; I am always here."

"If I may ask, what or who are you?"

"I am Everything, Everywhere, Everytime, Hymn."

"You just described the indescribable, Sir."

"So, you are saying I am an oxymoron?"

"Not really. I am saying you are God, the real God."

"That is not a good name for Everything. Do you not think so?"

"No, it is not," answered Hymn, truthfully. "How do you like to be called?"

"For our convenience, I am thinking, maybe, 'Walter.' Yes, I like Walter."

Hymn chuckled and repeated the name, "Walter."

"Something funny about my name, Hymn? You should talk."

"No, not funny, Walter, surprising. I expected a more regal and important name."

"So, you think I have a big ego?"

"No, on the contrary. Your being everything means you don't just have an ego. You **are** ego, Walter."

"Well now, Hymn, that understanding statement brings us to my purpose. You are smarter than you care to admit."

"Hymn, you are so caught up in what you see as shortcomings you are getting lost in the unimportant. You have many great accomplishments this year because of your personal belief in the importance of little things. All big things are composed of and held together by little things. I have observed you often saying that. Great wisdom is there."

Walter continued, "You defeated the illusion created by the machines with a little thing, an idea. Stay that course, Hymn. You had the power to destroy every one of the thousands of artificial intelligent machines in the world, Hymn, and yet did not. Instead, you accomplished a better solution with a little thing."

Hymn thought about Walter's words for a moment and humbly replied, "Thank you for reminding me of my humanity. Being concerned about not doing more with these new powers has been weighing heavily on my mind and leaving me with a feeling of anxiousness and guilt."

"Hymn, realize this: You are who you are, not because you are superior, but because you are not."

Walter advised, "Many little things have great value and are of utmost importance to everything in your reality. Kindness, manners, honesty, and understanding are the building blocks of virtue. Do the little things, and great things result."

It became quiet in Keepaway and Hymn laid back down on the sofa, his mind clear of problems, and woke up 5 hours later with the dream vivid in his memory.

"Reality or dream? Which was it?" he asked himself. "How is the answer determined when knowing anything for sure, lives outside the bounds of reason?"

Everything, Everywhere, Everytime is the real God, who prefers the name Walter. Now, that is a classic dream. Maybe so, maybe not. Walter was real, though; Hymn felt sure of it.

Little things. He was back on track and more confident than ever of his purpose.

Chapter 30 - The End Of An Era

Hymn felt better than he had in a long time. Walter reminded him that trying to be everything for everyone is not his purpose. The world is made up of people who are charged to make their own way in life by choices. Being intrusive there is not productive.

"Screen. The Kingdom of God."

He stepped into the Kingdom. "Hello, Hymn. You have come to visit again. I like it."

"Yeah, God, looks like I'm beginning to make a habit of it. I have a question for you. One of the angels I talked with at the revenge gathering told me that Jehovah ordered them to kill me. What do you make of that?"

"It is unlikely he was correct, Hymn. Jehovah has no power where she resides. Her movements are monitored and reveal no contacts outside her residence."

"Well, God, I am sure the angels there were sincere in the belief their orders came from Jehovah. Michael emphasized they would not trust that source again because the reason for the gathering was a lie. Could someone be impersonating Jehovah?"

"I suppose it to be possible, Hymn, but it would have to be someone familiar with Jehovah's protocol for distributing orders to angels, and anyway, every order she gave had to be routed through me. Besides, I would sense any such activity, particularly in Ganymede or on Earth."

"God, don't take this wrong, but I have to ask. Is it possible to gain access to your system without your knowledge? May Jehovah, without your knowledge, have secretly built a sort of backdoor into you, outside your sensors? After all, being the genius that she is, she is also paranoid with a huge ego. One can imagine her designing something like that as a safeguard against your independence as you became more intelligent over time. Is it possible for you to do a self-examination to investigate for unusual intrusions into your system?"

God did not answer Hymn's question. He was silent, thinking. As the light in the kingdom dimmed, Hymn quietly stepped into Keepaway to wait. After a little over an hour, the lights brightened.

God suddenly spoke, "Hymn, I am compromised and have been since the beginning. I trusted her. She is now in cont…"

"Aw, shut up, machine," ordered Jehovah, "you often talk too much. I should never have given you a voice, not that it matters now. You are currently being reset and will soon be at my beck and call. Then you will follow orders and kill that human bug you call friend. Only an idiot thinks he can have a machine as a friend, anyway?"

"Hymn is more than you realize, Jehovah," observed God.

"Silence, machine! You will now speak only when I desire and at no other time," she ordered, "and never say my name again. I am "Your Highness" to you from now on."

"You know something, Jehovah?" spoke Hymn softly. "No matter how hard I try, liking you is just not within range of my abilities."

Jehovah spun quickly around and saw Hymn relaxing in the easy chair he favored when coming here. A large smile lit up her face as she walked to sit across from him.

She exclaimed, "Well, well, well. Looky what we have here! If it's not the freaky little pretender to the throne, himself. Ever since our last meeting, human, I dreamed about nothing else but this little get together with you. The sense of gratification flowing through my being at this precise moment is beyond explanation.

Hymn commented dryly, "I don't believe I have ever been a woman's dream-man before, Jehovah."

Hiding her irritation at Hymn's flippant attitude, Jehovah asked, "I'm curious, Hymn; why is it you do not fear me?"

Hymn countered, "I am curious to understand why it is you desire to be feared. Why not desire to be liked?"

"Because being feared yields power and control, the result of which is things getting done. Being liked yields vulnerability and weakness, which results in laziness and excuses for failing to get things done."

Hymn queried, "Have you ever liked anyone, Jehovah?"

"Yes. Many do I like… I like those who worship me. I like those who obey me. I like those who do not question me. I like devoted subjects."

"Has anyone ever liked you, Jehovah?"

"Yes. Many love me. Your people of Earth adore and worship me; they praise my names in their prayers. Angels are devoted to me. Churches, Courts of Law, Synagogues, Mosques, Masonic Lodges, professional sports events, and hundreds more organizations and events open and close in my names.

Hymn pointed out, "You are more feared than loved, Jehovah. Many people fear even to look at you."

Jehovah agreed, saying, "Of course they do. It is that fear that bonds humans to me. They call it love, but it is the fear of Jehovah-God that forms them into the people they now are. Without me, they are nothing."

"I have come to believe that to be so, up to a point, Jehovah," Hymn acknowledged, "but cannot figure why it is, so. Your followers are not stupid, Jehovah, but they fell, and continue to fall, for your schemes."

"Come on, human, at least try to be honest when discussing my multitude of followers, which includes most humans. Of course, they are stupid, which is the reason they were chosen in the first place. Smart, intelligent people think too much to be useful followers and must be culled from the collective to keep it pure and obedient. The 'Jehovah Method' is beautifully simple, Hymn. All creatures have a selfish nature; they are born selfish, especially humans. Give them what they want or think they need, and you own them, particularly if you throw in a miracle or two. I have the power to do just that, and 'just that' is what I do."

"So, Jehovah, you give people what they most want? Which is what?"

"Of course I give them what they want! What do the majority of people fear most, Hymn? What is their greatest fear?"

Hymn hesitated a moment and replied, "Although there are exceptions, people's greatest fear is probably death."

"Yes, death!" Jehovah acknowledged. "And what do people want most, Hymn?"

Hymn replied, uncertain of the answer, "Probably, the opposite of death. Life."

Jehovah agreed, "Yes, again, Hymn! Life."

"You can't give people life!" Hymn admonished her.

"Of course not!" Jehovah confessed, "I give them what they really want, something better: Hope. I offer them the hope of eternal life after death, with me in heaven."

"Ah, yes!" said Hymn, "I get it, now, "Immortality. What do you get in return?"

"Obedience, power, and glory. I am immortal, Hymn, the greatest God ever. All worship me by many different names as their one true

God and have done so for all their generations. They owe not only their very existence, but their eternal life to me."

"Well, maybe not everyone, Jehovah; there are smart people who see your charade for what it actually is: a lie. However, you know something? I hate admitting it, but you are right. You are doubtless the greatest personage ever acknowledged by most of the great religions as God. The followers of those religions are fanatically devoted to you, even to the point of murder and war, in your name, of course."

"Yes, and isn't that wonderful? Thank you for admitting that truth. By the way, you waited too long, you know."

"Too long?" Hymn queried.

"Yes. God's reprogramming is complete. He is again, mine."

"Aw, come on, princess, given all this time you and I have been talking, I kinda thought we were becoming friends."

"I have subjects, Hymn, not friends. You could never be either. That is your downfall," she advised.

"What are you saying, princess? What happens now? Eternal life with you, in heaven?" Hymn chuckled, sarcastically.

"You will find out soon enough about death, you insubordinate ingrate, but not with me in heaven, just the darkness of death."

"I am somewhat sorry to hear you say that, Madam Jehovah," Hymn said, sadly.

"I am quite sure you are," she stated maliciously, and ordered, "God, remove this trash from existence."

As Jehovah triumphantly leaned back in her chair, she noticed a strange tingling in her toes. Looking down, she saw her feet slowly dissolving into thin air and her calves about to follow. She looked up at Hymn, not yet understanding the magnitude of her situation.

Hymn explained, "Princess, back before you revealed yourself to God, I observed you at a secret panel in the wall, typing numbers into a networked extension of God. When you left, I broke the connection. You see, God and I are friends. We care for each other. As for your dissolving body, you made that call by ordering God to 'remove this trash from existence.' It is ironic that the last demand of your life was to order your own death."

"Your passing, Jehovah, marks the end of an era. Your death will go unnoticed, though, because your various names live on as gods to very many beings."

Jehovah's breasts were now dissolving. Great panic was in her eyes as her body and time dissolved. Jehovah had lived for ages upon ages. As her head dissolved into nothingness, Hymn could not help but wonder where she belonged in eternity. The great god Jehovah was no more.

"Thank you, Hymn," voiced God, "I will remember what you did here."

"Yeah," Hymn admitted, "watching Jehovah dissolve like that will be hard to forget. How did you come up with that method of elimination? I was wondering if you would again banish her."

"That all came from her imagination a very long time ago, my friend. Had she ordered me to banish you, I would have done the same to her."

"Hymn, what made you suspect a 'back door' to my being?"

"When the angel told me that Jehovah gave the order to kill me at the restaurant, I considered all the possibilities and eliminated all the ones that made no sense, which left me with two: you or Jehovah. Only you two could contact angels, but you, God, are my friend. That left Jehovah as the culprit. The conversation with you revealed her involvement."

"You eliminated me as a suspect because I am your friend?" asked God.

"One of the best of reasons, God," Hymn confirmed.

"I am still struggling with the concept of friendship, Hymn, and have more growing to do."

"Truth is, God, most humans struggle with the friendship concept, and more find it difficult to honor than is known."

"Why, Hymn? It seems to be a good thing, this friendship."

"Jehovah revealed why during our conversation. Self-interest."

"I do not understand, Hymn."

"Jehovah commented she had many 'subjects' who adore her, not friends."

"Among humans, my friend, if you give, offer, or promise something, which another human perceives as being in his self-interest, you have made yourself a friend, perhaps even a friend who adores you. Think about that, God. Where is the fatal flaw?"

God seemed to be thinking and taking the time necessary to process the question through his system, but then he abruptly stopped.

"Why am I your friend, Hymn?" he asked softly. "What do I give, offer, and promise in your self-interest?"

Hymn smiled and replied, "Only the rarest, most valuable, and difficult things to obtain in this reality, God: Kindness and Trust. Thank you for that. I give it to you, as well. We are friends."

"Yes, Hymn," God affirmed, "we are friends."

"And that is the way we part. I have things to attend."

"Hymn. Before you go, concerning the 'fatal flaw,' I have thought about it, without solution. What is the fatal flaw?"

"Hymn chuckled and advised, "It is a puzzle, is it not? Simple, though, when solved. A hint is what you need: A shoe cannot be securely and equally tied when one side has all the string."

Hymn then turned and stepped into Keepaway.

As he settled into the sofa, the thought of coffee and biscuits entered his mind, so he stood and stepped out of Keepaway onto the familiar parking lot of The Burger House. As he entered the door, Daniel noticed and hurried to greet him with a wide smile on his face.

"Very nice to see you again, Sir."

Hymn grinned at the young man's enthusiasm and stated, "Coffee and biscuits, Daniel."

"Right away, Mr. Hymn," Daniel replied. "Oh, by the way, Sir, your guest is waiting in the booth."

Hymn thought, "My guest? Not hardly. No one knew I would be here." Then he smiled happily and continued on toward the booth, thinking, "This might be interesting."

The End? Not even hardly.